MISS BUNCLE'S BOOK

MISS BUNCLE'S
BOOK

By

D. E. STEVENSON

FARRAR & RINEHART, INC.

PUBLISHERS   NEW YORK

CONTENTS

MISS BUNCLE'S BOOK

CHAPTER I

Breakfast Rolls

*O*NE fine summer's morning the sun peeped over the hills and looked down upon the valley of Silverstream. It was so early that there was really very little for him to see except the cows belonging to Twelve-Trees Farm in the meadows by the river. They were going slowly up to the farm to be milked. Their shadows were still quite black, weird and ungainly like pictures of prehistoric monsters moving over the lush grass. The farm stirred and a slow spiral of smoke rose from the kitchen chimney.

In the village of Silverstream (which lay further down the valley) the bakery woke up first, for there were the breakfast rolls to be made and baked. Mrs. Goldsmith saw to the details of the bakery herself and prided herself upon the punctuality of her deliveries. She bustled round, wakening her daughters with small ceremony, kneading the dough for the rolls, directing the stoking of the ovens, and listening with one ear for the arrival of Tommy Hobday who delivered the rolls to Silverstream before he went to school.

Tommy had been late once or twice lately; she had informed his mother that if he were late again she would have to find another boy. She did not think Tommy would be late again, but, if he were, she must try and

3

find another boy, it was so important for the rolls to be out early. Colonel Weatherhead, (retired) was one of her best customers and he was an early breakfaster. He lived in a grey stone house down near the bridge—The Bridge House—just opposite to Mrs. Bold at Cosy Neuk. Mrs. Bold was a widow. She had nothing to drag her out of bed in the morning, and, therefore, like a sensible woman, she breakfasted late. It was inconvenient from the point of view of breakfast rolls that two such near neighbours should want their rolls at different hours. Then, at the other end of the village, there was the Vicar. Quite new, he was, and addicted to early Services on the birthdays of Saints. Not only the usual Saints that everybody knew about, but all sorts of strange Saints that nodody in Silverstream had ever heard of before; so you never knew when the Vicarage would be early astir. In Mr. Dunn's time it used to slumber peacefully until its rolls arrived, but now, instead of being the last house on Tommy's list, it had to be moved up quite near the top. Very awkward, it was, because that end of the village, where the old grey Sixteenth Century Church rested so peacefully amongst the tombstones, had been all late breakfasters and therefore safe to be left until the end of Tommy's round. Miss Buncle, at Tanglewood Cottage, for instance, had breakfast at nine o'clock, and old Mrs. Carter and the Bulmers were all late.

The hill was a problem too, for there were six houses on the hill and in them dwelt Mrs. Featherstone Hogg (there was a Mr. Featherstone Hogg too, of course, but he didn't count, nobody ever thought of him except as Mrs. Featherstone Hogg's husband) and Mrs. Greensleeves, and Mr. Snowdon and his two daughters, and two officers from the camp, Captain Sandeman and Major Shearer, and Mrs. Dick who took in gentlemen paying guests, all clamouring for their rolls early—except, of course, Mrs. Greensleeves, who breakfasted in bed about ten o'clock, if what Milly Spikes said could be believed.

Mrs. Goldsmith shoved her trays of neatly made rolls into the oven and turned down her sleeves thoughtfully. Now if only the Vicar lived on the hill, and Mrs. Greensleeves in the Vicarage how much easier it would be! The whole of the hill would be early, and Church End would be all late. No need then to buy a bicycle for Tommy. As it was, something must be done, either a bicycle or an extra boy—and boys were such a nuisance.

Miss King and Miss Pretty dwelt in the High Street next door to Dr. Walker in an old house behind high stone walls. They had nine o'clock breakfast, of course, being ladies of leisure, but the rest of the High Street was early. Pursuing her previous thoughts, and slackening her activities a little, now that the rolls were safely in the oven, Mrs. Goldsmith moved the ladies into the Colonel's house by the bridge, and the gallant Colonel, with all his goods and chattels, was dumped into Durward Lodge next door to Doctor Walker.

These pleasant dreams were interrupted by the noisy entrance of Tommy and his baskets. No time for dreams now.

"Is this early enough for you?" he enquired. "Not ready yet? Dear me! I've been up for hours, I 'ave."

"Less of your cheek, Tommy Hobday," replied Mrs. Goldsmith firmly.

.   .   .   .   .

At this very moment an alarm clock started to vibrate furiously in Tanglewood Cottage. The clock was in the maid's bedroom, of course. Dorcas turned over sleepily and stretched out one hand to still its clamour. Drat the thing, she felt as as if she had only just got into bed. How short the nights were! She sat up and swung her legs over the edge of the bed and rubbed her eyes. Her feet found a pair of ancient bedroom slippers—which had once belonged to Miss Buncle—and she was soon shuffling about the room and splashing her face in the small basin which stood in the corner in a three-corner-shaped washstand with a hole in the middle. Dorcas was so used to all this that she did it without properly waking up. In fact it was not until she had shuffled down to the kitchen, boiled the kettle over the gas ring, and made herself a pot of tea that she could be said to be properly awake. This was the best cup of the day and she lingered over it, feeling somewhat guilty at wasting the precious moments, but enjoying it all the more for that.

Dorcas had been at Tanglewood Cottage for more years than she cared to count; ever since Miss Buncle had been a small fat child in a basket-work pram. First of all she had been the small, fat child's nurse, and then her maid. Then Mrs. Buncle's parlourmaid left and Dorcas had taken on the job; sometimes, in domestic upheavals, she had found herself in the rôle of cook. Time passed, and Mr. and Mrs. Buncle departed full of years to a better land, and Dorcas—who was now practically one of the family—stayed on with Miss Buncle—no longer a fat child—as cook, maid, and parlourmaid combined. She was now a small, wizened old woman with bright beady eyes, but in spite of her advancing years she was strong and able for more work than many a young girl in her teens.

"Lawks!" she exclaimed suddenly, looking up at the clock. "Look at the time, and the drawing-room to be done yet—I'm all behind, like a cow's tail."

She whisked the tea things into the sink and bustled round the kitchen putting things to rights, then, seizing the broom and the dusters out of the housemaid's cupboards, she rushed into Miss Buncle's drawing-room like a small but extremely violent tornado.

Breakfast was all ready on the dining-room table when Miss Buncle came down at nine o'clock precisely. The rolls had come, and the postman was handing in the letters at the front door. Miss Buncle pounced upon the letters eagerly; most of them were circulars but there was one long thin envelope with a London postmark addressed to "John Smith, Esq." Miss Buncle had been expecting a communication for John Smith for several weeks, but now that it had come she was almost afraid to open it. She turned it over in her hands waiting until Dorcas had finished fussing round the breakfast table.

Dorcas was interested in the letter, but she realised that Miss Buncle was waiting for her to depart, so at last she departed reluctantly. Miss Buncle tore it open and spread it out. Her hands were shaking so that she could scarcely read it.

ABBOTT & SPICER
Publishers.

BRUMMEL STREET,
LONDON, E.C.4.
-th July.

DEAR MR. SMITH,

I have read *Chronicles of an English Village* and am interested in it. Could you call at my office on Wednesday morning at twelve o'clock? If this is not convenient to you I should be glad if you will suggest a suitable day.

Yours faithfully,

A. ABBOTT

"Goodness!" exclaimed Miss Buncle aloud. "They are going to take it."

She rushed into the kitchen to tell Dorcas the amazing news.

CHAPTER II

"Disturber of the Peace"

*M*R. *ABBOTT* looked at the clock several times as he went through his business on Wednesday morning. He was excited at the prospect of the interview with John Smith. Years of publishing had failed to dim his enthusiasms or to turn him into a soured and bitter pessimist. Every new and promising author found favour in his eyes. He had given up trying to predict the success or unsuccess of the novels he published, but he went on publishing them and hoping that each one published would prove itself a best seller.

Last Friday morning his nephew, Sam Abbott, who had just been taken into the firm of Abbott & Spicer, suddenly appeared in Mr. Abbott's sanctum with a deplorable lack of ceremony, and announced "Uncle Arthur, the feller who wrote this book is either a genius or an imbecile."

Something stirred in Mr. Abbott's heart at these words (a sort of sixth sense perhaps), and he had held out his hand for the untidy looking manuscript with a feeling of excitement—was this the best seller at last?

His sensible, publishing, business-man self had warned him that Sam was new to the job, and had reminded him of other lamentable occasions when authors who had promised to be swans had turned out disappointing geese, but the flame which burned within him leapt to the challenge.

The manuscript had gone home with him that night, and he was still reading it at 2 a.m. Still reading it, and still in doubt. Making allowances for the exaggeration due to his youth and inexperience Sam had been right about *Chronicles of an English Village,* and Mr. Abbott could not but endorse his opinion. It was not written by a genius, of course, neither was it the babblings of an imbecile; but the author of it was either a very clever man writing with his tongue in his cheek, or else a very simple person writing in all good faith.

Whichever he was, Mr. Abbott was in no two opinions about publishing him. The Autumn List was almost complete, but room should be made for *Chronicles of an English Village.*

As Mr. Abbott turned out his light—about 3 a.m.—and snuggled down comfortably in bed, his mind was already busy on the blurb which should introduce this unusual book to the notice of the world. The author might have his own ideas about the blurb, of course, but Mr. Abbott decided that it must be very carefully worded so as to give no clue—no clue whatever—as to whether the book was a delicate satire (comparable only with the first chapter of Northanger Abbey) or merely a chronicle of events seen through the innocent eyes of a simpleton.

It was really a satire, of course, thought Mr. Abbott, closing his eyes—that love scene in the moonlit garden for instance, and the other one where the young bank clerk serenaded his cruel love with a mandolin, and the two sedate ladies buying riding breeches and setting off for the Far East—and yet there was simplicity about the whole thing, a freshness like the fragrance of new mown hay.

New mown hay, that was good, thought Mr. Abbott. Should "new mown hay" go into the blurb or should it be left to the reader to discover? What fools the public were! They were exactly like sheep . . . thought Mr. Abbott sleepily . . . following each other's lead, neglecting one book and buying another just because other people were buying it, although, for the life of you, you couldn't see what the one lacked and the other possessed. But this book, said Mr. Abbott to himself, this book must go—it should be made to go. Pleasant visions of bookstalls piled with neat copies of *Chronicles of an English Village* and the public clamouring for more editions passed dreamily through his mind.

The author must come and see him, thought Mr. Abbott, coming back from the verge of sleep. He would know then, once he had seen the man, whether the book was a satire or a straight story, and he must know that (the mystery intrigued him) but nobody else should know. John Smith must be bidden to the office at the earliest possible moment for there was no time to waste if the book was to go into the Autumn List—John Smith, what a name! An assumed name of course, and rather a good one considering the nature of the book.

Sleep hovered over Mr. Abbott darkly, it descended upon him with outstretched wings.

On Saturday evening, after a day's golf, Mr. Abbott read the book again. He took it into his hands with some trepidation—it was probably not so good as he had thought—things looked different at 2 a.m.—he would be disappointed when he re-read the thing.

But Mr. Abbott was not the least bit disappointed when he re-read the thing, it was just as good to-day as it had been last night—in fact it was better, for he knew the end and could now appreciate the finer points. It made him chuckle, it kept him glued to his chair till the small hours, it drifted along and he drifted along with it and time was not. It was the characterization Mr. Abbott decided, that made the book. The people were all so real, every single character was convincing. Every single character breathed the breath of life. There was not a flat two dimensional character in the book—rather unusual that! There were glaring faults of construction in the thing—in fact there was not much attempt at construction about it—obviously a tyro, this John Smith! And yet, was he? And yet, was he? Weren't the very faults of construction part of the book's charm?

The first part of *Chronicles of an English Village* was a humdrum sort of affair—it was indeed a chronicle of life in an English Village. It might have been dull if the people had not been so well drawn, or if the writing had not been of that amazing simplicity which kept one wondering whether it were intended to be satirical or not. The second part was a sort of fantasy: a golden boy walked through the village playing on a reed pipe, and his music roused the villagers to strange doings. It was queer, it was unusual, it was provocative and, strangely enough, it was also extremely funny. Mr. Abbott was aware, from personal experience that you could not lay it down until the end.

The name of the book was poor, Mr. Abbott thought. *Chronicles of an English Village* sounded dull; but another name could easily be found, a name that would focus light on the principal incident in the book, the incident upon which the whole story turned. What about *The Golden Boy* or *The Piper Passes?* Perhaps the latter was too sophisticated for such an artless (or was it an artful) story. It might be called *Disturber of the Peace,* thought Mr. Abbott. Yes, that was rather good. It had the right ring about it; it was easy to remember; it cast the necessary light upon the boy. He would suggest the title to John Smith.

It will have been deduced from the foregoing that Mr. Abbott was a bachelor—what wife would have allowed her husband to sit up till all hours for two nights running reading the manuscript of a novel? None.

Mr. Abbott *was* a bachelor, he lived at Hampstead Heath in a very pleasant little house with a small garden. A man and his wife—Rast was their name—"did" for Mr. Abbott and made him extremely comfortable. Their matrimonial differences were frequent and violent, but these were confined to the kitchen premises and were not allowed to interfere with their master's comfort. A slate hung upon a hook on the kitchen dresser, and if the Rasts were not upon speaking terms they communicated with each other through the medium of a squeaky slate pencil. "Wake him 7.30" Rast would write, and Mrs. Rast would glance at the slate on her way to bed

and appear at Mr. Abbott's bedside at 7.30 precisely with
a spotless tray of morning tea. Lucky Mr. Abbott!

The letter summoning John Smith was despatched
early on Monday—it was the first thing Mr. Abbott had
seen to on his arrival at Brummel Street—and now here
was Wednesday morning, and Mr. Abbott was expecting
John Smith. There was the usual box of cigars on Mr.
Abbott's table and two boxes of cigarettes—Turkish and
Virginian—so that whatever sort of man John Smith
might be, his taste could be catered for with the least
possible trouble or delay. Mr. Abbott was not quite his
usual self this morning, he was excited, and the typist
found him distrait. He was not giving his whole mind
to the drawing up of a water-tight contract with Mr.
Shillingsworth, who was a best seller and quarrelled with
every publisher in turn, and it was important, nay, it was
imperative, that Mr. Abbott's whole mind should be
given to the matter.

"I think you had better come back later," Mr. Abbott
was saying. "I must think it over carefully."

At this moment there was a knock at the door and
the small page boy announced hoarsely, "Miss Buncle
to see you, sir. Shall I bring her up?"

"Buncle!" cried Mr. Abbott. "Buncle—who's Buncle?"

"Says she's got an appointment at twelve."

Mr. Abbott stared at the imp while he rearranged his
thoughts. Miss Buncle—John Smith—why hadn't he
thought that it might be a woman?

"Show her up," he said sharply.

The typist gathered up her papers and departed with
the swift silence of her tribe, and a few moments later

Miss Buncle stood before the great man. She was trembling a little, partly from excitement and partly from fear.

"I got your letter," she said in a soft voice, and showed it to him.

"So you are John Smith," he announced with a humorous lift of his brows.

"It was the first name I thought of."

"It is an easy name to think of," he pointed out. "I rather thought it was too bad to be true."

"I don't mind changing it," she told him hastily.

"I don't want it changed," said Mr. Abbott. "There's nothing wrong with John Smith—but why not Buncle? A good name, Buncle."

Her face blanched. "But I live there!" she cried breathlessly.

Mr. Abbott caught her meaning at once. (How quick he was, thought Miss Buncle. Lots of people would have said, "Where do you live?" or, "What has that got to do with Buncle?" but this man grasped the point in a moment.)

"In that case," he said, and raised his hands a little, palm upwards—they both laughed.

Contact was now definitely established, Miss Buncle sat down and refused both kinds of cigarettes (he did not offer her the cigars of course). Mr. Abbott looked at her and wondered. How had she felt when she wrote *Chronicles*? Was it a straight story or a satire? He was still in doubt. She was obviously a simple sort of person—shabbily dressed in a coat and skirt of blue flannel. Her hat was dreadful, her face was pale and rather thin, with a pointed chin and a nondescript nose, but on the other hand her eyes were good—dark blue with long lashes—and they twinkled a little when she laughed. Her mouth was good too, and her teeth—if they were real—magnificent.

Meeting Miss Buncle in the street, Mr. Abbott (who was rather a connoisseur of feminine charms) would not have looked twice at her. A thin, dowdy woman of forty —he would have said (erring on the unkind side in the matter of her age) and passed on to pastures new. But here, in his sanctum, with the knowledge that she had written an amusing novel, he looked at her with different eyes.

"Well," he said, smiling at her in a friendly manner, "I've read your novel and I like it."

She clasped her hands together and her eyes shone.

This made him add—quite against his principles—"I like it very much indeed."

"Oh!" she exclaimed ecstatically. "Oh!"

"Tell me all about it," Mr. Abbott said. This interview was proceeding on quite different lines from what he had imagined, arranged, and decided; quite differently, in fact, from any other interview between an author and a publisher in which Mr. Abbott had ever participated.

"All about it!" echoed Miss Buncle helplessly.

"Why did you write it? How did you feel when you were writing it? Have you ever written anything before?" he explained.

"I wanted money," said Miss Buncle simply.

Mr. Abbott chuckled. This was a new kind of author. Of course they all wanted money, everybody did. Johnson's dictum that nobody but a donkey wrote for anything except money was as true to-day as it had ever been and always would be, but how few authors owned to the fact so simply! They either told you that something stronger than themselves compelled them to write, or else that they felt they had a message to give the world.

"Oh! I am quite serious," said Miss Buncle, objecting to Mr. Abbott's chuckle. "You see my dividends are so wretched this year. Of course I ought to have known they would be, after all the papers said, but somehow I didn't. The dividends had always come in regularly and I thought—well, I never thought anything about it," said Miss Buncle truthfully, "and then when they didn't come in—or else came in only about half the usual amount— it gave me rather a shock."

"Yes," said Mr. Abbott. He could visualise Miss Buncle sitting there in the midst of a crashing world waiting with perfect confidence for her dividends to come in, and the dividends failing to come in, and Miss Buncle worried about it and realising at last that *her* world was crashing as well as the outside world. He could visualise her lying awake at night with a cold sort of feeling in her heart and wondering what she had better do about it.

"So then you thought you would write a book," suggested Mr. Abbott sympathetically.

"Well, not just at first," replied the author. "I thought of lots of other things first—keeping hens for one thing. But I don't care for hens much. I don't like touching them, they are such fluttery things, aren't they? And Dorcas doesn't like them either. Dorcas is my maid."

"Susan?" enquired Mr. Abbott with a smile and a motion of his hand towards the manuscript of *Chronicles of an English Village* which lay between them on the table.

Miss Buncle blushed, she neither confirmed nor denied that Dorcas was Susan (or Susan, Dorcas). Mr. Abbott did not press the point.

"Well, so hens were definitely ruled out," he prompted.

"Yes. Then I thought of paying guests, but there is already an establishment for paying guests in Silverstream."

"You couldn't take the bread out of Mrs. Turpin's mouth."

"Mrs. Dick," corrected Miss Buncle quickly.

"Very ingenious," commented Mr. Abbott, "and of course Susan—I mean Dorcas—wouldn't have liked P.G.'s either."

"She didn't like the idea at all," Miss Buncle assured him.

"So then you thought of a book."

"It was Dorcas really," said Miss Buncle, giving honour where honour was due.

Mr. Abbott felt like shaking her. Why couldn't she tell him about the book like a human being instead of having to have everything dragged out of her by main force. Most authors were only too ready to discuss the inception of their books—only too ready. He looked at Miss Buncle, feeling that he wanted to shake her, and suddenly found himself wondering what her name was. She was Elizabeth in the book of course—Elizabeth Wade —but what was her real name—Jane? Margaret? Ann?

"And how does Dorcas like the book?" enquired Mr. Abbott.

"She hasn't read it yet," replied Miss Buncle. "She hasn't much time for reading and I wasn't very keen for her to read it. You see I don't think she will like it much, she likes something exciting. My book's not exciting is it? At least the first part isn't. But life in Silverstream is rather dull and I can only write about what I know. At least—" she added, twisting her hands in her effort to explain her limitations as an author and be perfectly truthful about it all—"At least I can only write about *people* that I know. I can make them *do* things, of course."

Somehow Mr. Abbott was sure that she was thinking of those passionate love scenes on the terrace in the light of the Harvest Moon. He was almost persuaded now that *Chronicles of an English Village* was a straight story— no satire intended—it did not matter in the least, of course, because nearly everybody would think otherwise, but he did want to be sure.

"How did you feel when you wrote it?" he asked her suddenly.

"Well," she replied after a moment's thought, "it was difficult to start, and then it went on by itself like a snowball rolling down a hill. I began to look at people with different eyes, and they all seemed more interesting. Then, after a bit, I began to get quite frightened because it was all mixed up in my mind—Silverstream and Copperfield—and some days I didn't know which was which. And when I walked down to the village to do my shopping it was sometimes Copperfield and sometimes Silverstream, and when I met Colonel Weatherhead I couldn't remember whether he had really proposed to Dorothea Bold or not—and I thought I must be going mad or something."

Mr. Abbott had heard this kind of talk before and it had never impressed him very much. Miss Buncle did impress him because she wasn't trying to, she was simply answering his questions to the best of her ability and with the utmost truthfulness.

"Copperfield is actually Silverstream?" enquired Mr. Abbott.

"Yes—you see I have no imagination at all," said Miss Buncle sadly.

"But the second part—surely the second part is not all true?" gasped Mr. Abbott.

Miss Buncle admitted that it was not. "That was just an idea that came to me suddenly," she said modestly. "They all seemed so smug and settled, I thought it would be fun to wake them up."

"It must have been fun," he agreed.

From this point they went on to discuss the name, and Mr. Abbott explained his ideas on the subject. The title was a trifle dull, not a good selling title. He suggested *Disturber of the Peace*. Miss Buncle was only too ready to bow to his superior knowledge of such things.

"And now for the contract," said Mr. Abbott cheerfully. He rang the bell, the contract was brought and with it came Mr. Spicer and two clerks to witness the signatures. Mr. Abbott could have cheated Miss Buncle quite easily if he had wanted to; fortunately for her he didn't want to, it was not his way. You make friends with the goose and treat it decently and it continues to lay golden eggs. In his opinion *Disturber of the Peace* was a golden egg but whether Miss Goose Buncle would lay any more was beyond the power of man to tell. She said herself that she could only write about what she knew, or rather—and wasn't this an important distinction—about *people* she knew. It was an admission made by no author that Mr. Abbott had ever met before—a staggering admission. But to take it at its worst there was no reason to suppose that Miss Buncle had exhausted the whole essence of Copperfield in one book. Mr. Abbott wanted other books from Miss Buncle, books about Copperfield or any other place provided that they had the same flavour.

This being so, Miss Buncle was asked to sign a very fair contract with Abbott & Spicer, Ltd., in which she promised the first option of three more novels to the firm.

"Of course I may not write any more," she protested, aghast at this mountain of work which had reared itself so suddenly in her path.

Mr. Spicer looked somewhat alarmed at this admission of sterility, but Mr. Abbott was all smiles.

"Of course you may not," he comforted her. "Sign your name just there—but somehow or other I think you will."

So she signed her name—Barbara Buncle—very neatly, exactly where she was told, with Mr. Abbott's very fat fountain pen, and the others put on their spectacles—at least Messrs. Abbott & Spicer did, the clerks were too young to require any artificial aid—and signed too, in a very business-like way, and soon after this Barbara Buncle found herself in the street, slightly dazed and exceedingly hungry, for it was long past her usual hour for lunch and she had breakfasted early.

Brummel Street was crowded and noisy, Miss Buncle was jostled by newsboys selling afternoon editions of various papers and by business men hurrying to unknown but obviously important appointments. Nobody took any notice of Miss Buncle except to say "Sorry" or "Pardon me" when they nearly bumped her into the road.

The open door of a small restaurant seemed a refuge; she found a table and ordered coffee and buns and chocolate éclairs for she had an unsophisticated palate and a good digestion. Then, laying her handbag with the copy of the contract on the table beside her plate she considered herself, and the strange sequence of events which had brought her to this pass.

"I'm an author," she said to herself. "How very odd!"

     .   .   .   .   .

Colonel Weatherhead was in the Silverstream train—he had been in town paying a visit to his tailor—he waved his paper at Miss Buncle as she came along the platform.

"Come along, come along," he said, quite unnecessarily, for Miss Buncle was coming along very well, and the train was not thinking of starting.

"I didn't know you were in town," said Miss Buncle as the Colonel took her umbrella and placed it on the rack.

"And I didn't know you were," he replied. "You have had a successful day, I trust."

Colonel Weatherhead had a gallant and slightly jocular manner with the fair sex which had come out very successfully in *Disturber of the Peace*. In spite of this he was really a very nice man, Miss Buncle thought. She had not been too unkind to him, she had merely drawn him as he was—and after all she had given him a very nice wife; Dorothea Bold was a dear.

Miss Buncle said she had had a very successful day.

"Hats or the dentist?" enquired the Colonel naming the two reasons which usually brought the inhabitants of Silverstream to town.

Miss Buncle said it was neither, and blushed. She was feeling a little guilty over her enormous secret.

"Aha—I see I must not enquire further," said the Colonel archly. "Some fellers have all the luck—by Jove they have!"

Miss Buncle looked down and smiled, she would not be drawn. If Colonel Weatherhead liked to think she had gone to London to meet a man he must just continue to think so. And of course I did, thought Miss Buncle to herself, but not in the way he thinks—or pretends to think, for of course he doesn't really think I went to meet a man, but he thinks I would like him to think so.

It was rather muddled put like that, but Miss Buncle knew what she meant herself which was the main thing.

The train started without anyone else invading their solitude.

"Would you like the window up or down?" asked

Colonel Weatherhead attentively. "This one up and that one down? How pleasant to get a little fresh air. I can't think how anyone can live in London and breathe."

Miss Buncle agreed, and added that it was the noise she disliked.

"Dreadful!" said the Colonel. "Dreadful!"

Part of her hoped that Colonel Weatherhead would now settle down comfortably to the perusal of his papers and leave her in peace, but the other part hoped that he would continue to talk. He was such excellent copy, and, although *Disturber of the Peace* (such an excellent name suggested by that nice clever Mr. Abbott) was finished and done with, she had got into the habit of watching people and listening to them. It had become second nature to her.

Colonel Weatherhead did not continue to produce copy for Miss Buncle, he took up a paper and scanned it but without seeing anything to interest him. The visit to his tailor had disturbed him, and he was still smarting under the disclosures of the tape. Two inches round the waist since January—quite horrible! An hour's digging in the garden before lunch might help, and perhaps an extra ten minutes' physical jerks before breakfast.

Miss Buncle was also immersed in secret thoughts, but hers were pleasant. The houses sped by, and were gradually replaced by orchards and fields.

CHAPTER III

Mrs. Greensleeves

MRS. GREENSLEEVES lay in bed enjoying her breakfast and looking at her correspondence. She was a pretty woman and she liked pretty things. The pink satin quilt, the frilled pillows with their pink silk bows, the breakfast tray with its white cloth and pink china were all carefully chosen. Mrs. Greensleeves liked to think that they expressed her personality, and perhaps they did. Nobody saw her in bed except her maid—for Mr. Greensleeves had departed from this cold and weary world some years ago—but the mirror was adjusted so that she could see herself and she enjoyed the picture.

On this particular Summer's morning Mrs. Greensleeves' correspondence consisted of two horrible bills—which she didn't see how she could possibly pay—and a chatty letter from her greatest friend, Iris Stratton.

"My dearest one [Iris had written], Fancy that Ernest Hathaway appearing at Silverstream! Too intriguing! I've been making enquiries as you asked me—you know I'd do anything for my beloved Vivian—my dear, the man is rolling. He was at Oxford with Bob and Bob knows all about him. You can take it from your little Iris that he's full of ill-gotten gains. His father was in oil, or something, anyway he left thousands. His mother's dead too and Ernest was brought up by an old uncle, a clergyman in the North. Bob doesn't know why he has gone and buried himself at Silverstream unless he is writing a book—he's brainy of course and frightfully serious and goody goody.—Not Bob's style at all and not yours either—what? Bob's still potty about you. I've trotted out some nice girls for him but he won't look at them. He's very jealous of you taking an interest in E.H. I wish you would think seriously of Bob, you know I would like you as a sister-in-law. I believe you quite like Bob only he hasn't enough money for you—nasty little treasure-hunter that you are!— I bet you would be happier with Bob on twopence-halfpenny than buried with E.H. in a country parish. I don't see *you* in a country parish taking round soup and blankets to the sick and the needy. Perhaps you think you could dig him out of it. Tell me what he's like when you write and whether you are *really* interested in the creature: Why don't you come up to town and have a binge, you must be getting positively mouldy at Silverstream. There's nothing much on just now of course, but it would be fun.—Iris."

Vivian sighed and the letter fluttered on to the pink silk quilt—she had let her tea get cold while she read it. If only I could sell up the house and take a flat in town, she thought, but town's no fun without money. Nothing is any fun without money, I must have money somehow.

She lay back and considered ways and means. Iris was right, she was growing mouldy in Silverstream; it was dull as ditchwater, nothing ever happened. There was such a dearth of men in the place that she had actually made friends with one of Mrs. Dick's paying guests. He was amusing and admiring—though common—and he would be late before she had cleared the lunch and washed up.

"I suppose you'll want coffee," she said sullenly.

"Of course I shall want coffee," replied Mrs. Greensleeves.

She was perfectly aware that Milly was in a bad temper, but not in the least worried about it. She hummed a little song as she tripped off to church in her high-heeled shoes.

The Snowdons were coming out of their gate as she passed, they were all dressed up in their Sunday clothes. Mr. Snowdon lifted his hat to Mrs. Greensleeves and remarked in a cheerful voice that it was a fine day. The Misses Snowdon greeted Mrs. Greensleeves with cries of delight. They were no longer young but they were full of skittishness. Miss Olivia was fat and red, she was the musical one. Miss Isabella was thin and pale, she was the poetical one. They admired each other with a great admiration, and Mr. Snowdon admired them both, and they both admired him. They were an extremely happy family, but perhaps somewhat annoying to their friends; for they were all so full of each other's excellences that they had no admiration or interest for the excellences of outsiders.

On this particular Sunday morning Olivia was full of Isabella's latest poem; it was about a violet, and she had sent it to *Country Lore* and it had been accepted. Vivian Greensleeves was obliged to walk along with the Snowdons and listen to all this. Few of us have the necessary unselfishness to hear with gladness the talents of others extolled or to listen with patience to the successes of

had a car. He was better than nothing, that was
could be said. Unfortunately he had begun to get
troublesome just lately, Vivian would have to p
in his place and there would be no more joy-rides
Fortnum's car. What a nuisance it all was! She s
again and her eyes fell on the bills—something v
have to be done about it. She took up the letter a
and read the parts concerning Ernest Hathaway
carefully.

The next day was Sunday. Vivian Greensleeves r
from her pink bed much earlier than usual, she h.
mapped out her campaign and decided that there was n
time to be lost. When she was dressed she surveyed her
self in the glass. The effect was charming but rather
too—well *too smart*. Perhaps the black hat would be
better for the occasion. She changed her hat and rubbed
some of the red off her lips.

On her way down she looked in at the kitchen door
and said,

"I'm going to church, Milly. There may be a gentleman to lunch. Make a cheese soufflé in case."

She was inconsiderate and overbearing, but Milly
stayed with her because she was generous in a careless
way. She let Milly out a good deal, when it suited her,
and gave Milly her frocks and hats when she was tired
of them (which was long before they showed any signs
of wear).

Milly was annoyed about the gentleman coming to
lunch for it was her afternoon out, and it was doubtful,
now, whether she would get out at all. At the best it

those whom we despise—Vivian hated it more than most people.

"I must speak to Barbara Buncle," she said, and hurried on in the middle of the story. It was rude, of course, and the Snowdons were annoyed; they discussed the bad manners of Vivian Greensleeves all the way to church.

Meanwhile Vivian had hurried on and nearly overtaken Miss Buncle, but not quite. She did not really want to speak to Miss Buncle, nor to be seen walking with her—dull, frumpy creature! She was wearing a brown silk dress that had seen its best days long ago, and a light blue hat. It almost made your eyes water, Vivian decided. She slackened her pace a little, but not too much, for the Snowdons were behind.

The little Church of St. Monica was cool and dim—very pleasant after the bright glare outside. Vivian took up a strategic position beneath the pulpit. He was nice looking, she decided. She liked his thin, ascetic face, his sleek black hair and his dreamy grey eyes set wide apart. His forehead was high and his head beautifully shaped. The choir sang better than usual, and not so slowly; he seemed to have made a difference already in the church.

There was the usual gathering in the churchyard after the service. Vivian saw the Bulmers, with their two small children, talking to Mrs. Bold. Miss Buncle was walking across the fields with old Mrs. Carter—they lived next door to each other. The Snowdons were in animated conversation with Mrs. Walker, the doctor's wife.

Vivian avoided them all and strolled about by herself looking at the grey tombstones with their worn inscrip-

tions—some of them were so worn as to be illegible—
Vivian was glad that she was alive.

Colonel Weatherhead passed her, looking very smart
in a new grey flannel suit. He waited for Mrs. Bold at
the lych-gate and they walked away together—they lived
opposite each other at the far end of the village near the
bridge.

She'll never get him, thought Vivian, looking after the
two figures with a malicious smile. He's far too much of
a bachelor and too set in his ways—what a pair of fools.

The choir boys came tumbling out of the vestry, with
their hob-nailed boots clattering on the steps. They threw
on their caps and went tearing home over the fields.
Would the man never come? Vivian wondered. What
on earth could he be doing? Ah, there he was!

He walked quickly with his eyes on the ground, immersed in his own thoughts. Vivian had to touch him on
the arm as he passed her.

"I'm Mrs. Greensleeves," she said, smiling sweetly.

Mr. Hathaway took off his hat and shook hands with
her. "What a lovely day!" he said. She was sure he said
that to everybody.

"I wondered if you would come and have lunch with
me, Mr. Hathaway," she said in a friendly manner. "It
would give me so much pleasure." She saw refusal in
his face, and added quickly, "I knew Mr. Dunn so well.
I should like to get to know you. It is such a *help*—"

She saw that she had said the right thing and left it at
that—she was very cunning.

"I have got the Children's Service," he told her doubtfully.

"Not till three," she pleaded. "And my house is not far."

Mr. Hathaway would rather have gone home; he was still new to his work and he found it took a lot out of him, but perhaps it was his duty—it *was* his duty to make friends with his parishioners, of course.

Vivian was thinking what a pity he's not tall! He looked taller in the pulpit, but he can't be more than five feet six. He looks strong and athletic though. Vivian sighed, she liked tall men.

"Well, it's very kind of you—" said Ernest Hathaway, with a smile.

They left a message at the Vicarage and walked up the hill together. Vivian began to talk about the sermon, and asked one or two fairly intelligent questions about it. Mr. Hathaway answered them conscientiously. He was rather dull, she decided. For one thing he seemed quite unconscious that he was walking with a pretty woman. He's never once looked at me—she thought—I might have been Barbara Buncle for all the impression I have made on him.

Vivian's eyes were not so useless, she had noted the cloth of his black suit, it was fine and smooth; his shoes were hand-made and beautifully shiny. Fancy him having all that money, she thought—what a waste!

In spite of her bad temper Milly produced a good lunch. The cheese soufflé was a trifle curdled and lumpy, but it was quite eatable. Mr. Hathaway did not notice its deficiencies for he was talking about himself, and his ambitions. Like most people he enjoyed talking about himself to a sympathetic listener. It crossed his mind that Mrs. Greensleeves was a nice woman.

"I'm afraid I've talked all the time," he said as he went away to take the Children's Service.

"It has been *so* interesting," said Mrs. Greensleeves, hiding a yawn. "Come and have supper with me on Wednesday night—just a little plain supper—then you can give me an innings," she smiled at him.

Mr. Hathaway reminded her, a little sternly, that Wednesday night was a Saints' Vigil and that there was a service at St. Monica's at 8 o'clock. She looked suitably chidden, and asked him to come on Thursday instead.

"I'm afraid I have been rather naughty about Saints' Days lately," she told him, veiling her brown eyes with long black lashes.

There was no time now to point out the enormity of being lax, for the children would be waiting. Mr. Hathaway decided as he strode off down the hill that here was a soul to be saved. He had already suspected that his predecessor had been a somewhat careless shepherd. Mrs. Greensleeves was obviously a sweet, good little woman by nature—a trifle worldly perhaps, but fundamentally sound. She must be gathered into the fold. It was exactly what Mrs. Greensleeves intended him to think.

On Thursday night Mr. Hathaway appeared looking very smart in a well cut dinner jacket. Vivian Greensleeves had taken a lot of trouble over the "little supper" —it was just right. There were shaded candles on the table which shed a very pretty soft light on Vivian's beautiful arms. She leaned her elbows on the table and told her guest a great deal about herself. The greater part of the story came directly from a book which Vivian had just read, it was called *A Brand from the Burning*. Vivian softened it down a good deal, she did not want to appear too flaming a brand, or Mr. Hathaway might be afraid of having his fingers burned. Vivian was, of course, more sinned against than sinning, but she was definitely a strayed sheep. They sat on the sofa together afterwards and Mr. Hathaway did his duty by her. He showed her the error of her ways and besought her to repent. Mrs. Greensleeves repented very prettily with tears. Mr. Hathaway was forced to comfort her. He rather enjoyed the experience. It was impossible to complete the saving of Vivian's soul in one evening, and Ernest Hathaway was not one to grudge his time when the saving of a soul was in question. He promised to come again. He came again, quite often. It was soon rumoured in Silverstream that Mrs. Greensleeves had become an enthusiastic church-goer, Milly Spikes may have had something to do with the spreading of the news. Milly did the shopping in the village for Mon Repos.

"It 'asn't done 'er any good so far," Milly said, in answer to a piously expressed hope of her aunt, Mrs. Goldsmith, at the bakery. "More cantankerous than ever, that's wot she is. It's the Vicar she's after, if you ask me."

"Not really?" Here was a piece of news worth having, and straight from the horse's mouth, so to speak. Somebody came in at that moment for a cutting loaf—they would have to wait, that was all. Aunt and niece had their heads together over the counter. "And she said . . . and he said . . . and in comes Mr. You-know-who . . . and she said . . . but don't you say I told you, for Mercy's sake." It was all very thrilling.

CHAPTER IV

Mr. Hathaway

*I*T was not only Vivian Greensleeves who found in the new Vicar an acquisition to Silverstream, the Tennis Club also benefited from his presence, and benefited very considerably. Mr. Hathaway played an excellent game of tennis, he was streets ahead of anybody else in the club; but a fairly even match could be made if the Vicar were given an absolute rabbit as a partner—and there were plenty of rabbits to choose from.

Barbara Buncle was one of the most frequent of the Vicar's partners, she was a keen player, but her game never seemed to improve. The more she tried the worse she seemed to get, it was really very discouraging.

One fine afternoon in September, towards the end of the tennis season, Barbara Buncle walked down to the club. There was a match in progress, and those who were not taking part in the struggle were watching it from the verandah of the small pavilion. Barbara changed her shoes and joined the audience. It was an exciting game to watch, Mrs. Bulmer and the Vicar against Mr. Fortnum and Olivia Snowdon. They should have been evenly matched, for Miss Snowdon was one of the best players in the club, and Mrs. Bulmer one of the worst, and this should have counterbalanced the Vicar's superiority over Mr. Fortnum; but this was mere theory, and

35

did not allow for the psychology of the players at all. Barbara Buncle perceived that the Vicar and Mrs. Bulmer were going to win. The Vicar was in great form and he had managed to inspire his partner with unusual confidence. She was playing several degrees above her usual form, whereas their opponents were getting on each other's nerves and in each other's way and becoming more and more annoyed with each other. Miss Snowdon —in spite of her obesity—was a most energetic performer on the tennis court, she swooped here and swooped there, poaching in Mr. Fortnum's court and getting extremely red and hot. Mr. Fortnum was annoyed at having his strokes interfered with, he withdrew to a corner and left Miss Snowdon to do as she liked— if she wanted to play a single, let her. He sulked and became careless. Miss Snowdon glared at him every time he missed the ball.

Barbara watched it all with interest, it was such fun to watch people and see how they reacted to one another's personality. Vivian Greensleeves was watching it too, she did not care for tennis, but she had begun to come down to the courts in the late afternoons, nobody quite knew why. She sat in a deck chair with a good deal of very neat leg clad in beige silk stocking exposed to view. She looked cool and graceful and very pretty. The women members did not take much notice of Vivian, if she liked to come down she could come, they didn't mind much either way, but some of the men were quite pleased to sit and talk to her between the sets. The women members felt that she was not really a Silverstreamite, not really one of themselves. Miss Snowdon declared that she was "not good form," and Miss Isabella Snowdon added that her clothes were "ootray." Vivian was fully aware of their opinions; she, on her part, despised the whole lot of them. She thought them frumpy, and dull, and incredibly stupid. Her sole reason for appearing at the tennis club was to keep an eye on Ernest Hathaway. If he came, so must she; but she was bored stiff by the whole performance; she felt, and looked, as alien as a bird of paradise in a murmuration of starlings.

The game was almost finished—it *was* finished to all intents and purposes, for Mr. Fortnum was beaten and not all the energy and vim of Miss Snowdon could pull him through.

"Olivia has such beautiful style," announced Miss Isabella Snowden to all who cared to hear. She merely wished to point out, in a thoroughly ladylike manner, that it was not dear Olivia's fault if her side was losing.

"It would have made a better game if they had had Dorothea Bold instead of Olivia," said Miss King firmly.

"Oh, Miss King, how can you say such a thing?" cried Miss Isabella in horrified tones.

"Merely because it happens to be true. Dorothea is a more reliable player than Olivia," replied Miss King firmly, and moved away.

"Horrid old thing!" said Miss Isabella to Barbara Buncle who happened to be sitting next to her. "It's just jealousy, that's what it is. She may dress herself up like a man, and talk and smoke like a man, but she's nothing but a cat—that's what she is."

"I rather like Miss King," said Barbara placidly, and she looked at Miss King's tall commanding figure as it strode off across the court with some affection. Of course she *was* rather funny with her deep voice, and her short hair, and her strange habit of wearing tailored coats and skirts with collars and ties like a man, and very often she was to be seen with a cigarette in the corner of her mouth, and her hands in her pockets; but, after all, these little peculiarities did nobody any harm, and there was something rather nice about the woman. At any rate she would never say behind your back what she would not say to your face (like some people one could name). You always knew exactly where you were with her, she said what she thought without fear or favour.

Miss Isabella looked at Barbara with contempt—fancy standing up for Miss King! But of course nobody in Silverstream cared what Barbara Buncle thought, the woman was nothing but an idiot. She wondered idly what Barbara Buncle was thinking about now, sitting there with that silly vacant smile upon her face. She would have been surprised if she could have read the thoughts that prompted the silly smile.

The truth was that Barbara was feeling somewhat pleased with life to-day, and she had good reason to be pleased, for only that morning, a parcel of books had arrived from Messrs. Abbott & Spicer,—six neat copies of *Disturber of the Peace* with the firm's compliments. She had spent the whole morning reading her book, and marvelling at the astounding fact that she had written every word of it, and here it was, actually in print, with a smart red cover, and a jacket with a beautiful picture of a Golden Boy playing on a reed pipe.

The jacket was just a *little* disappointing because the Golden Boy was quite different from Barbara's conception of him. For one thing he seemed to have goats' legs and his ears were pointed in a peculiar way—Barbara had imagined quite a human, ordinary sort of boy—but that was, after all, a mere detail and you could hardly expect a strange artist to depict a Golden Boy exactly as you had imagined him.

The set was over now, and the players were returning to the pavilion talking about the various strokes which had made or marred their fortunes in the game. Mr. Hathaway was illustrating a back-hand-drive to Mrs. Bulmer. He was a kind man, always ready to help the rabbits to improve their status.

"What about a men's four?" suggested Dorothea Bold, "Here's Dr. Walker coming—it would be splendid to watch."

"Awfully sorry, I must go now," said the Vicar, struggling into his blazer, "The truth is my uncle is coming for two nights—"

He said good-bye to everybody and strode off. He was late, for the set had lasted longer than he had expected, he wondered if it would matter much if he broke into a run. Would it do Silverstream any harm to see its Vicar doubling along the High Street like an ordinary young man? Perhaps it was better just to walk quickly. When you became a Vicar it seemed necessary to stifle so many natural impulses.

Uncle Mike wouldn't mind him being a bit late—there was no foolishness of that kind about Uncle Mike—but Ernest was longing to see Uncle Mike after all these weeks, and to add to his pleasure it was delightful to be going to entertain Uncle Mike in his very own house.

The Reverend Michael Whitney was Ernest Hathaway's uncle, guardian, tutor, his father in God, and general confessor. He had looked after Ernest ever since the latter had been left an orphan at eleven years old. Ernest had spent all his holidays at the big old-fashioned country rectory, a corner of which was amply sufficient for the bachelor Rector's needs. Uncle and nephew—an oddly assorted couple—had walked and talked together and fished various small streams in the neighbourhood with more or less success. Uncle Mike had devoted one entire summer holiday to the important task of teaching Ernest to hold a straight bat, to keep his eye on the ball and step out to it. There was a certain telling pull to leg which Uncle Mike had imparted to Ernest and which had brought that young man laurels on more than one occasion.

Ernest owed everything to Uncle Mike, and he knew it and was grateful. It was nice to be able to entertain Uncle Mike in return. He was only coming for two days, of course, but Ernest had managed to include most of Uncle Mike's favourite dishes in the two days' menu. He hoped Mrs. Hobday would make a success of the dishes and not forget the orange salad, nor make the curry too hot.

As Ernest put his hand on the gate and vaulted lightly into his own garden he saw Uncle Mike had arrived, and had established himself in a deck chair on the lawn beneath the chestnut tree. Ernest waved his hand, and shouted, "Don't get up."

"I can't," said Uncle Mike (his figure was not of the type that rises easily from deck chairs), but his round fat face beamed with pleasure as Ernest came towards him across the lawn.

"Been teaching your parishioners to play tennis?" asked Uncle Mike chuckling.

"Trying to," smiled Ernest.

"Not getting stuck up, are you?"

"Trying not to," smiled Ernest again.

"How often have I warned you against the Sin of Pride?" demanded Uncle Mike with mock severity.

"Hundreds of times," Ernest agreed with mock humility.

They both laughed. It was very pleasant to joke with somebody who understood. Ernest was happy, the garden was full of the late afternoon golden sunshine and the song of birds, it was quiet and peaceful after the chatter of the tennis club. He sat down on the grass beside Uncle Mike and took off his hat.

"You're very comfortable here," Uncle Mike told him, "I like the look of that woman you've got—Mrs. Hobday, isn't it? Your book-case fits into the library nicely, doesn't it?"

"I'm too comfortable," Ernest replied tersely.

"You said so in your letter," agreed Uncle Mike, "I didn't know what you meant. How can a person be too comfortable? I suppose you have got one of your wild cat ideas—"

"Yes, I have," Ernest owned smiling a little, "at least you will probably think it is a wild cat idea."

"I have no doubt of it. Let's hear the worst."

"It's like this, Uncle Mike," Ernest said, clasping his hands round his knees and looking up at the other man with his frank gaze, "I've got too much money."

The fat man began to laugh, he laughed and wheezed and laughed again.

"You've got your asthma—" said Ernest anxiously.

"You're enough to give anyone—asthma," gasped Uncle Mike. "Absolutely unique in this planet—don't you know that the—whole world is on the verge of bankruptcy?"

"I'm not talking about the whole world," replied Ernest, "I'm talking about myself. Here am I, a strong healthy man, living in luxury—it's not right."

"You can help people, Ernest."

"There is nobody here that needs help," Ernest replied, "nobody really poor. Of course I can give money away to people, but it doesn't do much good—in fact I'm beginning to see that it does harm. People here think that I've got plenty of money and they come to me with tales —not always strictly true—and expect me to help them."

"Human nature," suggested Uncle Mike who had seen a good deal of human nature in his time.

"It's doing harm," Ernest told him, "my money is doing harm in this parish. Instead of giving, they take. It's not right. St. Paul said people should give to the church and support their priests."

"You find them grasping?" enquired Uncle Mike.

"Only because I'm well off—I'm sure of that, or at least nearly sure— They are only grasping because they think I can afford to give."

"Well, you can."

debasing the church—no living should be so poor that a single man couldn't live on it."

"The world is far from perfect," Uncle Mike said (he had lived in the world a long time and had learnt to take the bad with the good like a Gregory Powder in jam). "The world is far from perfect. There are lots of things wrong but you can't change the world."

"I don't want to change the world—at least perhaps I do want to, but I'm not such a fool as to think I can—that isn't the point. The point is that there's something wrong *here,* something wrong in my life and I've got to change it. I'm going to try and live on my stipend, Uncle Mike. After all a man should be able to live on very little. Look at St. Francis—"

"Well, go ahead then," said Uncle Mike who was beginning to feel rather weary, and had no wish to hear any more about St. Francis at the moment. "Go ahead and try to live on it for a bit. I don't suppose it will do you any harm. Try to keep your expenses down to three pounds a week—"

"That wouldn't be any good," interrupted Ernest, shaking his head, "I wouldn't be able to do it."

"Of course you wouldn't. Isn't that just what I've been telling you," asked Uncle Mike in exasperation. And how could he? How could Ernest, who had always had as much money as he could spend, suddenly start living on three pounds a week? (Especially when there was no real necessity for it. If you had to do a thing you just had to, and there was the end of it.) It was not that the boy was extravagant, exactly, but he always liked the best of everything, and, since his father had left him well pro-

"Yes, but the system is all wrong. The ⟨…⟩ back to front—oh it's so difficult to expla⟨…⟩ cried, waving his arms, "My mind is so full ⟨…⟩ I simply can't put it into words. Look at t⟨…⟩ look at St. Francis! They stripped themselve⟨…⟩ worldly goods (perhaps it was to teach people⟨…⟩ and they didn't starve, did they?"

"People fed them," replied Uncle Mike. "Peopl⟨…⟩ feed saints nowadays, they ask them why they a⟨…⟩ on the dole, and advise them to apply for parish re⟨…⟩

"Now don't be horrid, Uncle Mike," said Ernest, a⟨…⟩ he were, once more, only eleven years old. "You ⟨…⟩ understand if you want to. It's really quite simple—he⟨…⟩ am I living in luxury and getting fat and lazy. It's fright⟨…⟩ fully bad for me, and it's bad for other people too. Mrs. Hobday is wasteful and extravagant, and I don't care— why should I?—People come and ask me for money and I give it to them because it's less trouble to give it to them than to refuse—it's bad, bad, bad."

"Well, supposing it is bad—what is the remedy?" enquired Uncle Mike uneasily.

"I ought to be able to live on my stipend."

"You couldn't," replied Uncle Mike, "we went over all that before you came here. The living was offered to you because you had private means. It is such a poor living that no man who had not private means could take it—"

"That's another wrong thing," said Ernest excitedly. "A living shouldn't be offered to a man because he has private means—the labourer is worthy of his hire—it is vided for, there seemed to be no reason why he should not have the best of everything. Mr. Whitney had nothing to complain of about Ernest's spending. The boy spent wisely, and he had always been generous in a wise manner, but up to now, he had managed to go through his large yearly income without the slightest difficulty.

"I shan't be able to live on three pounds a week unless I have only three pounds a weeks to live on," Ernest was saying. "If I have only three pounds to spend, I can't spend more."

"Can't you?" enquired Mr. Whitney.

"Well, I shan't, anyhow," returned Ernest, "and what I want to do is this, I want to arrange for all my money to go to various charities, to go to them straight off just as it comes in, so that I shan't have it at all, even if I want it. You can get a deed of gift made out, or something like that, I suppose."

Mr. Whitney gasped.

"Here's a list of charities I've thought of," Ernest continued taking the list out of his pocket and handing it over. "You can probably suggest others. Of course the capital is tied up in the trust or I could have got rid of it much more easily—it's a pity."

"It is indeed," replied Mr. Whitney with deplorable sarcasm.

"I'm afraid it's going to be a bit of a nuisance for *you*," continued Ernest. "But I don't see how else I can arrange it, or who else I could get to do it for me—"

At this point Mr. Whitney ceased to listen, he knew Ernest sufficiently well to know that when Ernest got an idea into his head nothing would remove it. The only thing to be done was to safeguard the rash youth from the consequence of his wild cat scheme. If Uncle Mike took the management of the wild cat scheme into his own hands he could keep part of the money in reserve for Ernest when he wanted it—as he most assuredly would want it. Yes, that would be the best way—he would fall in with Ernest's plan and agree to distribute the money, and of course he would distribute the greater part of the money as Ernest wished; but part of it—say five hundred pounds—he would bank safely in Ernest's name so that it would be there if required, and if not required, it could be distributed at the end of the year. A year of poverty would do Ernest no harm—no harm at all. In fact it would be quite a valuable experience for Ernest. He had always had too much money, and too much money was bad—not that it seemed to have done Ernest any harm— Mr. Whitney had been worried about Ernest's affluence at one time, but when he saw that the boy was turning out all right in spite of the money, he had ceased to worry. It was strange how things worked out. Mr. Whitney had wished that Ernest might have the experience of poverty, and now Ernest had chosen to have it, and Mr. Whitney was worried. But there was really nothing to worry about, thought Mr. Whitney, comforting himself—he hated having to worry about things—because everything would be quite all right, and it would do Ernest good to count the pennies for a year. As long as the boy did not starve himself it would be all right, he must keep an eye on Ernest and see that he did not do that, of course.

They discussed the whole matter again after dinner—

the dinner had been very satisfactory—and it was decided that Ernest should sign a paper making over his year's income to Uncle Mike. Uncle Mike would then distribute the money to various charities as he thought best. Ernest didn't mind very much who got the money as long as he was rid of it—he had begun to look upon it as a burden—perhaps the burden that Christian had carried strapped to his back. At the end of a year the matter would be reconsidered. Mr. Whitney insisted on the year's probation—Ernest might want to marry, or he, himself, might die, anything might happen in a year—

"Good," said Ernest at last, stretching his arms, "I'm free."

"You are bound," thought Mr. Whitney but he was too wise to say so.

.   .   .   .   .

The next morning was a Saint's Birthday. Ernest and Uncle Mike walked down through the garden to the little church. The dew glistened on the grass like millions of diamonds, a lark was singing blithely.

Ernest thought that he had never enjoyed anything more deeply and perfectly than that Early Celebration, his heart was full of peace and happiness. It was too wonderful to talk about. After it was over they walked back through the sunlit garden, very near together in spirit.

"Do you think I'm a fool, Uncle Mike?" asked Ernest suddenly.

"If you think it the right thing to do you are right to do it," replied Uncle Mike quietly, "I believe the experience will be valuable."

CHAPTER V

Mrs. Walker

MRS. WALKER—the doctor's wife—was the first person in Silverstream to read *Disturber of the Peace*.

It was a foggy evening in October, very raw and damp for the time of year. Incidentally it was the fifth anniversary of the Walker's wedding day, and Sarah Walker had arranged a nice little dinner with all the doctor's favourite dishes to celebrate the occasion. But woman proposes and God disposes. Sarah knew when she heard the telephone bell that it was an urgent call.

It was quite absurd that she should know from the way the bell rang that it was an urgent call (it might just as well have been a telegram from her father remembering, belatedly, the occasion; or a message from Mrs. Featherstone Hogg bidding her to tea; or half a dozen other things of no importance whatsoever), but Sarah always declared that she knew the moment the telephone bell rang whether or not it was the hand of God summoning John from her side, and the strange thing was that she was very often right.

So, to-night, when the bell rang, and John ran downstairs to answer it, and returned to say, "It's the Sandeman baby arriving," she had already got over her disappointment about the anniversary dinner and had decided

to counter-order everything. She saw that the feast would
be but an empty farce without John, and besides, she did
not really enjoy salmon and oxtail herself, but only liked
to see John enjoying them. She would have a poached
egg and a cup of cocoa on a tray in the study.

"I'm frightfully sorry," said Dr. John, "but it can't be
helped. Don't wait up for me, Sally. Dear knows when
I'll be home—have you seen my rubber gloves?"

"There's a new pair in the drawer in the Surgery,"
Sarah said, "the others split. Never mind, we'll pretend
it's to-morrow. Be sure to make it a boy."

This was a recognised joke, so the doctor chuckled
dutifully.

"Take your muffler—the big grey one," Sarah added,
"it's a horrible night."

He kissed her and tore himself away.

The study was a cosy, rather shabby room with red
curtains, shaded lights, and a few good prints on its plain,
cream-coloured walls. Two deep leather arm-chairs stood
on either side of the fire.

Sarah sighed, drew back the curtains and peered out
at the night. She could not make out whether it was raining or not, the mist was heavy, and the street lamps
were surrounded by an orange-coloured nimbus. She felt
glad that she had made John take his muffler. She wondered how long Mrs. Sandeman's baby would take to
arrive. Her mind strayed back three years, it was on a
night like this that the twins had made their unexpected
appearance in the world—how horrible it had been! She
had never appreciated John at his full value until that

dreadful night, his kindness, his gentleness, his marvellous strength.

The parcel of books from the library was on the table. Sarah undid the string and turned them over with her long thin fingers. What had they sent this time? She rejected a fat biography, and dipped into a historical *réchauffé*—too dull. She was not in the mood for improving literature to-night, something light and amusing would pass the time better. What about this one—*Disturber of the Peace* by John Smith? She took it up and sank into the doctor's chair (it was the more comfortable of the two for John's weight had broken some of the springs, and flattened out the others, whereas Sarah's chair was still in its pristine state of bulgy hardness despite her five years' occupancy). Nell, the setter—who had never set at anything more exciting than a crow— lay down comfortably at Sarah's feet.

"I shall wait up for him however late it is," Sarah told her. "He can't be later than twelve, can he, Nell? I shall make him a cup of Benger's, and you shall have some too."

Nell wagged her tail, it was a pity she couldn't talk, but she understood every word you said—at least the Walkers declared that she did.

Sarah turned on the reading lamp and opened the book; quiet fell in the room as she began to read. She read quickly, for, since the advent of the twins, she had not been very strong, and people who are not very strong usually read a great deal, and people who read a great deal read quickly—besides the book ran along so easily, it swept you along—

Sarah laughed softly, and Nell stirred in her sleep and raised her beautiful head.

"You know, Nell, you miss a lot by not being able to read," Sarah told her. "These people are real live people—they are quite delicious."

Nell wagged her feathery tail, it was good when the goddess descended from the clouds and spoke to you, it gave you a cosy safe feeling in your inside.

Sarah read on. You couldn't help reading on. She read on till the fire died down and she had to rouse herself to mend it—dreadful if John returned cold and wet to find a half dead fire! As she put on a piece of coal, her mind, freed from the witchery of the printed page, swept back over what she had read. It might be Silverstream, she thought. Copperfield—Silverstream—how queer! And Major Waterfoot is exactly like Colonel Weatherhead, and Mrs. Mildmay might easily be Dorothea Bold—

She knit her brows and turned back the pages, growing more and more suspicious that this was no mere coincidence of names and personalities. She was looking for that bit about the doctor who had been sent for by Mr. Gaymer. Here it was—

"Dr. Rider was a tall, broad-shouldered Scotsman with a whimsical mouth and a pair of shaggy eyebrows; he brought a cheery atmosphere of health and vigour into the most hopeless of sickrooms. Children loved him and he could do what he liked with the most unmanageable mother's darling in Copperfield. But for those with imaginary ailments he had short shrift, and was apt to pre-

scribe castor oil for malingerers, a peculiarity which did
not endear him to their hearts."

It was John to the life. Sarah lay back in her chair and
laughed and laughed. Who on earth could have written
this book? Somebody in Silverstream obviously; somebody who knew everybody in Silverstream; one of John's
patients. She turned to the cover and saw that the author
called himself John Smith—it did not help very much,
anybody might be John Smith. Well, she thought, let's
go over all the people in Silverstream who might have
written it, and eliminate the impossibles, there aren't so
very many people in Silverstream. Could it be Colonel
Weatherhead? No, not his style at all, besides he could
never have written such a true and penetrating description of himself. Could it be Mr. Dunn? Too old and
dull. The new Vicar? Hardly, he was too busy with his
saints, and besides he had not had the time to get to know
the people of Silverstream as this man knew them. Mr.
Fortnum? No, the book was too unkind to him. Mr.
Snowdon? No again, and for the same reason. That left
the military people and Mr. Featherstone Hogg. Sarah
eliminated the military people, they were too taken up
with themselves and their own affairs, they were birds
of passage and scarcely knew Silverstream. Mr. Featherstone Hogg was far too much in awe of his wife to draw
her as she was drawn in this amazing book, for Mrs.
Horsley Downs was Mrs. Featherstone Hogg to the life.
Her languid elegance and her assumption of superiority
were touched in with inimitable skill. There was even
a description of one of her musical evenings when all

Copperfield had been bidden to listen to Brahms, and to partake of lukewarm coffee made of coffee essence and anchovy paste sandwiches— Mr. Featherstone Hogg would never have dared—

There was Stephen Bulmer of course, everyone in Silverstream knew that Mr. Bulmer was engaged in writing a book about Henry the Fourth. But this book was not about Henry the Fourth, and Sarah was pretty sure that Stephen Bulmer had not written it. She visualised his long thin face and the unpleasant lines upon it—deep lines from the base of his nose to the corners of his cynical mouth, and deep vertical lines between his brows.

Horrid thing!—thought Sarah—horrid, selfish, bad-tempered thing! She felt very strongly about Stephen Bulmer because Margaret Bulmer was her friend, and Meg had been such a gay, pretty little creature before she married him, and now she was neither pretty nor gay. Meg was a loyal soul and said very little about Stephen—even to Sarah—but Sarah knew that she was unhappy. As for the children, they were like two little mice, unnaturally quiet and subdued. They came to tea with the twins, sometimes, and were alarmed by the noise these robust infants made. "We're not allowed to play noisy games at home, it disturbs Daddy," small Stephen had said. She had told John what he had said, and John had been quite violent about it—John adored children.

Sarah had now exhausted the masculine element in Silverstream.—It might easily be a woman, she thought, perhaps if I read on I shall see—

She read on.

The book was doubly amusing now, she was always stopping to say, "It's Miss King, of course—Miss King *exactly*. And this is Olivia Snowdon. Oh, *what will* she say when she reads it?" Stopping to laugh, or to clap her hands softly, or to re-read some specially spicy description of a well known person.

It was midnight when she finished the first part of the book, a complete picture of the village; quiet and uneventful, very busy in its own estimation, the people full of gossip and curiosity about the affairs of their neighbours. So far not a thing had happened in Copperfield that could not have happened quite easily in Silverstream. The book was as uneventful as that, and yet it had not been dull. The first part occupied two thirds of the book and ended with the words, "And so the village of Copperfield slept beneath the stars."

Sarah looked up at the clock, it was midnight and John had not returned. She hoped there was nothing wrong. It was a first baby, of course, and first babies were apt to keep people waiting. Mrs. Sandeman was a nice little thing. Captain Sandeman was nice too. Quite young and very devoted to his wife—he would be having a wretched time, poor soul.

Sarah sighed, turned over the page and read on.

"Down the path from the hills came a boy playing on a reed pipe. He was a tall slim youth, barefooted, with a tattered goat-skin round his body. The sun shone upon his golden hair, and on the fine golden down which clothed his arms and legs. He came into Copperfield over the bridge. The clear notes of his pipe, mingled with the song of the river, came to the ears of Major Waterfoot who was digging in his garden. He straightened his back and looked up. The clear notes stirred something in his heart, something deep and elemental that had been slumbering for years. Mrs. Mildmay —on the other side of the road—heard the music also. It was music only in the sense that bird-song is music. It was—if such a thing can be imagined—the essence of bird-song. There was in it the love song of the male bird courting his mate, showing off his voice and boasting of brave deeds; and there was the call to adventure and the violence of battle; and lastly there was the satisfaction of mating, and the joy of the first egg. Mrs. Mildmay felt that her life was very empty. She looked across the road at the chimneys of the Major's house which could be seen above the treetops, and she sighed."

(Unlike Mrs. Mildmay, Sarah chuckled. She wondered if John Smith had meant her to chuckle—or not.)

The golden boy piped on through the High Street and up the hill, and then down again past the Vicarage and the old church which slumbered quietly by the river. Wherever he went he left behind him unrest and strange disturbance. People woke up, cast aside the fetters of conventional behaviour and followed the primitive impulses of their hidden natures. In some hearts the clear sweet music woke ambition, in some it woke memories of other days and prompted kind actions. Some of its hearers were driven to acts of violence, in others it kindled Love.

At least John Smith said that the music kindled love, but Sarah Walker—who knew something about that commodity, something more, she suspected, than John Smith—would have said that the emotion which the boy's pipe kindled in the hearts of its hearers was not love at all, but passion.

After this things began to happen in Copperfield—incredible things—Major Waterfoot discovered that he had loved Mrs. Mildmay for four years without ever having suspected it, so he rushed across the road and found Mrs. Mildmay in her garden, and proposed to her with a fervour which almost made Sarah's eyebrows disappear into her hair. (It may be remarked in parenthesis that Sarah's eyebrows were a distinctive feature, darker than her hair and beautifully arched.) This was the love scene which had made such an impression upon Mr. Abbott. It was a passionate scene, and had either been written by somebody who knew very little about such matters or somebody who knew a great deal. It was either very innocent—or else it wasn't.

Sarah read it twice and was still undecided about it, she left it and hastened on in the wake of the piping boy. Copperfield seethed with emotion. The very buns on Mrs. Silver's spotless counter were charged with electricity. Mr. Horsley Downs, who had never been capable of saying boo to a goose, developed a superiority complex, and, not content with bullying his wife in private, actually went the length of inserting a notice in the *Copperfield Times* to say that he would not be responsible for his wife's debts, and that she had been a chorus girl when he married her. Mrs. Nevis rose from her grave where she had been reposing peacefully for three years and turned up at her old home in the middle of a dinner party to the consternation of her husband and daughters (the Snowdons of course). She had always been a thorn in their flesh on account of her plain homely Yorkshire accent and habits, which she had never been able to eradicate on her elevation to a higher sphere of life. Her appearance at the feast, all smiles and affection after her three years' absence; and the horror-stricken family and embarrassed guests were drawn with the pen of a master. Then Edith Gaymer (Margaret Bulmer of course) eloped with old Mrs. Farmer's son (Harry Carter of course), and Mr. Mason (who was obviously Mr. Fortnum) serenaded Mrs. Myrtle Coates, playing all night long on a mandolin in her garden, and breathing his last beneath the firmly closed windows of his cruel charmer. In fact everyone did something queer, even Miss King and Miss Pretty (they were called Earle and Darling in the book but Sarah had got beyond troubling her head with such details) were seized with the spirit of adventure and decided to start upon an expedition to Samarkand. They each ordered a pair of riding breeches from Sharrods, and the book closed—very suitably—on that high note.

Sarah heard John's key in the front door as she raced through the last page.

. . . . .

"You don't mean to say you waited up!" Dr. John exclaimed, filling the doorway of the study with his huge bulk. He was half annoyed with her for disobeying orders, and wholly pleased to find a smiling and wide-awake Sarah.

"Was he a tired, cold boy, then?" she enquired twining her arms round his neck and kissing the wrinkles at the corners of his eyes.

"He was, rather," admitted John Walker laughing, but, strange to say, he felt—all at once—much less tired, and quite warm and comfortable.

He sat down by the fire, which, thanks to Sarah's care, was full of leaping, warming, cheering flames, and listened to her light footsteps going down the passage to warm his Benger's for him. What a blessed darling she was—thought Dr. John—and how lucky he was, and how unworthy of her dear warm love! There had been a time, after the twins were born, when he thought he might lose her. She seemed to be going downhill—down, down, down—and nothing that he could do, or think of, seemed to stop that steady decline. Not prayer, nor cod-liver oil, nor iron injections had seemed of the slightest avail, and he knew only too well where that hill ended. And then, quite suddenly and for no reason that he could see, she had begun to climb up again, and here she was, still with him; still spoiling him; still making him love her more and more and more every day.

He stretched his arms and yawned luxuriously—"Nice fire, Nell," he said. Nell agreed fervently.

The steps were coming back now along the passage—not quite such light careless steps this time, for Sarah was carrying the tray, and there were three bowls of Benger's on the tray and a tin of Marie biscuits—

"You don't mean to say—" said Dr. John.

"I promised her," replied Sarah gravely. She gave Nell her Benger's and put down the tray in front of the fire on a small stool. The doctor took his and stirred it slowly.

"Have a biscuit," Sarah said.

They sat in the two big chairs with their bowls of Benger's and the tin of Marie biscuits between them, and he began to tell her about his case. She was completely trustworthy and tremendously interested in all his cases.

and Dr. John had discovered long ago that it was not only a pleasure to talk to his wife about his work, but also that it was actually a help to him to put his difficulties and doubts before her. It helped to clear his mind and to make things plain to himself, and her intelligent questions often served to throw light upon puzzling problems. Sometimes Dr. John teased his wife about her interest in his work, and told her that she had picked his brains for five years, and that she thought she was as good a doctor as he was; and then, just to learn her, he would break into technicalities of medical jargon and Sarah would toss her head and say, "What's the good of all those silly Latin names? It doesn't help to cure people to call their diseases by names of five syllables. Of course you only do it to bamboozle the poor things and make them think that you are a great deal cleverer than you really are."

To-night he had a lot to tell Sarah, and Sarah listened with a little frown of concentration (she understood most of it, and wildly guessed at the rest, for she had read some of John's books on the sly, so that she might follow with a reasonable amount of intelligence when John talked to her). He told her what a ghastly time he had had, and how anxious he had been, and how they had telephoned to London for a specialist to come at once, but the baby decided to come first, and to come in a very unusual manner—a very eccentric troublesome sort of baby it had been. But everything was all right now, except that the Sandemans would have to pay the specialist for coming down from London in the middle of the night, and looking at Mrs. Sandeman and saying, "You all right? That's right," and looking at the baby and saying, "Nice little chap—he's all right," and going home again in his car.

"They won't mind," said Sarah wisely.

"Perhaps not, but I do," replied the doctor.

"Why? Would you rather he had come and said they were all wrong?"

He laughed, it was no use arguing with Sarah, she always got the best of it. Her dancing brain could make circles round his big, sure, slow-moving mind—

"You were very naughty to wait up," he told her, changing the subject. "I might have been there all night."

"It was that book," Sarah said. "I meant to sit up until twelve—and then I simply had to finish it. My dear, *you are in it.*"

"Me? Nonsense," he said, smiling at her excitement.

"It's not. You are," she told him eagerly. "Everyone in Silverstream is in it. It's all about Silverstream—"

"Well then, you are in it too, I suppose," he replied, humouring her, but not believing that it was actually true. "I can't be in it without you, or there would only be half of me—less than half of me—" he laughed comfortably.

"I'm not in it," she said, wrinkling those eyebrows of hers, for it had not struck her until this moment that she was about the only person in Silverstream who did not figure in *Disturber of the Peace*. "But of course you are only mentioned once or twice—just as a doctor who goes about giving his malingering patients castor oil—"

He shouted with laughter at that, and she had to remind him that the twins were sleeping overhead.

"—But you must read it, and then you'll see for yourself," she added, when he had moderated and apologised for his unbridled mirth, "Just you read it, Dr. John."

He took the book in his hands and looked at it idly.

"Not *now,* for Mercy's sake," she gasped, seizing it from him and hiding it behind her back. She had experienced the strange allure of *Disturber of the Peace,* and had no wish to see him start upon it at this hour of the morning.

"You silly kitten!" he exclaimed humorously, "you don't really suppose I would sit up all night reading a novel? Tell me about it while I finish my Benger's."

She complied, knowing that it was good for him to take his mind off his work before he slept. He was such a conscientious old darling, worrying himself to death about every case, heartbroken if one of his patients slipped through his fingers, taking all the blame if things went wrong, and giving all the credit to Nature or nursing if things went right.

"Well, you're Dr. Rider," she told him, clasping her lovely hands round one knee, and looking up at him with a whimsical smile. "You've gone up in the world, you see. And Colonel Weatherhead is Major Waterfoot—so he's come down. And Barbara Buncle is Elizabeth Wade —I can't see the connection there, but she *is.* And Dorcas is Susan—she's frightfully good. And Miss King and Miss Pretty are Miss Earle and Miss Darling, and Mrs. Featherstone Hogg is Mrs. Horsley Downs—she is screamingly funny— And the Bulmers are the Gaymers, and Mrs. Dick is Mrs. Turpin and Mr. Fortnum is Mr. Mason and the Sandemans—"

"Stop, stop!" cried the doctor.

She stopped and sat there smiling at him and swinging her foot a little.

"Is this all *true?*" he asked. The question was quite a legitimate one, for Sally had a puckish sense of humour, and more than once she had spun him tales of amazing events full of the most circumstantial details, and he had followed her, blundering along credulously in his elephantine way, only to be told at the end that the whole thing had been fabricated in her own busy head. So, to-night, the suspicion arose in his mind that this was merely one of Sally's "take ins," and that in a moment or two she would burst out laughing and tell him that he was a darling old donkey and that she had made it all up.

"It's all true, honour bright," Sally said, nodding at him gravely, too much taken up with the queerness of it all to resent the aspersions on her veracity.

"Well what do we *do,* then?" he asked, standing up and stretching himself. "It can't be a very exciting book if it is all about Silverstream—Silverstream's worst enemy couldn't accuse it of being exciting. What *happens* in the book? What do we all *do?*"

"Oh, my dear!" she cried, "that's just it—what you all *do.*"

"It seems to me there are breakers ahead," said Dr. John solemnly.

CHAPTER VI

Mrs. Carter's Tea-Party

THE first breaker broke a few days later at old Mrs. Carter's tea-party, and the full force of the wave fell upon the head of Barbara Buncle. They were all sitting in the drawing-room round the Jacobean gate-legged table, and there was a bowl of chrysanthemums—the very last, Mrs. Carter assured them—in the centre. Barbara knew when she saw the china that Mrs. Featherstone Hogg was expected, and her spirits fell a degree for she did not like Mrs. Featherstone Hogg. Barbara had met Dorothea Bold on the door-step and they had gone in together, Miss King and Miss Pretty were there already. But not for these would Mrs. Carter have produced her best eggshell cups and saucers, that filmy drawn-thread-work tea-cloth, those lusciously bulging cream-buns.

"Agatha said she would look in later," said Mrs. Carter in confidential tones. "She's such a busy bee we must take her when we can get her."

Mrs. Featherstone Hogg was less like a busy bee than anybody Barbara could think of. She was tall and willowy and tired, so tired that you could not help feeling it was good of her to trouble to speak to you at all. She did not speak much of you, of course, if you were an unimportant person like Barbara Buncle. Barbara sometimes wondered what it was that gave Mrs. Featherstone Hogg her social position in Silverstream. Why did everyone flock to her dull parties and consume the poor fare provided for them there? Why did everybody do what she told them to do? Why did old Mrs. Carter produce her best china and linen for Agatha's delectation? Was it because of her rude manner? or was it because she bought her clothes from the most expensive place in London?

It was this tired and languid lady that Mrs. Carter compared to a busy bee and something shook in Barbara's interior at the ineptness of the description; but it would never do to laugh, nobody in Silverstream laughed at Mrs. Featherstone Hogg. Barbara turned quickly to her nearest neighbour, who happened to be Angela Pretty, and asked her if she had put in her bulbs yet. Of course it was just like Mrs. Featherstone Hogg to say she would "look in later"—she was not like an ordinary mortal who was expected to arrive at the time appointed for her arrival—Barbara made a mental note of the phrase and then remembered with a twinge of disappointment that *Disturber of the Peace* was finished, and that nothing more could be added to its teeming pages. Perhaps I *will* write another, she thought to herself in surprise.

Angela was twittering on about her bulbs—the exact amount of moisture they required and the exact number of days one should keep them in the dark to promote the growth of healthy roots—it was very dull. Barbara detached one ear from Angela to listen to what the others were talking about.

"She is coming to me to-morrow," Mrs. Carter was saying. "Such a sudden decision, but of course I am delighted to have the dear child. I am putting her in the old nursery, it is the pleasantest room on that floor, and has a delightful view over the river. It gets all the morning sun, and sunshine is just what she requires after her operation—plenty of sunshine and fresh milk, the doctor said—so of course dear Harry thought of me at once."

Barbara could not see why he had thought of old Mrs. Carter in connection with the doctor's prescription. Sunlight and milk were no part of the good lady's *régime*. She hardly ever went out of doors even in the summer, unless to go to Church or to tea with a friend, and Barbara had never beheld her neighbour imbibing milk except as an accompaniment to a cup of tea. But of course Harry was her son, so he must know her better even than Barbara did; or, perhaps, his thoughts went back to his childhood and milk puddings, and he connected his mother with these—it was rather far fetched—but the subconscious mind was so marvellous nowadays—

"I don't think you heard that, Barbara, dear," said Mrs. Carter kindly, "you were talking to Angela. Harry is going out to India with his regiment and dear little Sally is coming to me to be built up after her appendicitis. *Built up,*" repeated Mrs. Carter obviously delighted with the term, and nodding her beautifully waved grey head with solemn emphasis.

"How nice for you—and for her of course," exclaimed Barbara. She had lived for so long amongst these people and had suffered so many afternoon teas that she was able to say the expected thing without thinking about it at all. You simply put a penny in the machine and the expected thing came out at once, all done up in a neat little packet, and suitably labelled. The machine worked without any effort on Barbara's part, it even worked when the real Barbara was absent and only the shell, dressed in its shabby garments, remained sitting upright upon its chair. The real Barbara often flew away like that and took refuge from the dullness and boredom of Silverstream in the scintillating atmosphere of Copperfield.

"It will be nice for us all in Silverstream—there are so few young people here," said Angela Pretty prettily.

At this moment—Barbara was just handing Mrs. Carter her cup for some more tea—the door opened and Mrs. Featherstone Hogg burst in. She appeared to be carrying something in one hand, holding it away from her as if it were a poisonous reptile or a loathsome toad.

"Filth!" she cried. "Filth!" and flung it on to the table all amongst the cakes and china and chrysanthemums. It lay there, half resting upon a dish of cream-buns, and half propped up against the damson jam—it was a copy of Barbara Buncle's book.

"My dear Agatha!" exclaimed Mrs. Carter with pardonable surprise. The rest of the party was too aghast for speech, it was as if a bomb-shell had burst among them; even Barbara was amazed and pained at the transformation which her simple story had wrought upon the elegant, languid personality of Mrs. Featherstone Hogg.

"You are in it too," said "dear Agatha," incoherently to her hostess. "You haven't read it, I suppose, or you wouldn't be sitting there like a graven image. You wear a wig, you know, and false teeth, and you put pectin in your damson jam to make it set, and your son elopes with a married woman—Mrs. Farmer is your name."

"She's mad," whispered Mrs. Carter white to the lips.

Mrs. Featherstone Hogg laughed shrilly. "Oh no, I'm not mad," she said, "I'm quite sane, I assure you. I intend to have the man up for libel. Edwin has gone up to town to see our lawyer about it—I sent him straight up in the Daimler. The man will find he can't trifle with *me*. He'll be sorry he was born before I've done with him.—You're in it too," she added, pouncing upon Dorothea Bold so fiercely that the poor woman nearly choked on a piece of dry seed-cake. "And you—and you—and you," she continued, pointing with her heavily ringed fingers at the remaining three guests.

Miss King found her voice first. Perhaps it was the manliness of her attire that gave her confidence in her own capabilities, or perhaps it was her confident and capable nature which promoted the manliness of her attire. It does not really matter which, the important thing is that Miss King believed she was a capable sensible person and this belief was a great help to her in emergencies such as the present one.

"Do you mean that we are all described in that book?" demanded Miss King in her deep quiet voice, and she pointed to the somewhat battered copy of *Disturber of the Peace* which still lay dejectedly upon the buns.

"I've told you so, haven't I?" shrieked Mrs. Featherstone Hogg. "Are you all deaf or imbecile that you can't understand plain English?"

Barbara Buncle never knew how she got away from that dreadful tea-party. She had a vague idea that she had made her exit in the wake of Miss King, and that Miss King had remarked upon the beauty of the night and added that Mrs. Featherstone Hogg had rather given herself away, hadn't she? Some people's elegance was only skin deep, scrape off a little bit of the veneer and you got the real wood—common deal in this case, Miss King suspected. Barbara made some non-committal reply, and staggered home—fortunately it was only next door— she sat down in her comfortable chair beside her own cheerful fire and held her head.

Presently she rose and went to the telephone. She must speak to Mr. Abbott. If anyone could help her he could, but she did not think anyone could help her. It was a sort of blind instinct that made her fly to Mr. Abbott.

They told her at the office that he had gone home some time ago, and, after an agonising delay, and much consultation among themselves, they consented to give her the telephone number of his private residence. Barbara was almost in tears when she got on to him at last.

"It's going splendidly," his cheerful voice proclaimed. "Nothing to worry about. I've put a second impression in hand—we shall probably need a third—"

"But they *know*," she squeaked. "They know it's them —they are going to start libel actions—"

"They won't do anything of the sort," he assured her in his comforting deep voice. "No lawyer would look at it. Now don't worry, and don't say another word over the telephone. I'll come over and see you to-morrow afternoon and you can tell me all about it."

Barbara put down the receiver and stood there for a few minutes looking at it thoughtfully.

CHAPTER VII

First Fruits

"*THERE'S* absolutely nothing to worry about," said Mr. Abbott. He was standing in front of Miss Buncle's fire in Miss Buncle's comfortable, though rather shabby, and old-fashioned drawing-room and smiling at her cheerfully. "Any respectable lawyer would turn down the case. He would look a fool appearing in court with a case like that, and his clients would be made to look worse fools. We have only got to say, 'The portrait which you find so ugly was never intended to be a portrait of you. If you really think you are like that we are sorry for you and offer you our sincere sympathy.'"

Barbara actually smiled. It had taken Mr. Abbott half an hour's hard work to obtain that smile. Now that he had obtained it, he liked it immensely, and he liked her teeth—he had decided quite definitely that they were real.

"Of course they don't know it's me," Barbara said hopefully.

(It was curious, Mr. Abbott thought, that a woman who could write good English should be unable to speak it, he had noticed this little peculiarity of Miss Buncle's before, it amused and intrigued him.)

"No," he agreed, "and you are perfectly safe with *us*."

"Oh, I hope so," cried Barbara, "I should have to leave here if they found out who it was."

"Surely it is not as bad as all that!"

"Quite as bad," Barbara told him nodding emphatically, "of course they haven't all read it yet but Mrs. Featherstone Hogg is furious, and Mrs. Carter doesn't like the bit about her wig and the pectin in her jam. She is frightfully proud of her damson jam, you see, but I'm sure there is pectin in it, I'm sure it would never set like that without pectin—mine won't— Besides I saw the packets in the grocer's basket."

She was beginning to talk now. Mr. Abbott urged her on with encouraging noises and nods. He had already noticed that Miss Buncle was either monosyllabic and completely inarticulate, or else overpowered by a stream of words which forced themselves between her lips like water from a bursting dam.

"I suppose I should never have written it," continued Miss Buncle sadly. "But you see I had to do *something*— I told you about the dividends, didn't I?—and the only thing I could do was to write a book, and the only kind of book I could write was about people I knew. And then another thing was that I never really thought or believed *in my bones* that the book would be published. I just finished it and sent it up—"

"And why to *me?*" enquired Mr. Abbott with much interest. "I mean why did you send the book to *me?* Perhaps you had heard from somebody that our firm—"

"Oh, no," she exclaimed, "I knew nothing at all about publishers. You were the first on the list—alphabetically —that was all."

Mr. Abbott was somewhat taken aback—on such trifles hang the fates of best sellers!

"And then when you took it," continued Miss Buncle, quite obvious of his reaction to her naïve admission, "when you actually said you would publish it, I was so excited that I forgot about the people being so like the people here. It seemed so funny to be a real author—so important somehow. When I thought about it all (which wasn't often), I thought, perhaps they'll never see it or read it at all. Heaps of books are published and you never hear about them. And even if they do read it they'll never think it could possibly be them—in a book I mean. But really and truly I scarcely even thought about it at all," said Miss Buncle, trying hard to be absolutely exact, and to explain her extraordinary density in the matter.

"It was quite natural," Mr. Abbott told her.

"But of course I see now that I should never have written it at all."

"That would have been a pity," said Mr. Abbott with his mind on the mounting sales of *Disturber of the Peace*. "A pity for me, and a pity for you. The book is doing so well." He took out his pocket-book and produced a large white note which he laid down beside her on the table. "Just a little something on account," he added, smiling at her surprise. "I thought perhaps you might be glad to have it with Christmas coming on. I shall want a receipt of course."

Barbara looked at it—she could not believe her eyes—and then she looked at Mr. Abbott.

"But I couldn't—" she said tremulously.

"My dear girl, I am not a philanthropist. You've earned

it," said Mr. Abbott. "I didn't bring you a cheque, because if a cheque from us goes through your bank it might give the show away. Banks are supposed to be sound-proof," said Mr. Abbott talking on to give this extraordinary woman time to get over the shock of receiving a hundred pounds. "But my experience is if you want to keep a thing dark the fewer people who know about it the better. So you can pay that in, and nobody will know where it has come from. . . . You can say it is a present from your uncle in Australia," added Mr. Abbott chuckling. "Make him a sheep-farmer with a benevolent disposition, or a gold digger who has struck lucky if you like."

It took him ten minutes to convince the extraordinary woman that this was her own money which she had earned by the sweat of her brow, and that there was more coming which she would receive in due course.

Mr. Abbott had said that he was not a philanthropist, and he was not. He was merely a man who did business in his own way. He called himself a student of psychology. Authors—he was wont to say—were kittle cattle. He prided himself on his management of authors. Mr. Abbott had produced the hundred pound note for several reasons. To begin with, *Disturber of the Peace* had earned it and was well on its way to earn more. Of course he need not have paid Miss Buncle anything on account, there was nothing about it in the contract. If he had wanted to be strictly business-like he would have waited until February—when his books were made up—and sent her a cheque for what was due, but he did not want to be strictly business-like. It amused him to surprise and please people, and perhaps especially to surprise and please Miss Buncle. Then Miss Buncle was distressed about the stir caused by her book and Mr. Abbott knew of nothing more soothing to worry or distress than a nice round fat cheque (or bank note). Lastly—and this was the most subtle reason of all—lastly he wanted another book from Miss Buncle, and he wanted it soon, before the *éclat* of *Disturber of the Peace* had died away and John Smith had faded out of the fickle memories of the great British Public, and he knew that—paradoxical as it might sound—a nice fat cheque (or bank note) was not only a soothing and comforting balm to troubled authors, but it was also a spur.

Miss Buncle signed the receipt for a hundred pounds on account of her novel with a trembling hand. It was not nearly such a neat signature as that which had appeared upon the contract. He didn't know—he couldn't possibly have known—that in spite of all her economies, in spite of stinting and scraping, of eschewing meat, and eating margarine instead of butter, and diluting the milk, and buying the very cheapest tea that floated like dust on the top of your cup, Miss Buncle's account at the bank was overdrawn by seven pounds fifteen shillings and would soon have been overdrawn by more; for the dividends, which had been steadily decreasing, had now practically ceased.

There were tears in Miss Buncle's eyes as she signed the receipt and folded up the amazing note. Fancy that tiny piece of paper representing so much! It really *was* rather astonishing (when you come to think of it) what that tiny piece of paper represented—far more than a hundred sovereigns (although in modern finance less). It represented food and drink to Barbara Buncle, and, perhaps, a new winter coat and hat; but, above all, freedom from that awful nightmare of worry, and sleep, and a quiet mind.

CHAPTER VIII

Miss King and Mr. Abbott

*M*R. *ABBOTT* was very busy when Miss King called to see him, but he agreed to "give her ten minutes." The truth was Mr. Abbott could not resist the temptation of seeing Miss King, for she had written on her card "re *Disturber of the Peace.*"

Miss Buncle's book intrigued Mr. Abbott, and Miss Buncle herself intrigued him. She was such a queer mixture of simplicity and subtlety (at least he thought she was). She spoke bad grammar and wrote good English. She was meticulously truthful in all she said (it was almost as if she were on oath to speak the truth, the whole truth and nothing but the truth all day long and every day of the week). She lived her solitary life amongst all those people, with her tremendous secret locked up in her breast; going about amongst them looking as if butter wouldn't melt in her mouth, but taking careful note of all they said and did, and then going quietly home and writing it all down. They were after her now like a pack of hounds, but they didn't know that the fox was in the very midst of them, under their very noses, disguised as one of themselves—it was a piquant situation and Mr. Abbott fully appreciated it.

"But I must be very careful," said Mr. Abbott to himself, as the imp went away to fetch Miss King for the ten minutes' interview, "I must be very careful."

Miss King accepted the chair which Mr. Abbott offered her with his pleasant old-fashioned bow, but declined a cigarette. You couldn't smoke a man's cigarettes and then threaten him with a libel action.

"I have only a very few minutes to spare, Miss—er—" —he glanced at the card which lay on the table—"Miss King," said Mr. Abbott blandly.

"A very few minutes will be sufficient for my purpose," replied Miss King in her most capable manner. "I have merely called to request you to withdraw *Disturber of the Peace* from circulation."

"Dear me!" said Mr. Abbott, blinking, "that is surely very—er—drastic."

"Desperate diseases demand desperate remedies," said Miss King sententiously.

"And what is your objection to the novel?" enquired Mr. Abbott gently. "It seems to me a very harmless sort of novel. I would not compare it for a moment with a desperate disease. In fact I found it amusing—light reading of course, but distinctly amusing—"

"It is a horrible book," said Miss King, losing a little of her business-like calm. "It is causing a great deal of misery and trouble to innocent people—"

"How can that be?" wondered Mr. Abbott aloud.

"You will withdraw it immediately," continued Miss King, taking no notice of his interruption. "You will withdraw the book from circulation. I have been empowered by several people in Silverstream to come to-day and ask you to withdraw it."

"And if I refuse?" enquired Mr. Abbott softly.

"You will not refuse," Miss King told him, trying to make her voice sound confident, "you do not wish to— to be had up for libel, I suppose."

"No," said Mr. Abbott simply.

"Well, you will," declared Miss King. She knew that she was putting her case badly. She knew—although she had not admitted it to herself—that her case was already lost. She was nervous, and her flow of language—business-like language—had deserted her. Coming up in the train she had overwhelmed Mr. Abbott with her eloquence and brought him to his knees. But Mr. Abbott was so different from what she had imagined, so quiet and calm and sure of himself, so benign looking. If he had been angry or rude she could have dealt with him much more easily. She had never imagined that a publisher was like this.

"I'm afraid you must be more explicit," said Mr. Abbott with unruffled calm.

"I thought I had been explicit."

"Oh, no," he said, shaking his head at her sorrowfully, "you have told me what you want, but surely you can't expect me to comply with the request of a complete stranger without any adequate reason being offered. My business is run on strictly business lines, I do it to make money," said Mr. Abbott, lifting his brows apologetically.

"So I supposed," said Miss King with some sarcasm. "And that is the reason I'm here. You will save money if you withdraw the book immediately. You ask me to be explicit and I will be explicit. My friends and I intend to put the matter into the hands of our lawyers and you will find yourself involved in a costly action for libel unless the book is withdrawn immediately—that is the position in a nutshell."

"Have you consulted your lawyer, Miss King?" asked Mr. Abbott, still with that peaceful smile.

"I fail to see how that affects the position."

"It doesn't, really," he admitted, "I only wondered if you had. In any case your suggestion is impracticable. The novel is selling well and—"

"I don't care how it is selling—if it is selling well that is all the more reason to stop it," cried Miss King incoherently. "How would you like to be pilloried in a horrible book like that? Every small detail of your domestic life laid bare—your most sacred secrets dragged into the limelight and trampled upon—how would you like it, I ask you?"

"My dear lady!" exclaimed Mr. Abbott, surprised and pained by her vehemence, "my dear lady, people often imagine that their personalities have been drawn upon in a novel. I put it to you that you are mistaken, that the secrets exposed in *Disturber of the Peace* are not your secrets at all. Authors must be credited with a certain amount of imagination, you know. They seldom draw their portraits from life—"

"Portraits!" she cried. "This is not a portrait, it's a photograph."

Mr. Abbott looked at her and decided that it was. She was Miss Earle of course. Miss Buncle had drawn her with a faithfulness which was almost staggering. He felt a little annoyed with Barbara for a moment—it was scarcely necessary, for instance, to have mentioned that small mole upon her chin and the three longish hairs which grew from it. The mole would have been omitted from a portrait of Miss King, or else idealised and made to look like a beauty spot, but in a photograph there was no such evasion of the truth—

He realised suddenly that Miss King had changed her tactics; she was appealing now to his better nature; she was throwing herself on his mercy; she had begun to tell him her life-story—or at least that part of it which she considered relevant to the occasion.

"So there we were," she was saying, "both orphans, without anybody dependent upon us, nor any near relations. I had a house, larger than I required. Miss Pretty was homeless. We both possessed small incomes, too small to enable us to live alone in comfort. I was about to sell my house (for I could not live in it alone) when the suggestion was made that we should pool our resources and live together—what more natural? By this means we were enabled to live comfortably in my house. The companionship was pleasant, the financial problem was solved. There was a book some years ago," continued Miss King incoherently, "it distressed us very much at the time, but it had nothing to do with us, and I decided to ignore it—this book is far worse—it's all about us— it's far far worse—"

"You have misread the novel entirely," said Mr. Abbott uncomfortably. "I assure you that you have misread it. There is nothing in it to cause you the slightest distress. The author is a particularly simple-minded—er—person."

"But Samarkand!" exclaimed Miss King, trying to

keep the sound of tears out of her voice. "Why Samarkand of all places?"

"I don't know anything about Samarkand," said Mr. Abbott truthfully, "but to me it has an adventurous sound, and I feel convinced that that was what it was intended to convey—"

"A dreadful Eastern place—full of vice and—and horribleness," cried Miss King.

"No, no. *Adventure*," replied Mr. Abbott, waving his hands wildly—"Deserts and camels, you know, and Sheiks and Arabs riding about on milk-white steeds, and oases with palms—all that sort of thing. But at the same time," he added retreating into safety again, "at the same time I feel sure you are mistaken and the characters are surely imaginary—purely imaginary. It is merely an unfortunate coincidence that they seem to bear some resemblance—"

"Who is this John Smith?" demanded Miss King suddenly, interrupting Mr. Abbott's flow of eloquence with a lamentable lack of ceremony, "Tell me that. Who is the man? He must be somebody living in Silverstream of course, but who? That's the question. Bulmer is the only man I know of who writes books, and he would not make his wife elope with another man—it's simply unthinkable—"

"I'm afraid our time is up," said Mr. Abbott, looking at his watch regretfully. "I have given you rather longer than I intended, but it has been a most interesting conversation—"

"I shall remain here until you tell me who John Smith

is," said Miss King firmly—he could scarcely throw her out, she reflected.

Mr. Abbott smiled and shook his head. "Quite impossible, my dear lady," he said. "Besides, why should you suppose that you would know him?"

"Because he knows me," replied Miss King with incontrovertible logic.

"I feel sure you are mistaken," said Mr. Abbott.

"I shall remain here until you tell me," said Miss King.

It looked as though they had reached an impasse, but Mr. Abbott was a man of resource—there were other rooms in his office. He rose quickly and reached the door before Miss King had perceived his intention. "By all means remain, here," he invited her with his courtly little bow. "You will excuse me if I leave you—I have an appointment" and was gone.

Miss King realised at once that she had been outgeneralled. She sat still for a few moments, looking round the cosy little room and wondering whether the clue to the mystery might be found here by a determined woman. Surely it must lie at her hand, here in the sanctum of the senior partner of Abbott & Spicer's firm. The walls were papered with light brown, the carpet was thick and soft and brown, the curtains were of dark brown velvet. On a small oak table in the corner stood a book-trough containing two large dictionaries, a copy of "Who's Who", and a London Post Office Directory. In the other corner was a small safe. A large glass-fronted bookcase took up the length of one wall. Above the mantelpiece there was an oak shelf containing Abbott & Spicer's latest publications. Miss King rose from her chair and took down *Disturber of the Peace*. She glanced through it with a shudder of distaste, but there was nothing to be learned from it—no clue to be gained as to who had perpetrated it—it was merely an ordinary copy of the book such as could be bought at any bookstall for the exorbitant sum of seven and sixpence.

Gaining confidence, Miss King now turned to the desk —it was a large oak desk and it stood in the middle of the room, carefully arranged so that the light from the window should fall over Mr. Abbott's left shoulder. The drawers of the desk were all locked except one, in which was an assortment of paper and envelopes. On the desk stood a telephone of the usual pattern. There was also a manuscript entitled, *The Flames of Hell,* by Hesa Feend. Mr. Abbott had been considering its merits and demerits when Miss King had interrupted his morning's work. Miss King glanced at it with disgust. The large sheet of blotting paper on the desk was virgin, save for a signature which Miss King decided was that of Mr. Abbott himself. The waste paper basket contained two circulars, and a review of Mr. Shillingsworth's latest novel just published by the firm. Nothing remained to be investigated but the safe. Miss King investigated the safe fruitlessly.

She glanced once more round the room—how tantalising it was to be here in this room with the clue so near and not to be able to find it! If I could only find out who it was, she thought, with a sigh. The room lay before her, perfectly open. Mr. Abbott had given her the freedom of the room, but she had found nothing. Was it any use waiting in case Mr. Abbott might return, or Mr. Spicer might come in to get something? She thought not.

She went over to the door and put her hand on the knob. Had he locked her in, she wondered suddenly? Mr. Abbott had done nothing so ungentlemanly, the handle turned, the door opened, Miss King was standing in the passage. With some little difficulty she found her way down various long corridors and iron steps, and in a few moments she had reached the street.

Miss King was in such a hurry to shake the dust of Abbott & Spicer's from her feet that she ran straight into the arms of a man—a tall thin man—who was about to enter the building.

"Mr. Bulmer!" she exclaimed in amazement.

Mr. Bulmer looked as startled as herself and somewhat sheepish into the bargain.

"If you have come to see that man it's no good," she told him breathlessly. "He's a perfect fool" (she had forgotten for the moment that he had outwitted her), "one of those stolid smiling fools that nothing will move or excite."

"I don't want to move or excite Mr. Abbott," replied Mr. Bulmer sourly. "I merely want to find out the name of the man who wrote that novel about Silverstream. Mrs. Featherstone Hogg lent it to me yesterday and I sat up reading it half the night. Have *you* read it?" he asked, looking down at Miss King with sudden suspicion.

"Of course—that's why I'm here."

"You don't like it—eh?" he asked, smiling in rather an unpleasant sort of way.

"No more than you do," retorted Miss King, who was always at her best if people turned nasty. She wondered if she should press home her point—men did not care to be deserted by their wives. It was not true, of course. Margaret Bulmer had not really gone off with Harry Carter—at least if she had, Miss King had not heard of it —but the book said that she had. The book had exposed Mr. Bulmer's selfishness and cruelty so frankly that you felt quite glad Margaret had escaped from him; you did not blame her for it. On the other hand Mr. Bulmer was angry about the book, he might be a good ally in the fight against Abbott & Spicer and the mysterious John Smith. Miss King decided not to press the point home.

"The book must be withdrawn from circulation," said Miss King firmly.

Mr. Bulmer laughed bitterly. "So that was your idea. Why don't you go to the zoo and ask the lion to give you his ration of meat? You would be more likely to succeed."

"What do you mean?" she enquired.

"I mean, *Disturber of the Peace* is a best seller. A publisher doesn't get hold of a best seller every day of the week. Abbott won't withdraw it—he'd be a fool if he did."

"What are *you* going to do?" she asked him. "You're going to do something, I suppose—you've come here to see the man, haven't you?"

"My idea was merely to get hold of the author's name and strangle him slowly," replied Mr. Bulmer with a nasty smile. "Quite a primitive idea compared with yours, isn't it? But more likely to succeed—"

"I asked him that too," said Miss King.

"Well, keep on asking," Mr. Bulmer replied sarcastically. "Perhaps in time he will get tired of saying no.

Come up and see him constantly—publishers love to have their mornings wasted for them—put off your visit to Samarkand for a few weeks, and sit upon Mr. Abbott's doorstep."

"Samarkand!" cried Miss King, goaded to frenzy, "I'm not going to Samarkand—why should I? What's it got to do with you where I go? I shall go to Samarkand if I like—"

She put up her umbrella and plunged away from him down the teeming street.

CHAPTER IX

Mrs. Bulmer

*M*ARGARET BULMER knew quite well that something had upset Stephen but she did not know what it was. He had said nothing to her about the book which had been lent to him by Mrs. Featherstone Hogg, nor had he offered it to her to read. On the contrary when Stephen Bulmer had finished the book he had looked about his study for some safe place to hide it, and, finding none really safe from the prying eyes of wives and housemaids, he had deliberately made up the fire, and, tearing the book to pieces in his thin claw-like hands, had fed it to the flames. Slowly and bit by bit *Disturber of the Peace* had been reduced to ashes in Mr. Bulmer's grate. He felt a sort of queer satisfaction in the rite. The copy belonged to Mrs. Featherstone Hogg, of course—she had paid seven and sixpence for it—but that didn't matter in the least. He was not afraid of Mrs. Featherstone Hogg, if she asked for the book it would give Mr. Bulmer the greatest pleasure to reply that he had burnt it—he hoped she would ask for it.

After he had finished burning *Disturber of the Peace* he went up to bed very quietly. Margaret had been in bed for hours. He took great care not to waken her, for somehow he did not want to face Margaret's clear gaze just now. He was not really like David Gaymer of course, but perhaps he had been just a little inconsiderate now and then.

Margaret was not asleep, she was merely pretending to be asleep because it was easier, and she was so tired. She was surprised when Stephen came up to bed quietly instead of stamping about in his dressing-room as he usually did, and throwing his boots on the floor. She was even more surprised when he crawled into bed without putting on the light and telling her that his hot-water bottle was stone cold. She wondered vaguely if Stephen were ill, but decided that he couldn't be ill, or he would have wakened her up to find the aspirin tablets and to warm some milk for him—she drifted off to sleep.

In the morning Stephen was still "queer." He came down to breakfast shaved and dressed instead of having breakfast in bed as he usually did, and, instead of immersing himself in *The Times,* he was quite conversational. He even spoke kindly to the children (who were too astounded at this unusual behaviour to answer him at all) and asked Margaret what she was going to do with herself—*he* was going to London by the ten-thirty. Margaret replied that she was going to give the children their lessons. She caught him gazing at her in a queer way when he thought she was busy with the tea-cups. She was relieved when he departed to catch his train.

Margaret thought about it all as she ordered the dinner and gave the children their lessons. Of course it was quite a usual thing for Stephen to sit up half the night; he said he could write better when the house was quiet. The house was as quiet all day as it was possible for any house to be. Everyone was provided with carpet slippers and there was soundproof felt on the stairs. If Stephen were not writing, he was asleep, or thinking, and, whichever of these pursuits he was engaged upon, the house had to be quiet. At the slightest sound the door of the study would fly open and Stephen would emerge white with fury and stamp up and down the hall raging like a maniac, and demanding of his Maker why he could not get a little peace in his own house. Sometimes Margaret took the two children out into the woods for a picnic lunch, and urged them to run about and make a noise. She tried to make them play games such as she had played in her childhood, and to shout and sing, but it was no good. The children were like two little mice. She couldn't get a loud sound out of them. Margaret worried about the children quite a lot, it was not natural for children to be so quiet, but she could do nothing. They were terrified of Stephen of course, that was the reason of it—terrified of his rages and his loud strident voice. They would creep past his door like ghosts, they would stop suddenly in the midst of their quiet games and listen with strange intent looks upon their little faces.

Now that Stephen had departed for the train the house woke up a little. Margaret could hear the two maids talking in the kitchen, a saucepan fell on the floor with a clatter, and one of them laughed.

Margaret wondered what was the matter with Stephen to-day, and last night. Why had he gone to town? What was it that he had burnt last night in the study grate? She was sure that he was upset about something. Stephen was frequently upset, either in mind or stomach, but the strange thing was that he had never been known to show it in this fashion. Usually when Stephen was upset he was *more* irritable and morose, not *less*.

"No, Stevie dear, this is an adding sum," said Margaret, "it's not subtraction like we did yesterday. You remember how to add, don't you? Take your pencil out of your mouth, Dolly."

It really was very queer about Stephen. The more she thought about it the more queer it seemed. She wondered whether she should give the children a holiday and run over to see Sarah Walker and tell her about it—Sarah was so wise. She would not say too much to Sarah—just that Stephen did not seem quite like himself. Of course Sarah could not advise her without knowing in what way Stephen was not like himself, but Margaret did not want advice, she wanted to be reassured, she wanted sympathy, she wanted a nice long talk with Sarah. It was strange that she should want sympathy and reassurance because her husband had been more considerate than usual—or less inconsiderate—but it really just meant that her world was shaking under her feet.

So Margaret gave the children a holiday, and told them to rush about and play hide-and-seek and make a lot of noise because Daddy had gone to London, and then she ran upstairs and pulled on a tammy, and caught up her last year's coat with the worn fur collar (because of course in these hard times she could not afford a new winter coat although she had noticed rather enviously that her maids had each afforded one), and sped along the streets to see Sarah, feeling guilty, and happy, and worried, all at the same time. Guilty because of the holiday, happy because she was going to see Sarah whom she loved, and worried because Stephen had been so queer.

The sky was blue and there was a lightness and brightness in the air due to a touch of frost. It really was a lovely morning. Margaret tripped along and her spirits rose because it was so lovely. Everything was bright and shining, the river was shining like polished silver, the trees were flaunting their Autumn colours in the clear sunlight. She passed Tanglewood Cottage and waved her hand to Barbara Buncle who was making a bonfire in her garden.

"Lovely smell!" she shouted to Barbara in a friendly manner, and Barbara waved her rake in reply.

.   .   .   .   .

The maid said that Mrs. Walker was in. That was one of the good things about Sarah, she always seemed to be there if you wanted her. And another good thing was that however busy she might be—and of course she must be busy sometimes—she never seemed to be busy when you wanted her, but could always sit down and chat in a comfortable leisurely manner whatever time of day it happened to be.

All this flashed across Margaret's mind as she was shown into the doctor's study, and Sarah rose from the desk where she had been adding up accounts and held out her hands.

"How lovely!" Sarah said, "I was just longing for some excuse to escape from those horrible things." They sat down beside the fire—Sarah poked it into a nice blaze—and talked about their children. Margaret complained that hers were too quiet, and Sarah declared that hers were too noisy, and they both laughed a little because they understood each other perfectly and were happy in being together.

"I can't think why we don't see each other more often," Sarah said, and Margaret agreed that *she* couldn't either, except, of course, that they were both busy with husbands and children and things.

Sarah was looking at her friend with new eyes borrowed from *Disturber of the Peace,* and she saw that what the mysterious John Smith said was true. Margaret was worn down by her husband's bad temper just as a silver sixpence is worn down by constant rubbing against coarser coins. Margaret's prettiness was almost gone, and her vivacity was almost gone. (To-day she was prettier than usual, and more vivacious, because she had come quickly through the brisk air to see her friend.) And Sarah thought—as all happy wives think—I would never have stood it all these years. I would have left the brute long ago. I ought to have thought about her more, and been kinder to her, for I am so blessed. And she thought of John (who had been called out in the middle of breakfast to succour Mrs. Goldsmith's youngest grandchild in convulsions, and had not yet returned) and smiled very tenderly.

Margaret said, "You know, Sarah, I really came because I was worried about Stephen."

"Is he ill?" enquired the doctor's wife.

"No, in fact he seemed particularly well," replied Margaret surprisingly. "He sat up half the night, but he wasn't writing—at least he wasn't writing his book—

and then this morning he got up early and went to London."

Sarah murmured commiseratingly—she was slightly fogged as to why she should commiserate, but commiseration was evidently required, so, like a good friend, she supplied it.

"I know it sounds silly put like that," Margaret owned, "but somehow Stephen was not like himself at all."

Sarah thought that any deviation from Stephen's usual self must be an improvement, but she did not say so. She said—"I know what you mean."

"Yes. He spoke to the children at breakfast instead of reading the paper. He was quite talkative, and more— more considerate," said Margaret. She had not meant to say that, because of course it implied that Stephen was not as a rule considerate; but somehow the words had popped out and there it was: Sarah knew now that Stephen had been considerate, and that it was such a very unusual thing for Stephen to be considerate that Margaret was worried about it.

Sarah wrinkled her brows and thought about the problem which had been presented to her. It would have puzzled Sherlock Holmes, she felt, for there were no clues at all to work on, and Margaret was not being frank with her. Margaret had only told her about half the story, and even that had come out by accident.

"Dear old Meg," said Sarah suddenly, laying a friendly hand on Margaret's arm, "if you are really worried, and really want my help you'll have to tell me the whole thing."

Margaret had seen that five minutes ago, and she was

torn in twain. She hated to be disloyal to Stephen, she hated women who told tales about their husbands; but on the other hand she really was worried—supposing Stephen had gone up to town to meet a *woman*—and Sarah was completely trustworthy. So after a moment's thought she told Sarah the whole thing—all about his quietness in coming up to bed, and his endeavour not to waken her, and how the morning had found him full of kindness and amiability, and she told Sarah about the very queer way he kept looking at her when he thought she was not looking at him.

Sarah was appalled at the revelation—not of to-day's kindness of course, but of previous brutality. Margaret seemed to think it was quite natural that Stephen should be selfish and morose, she seemed to think that husbands had a right to make everybody round them miserable. Sarah would have liked to say, "For Goodness' sake leave the man before he has utterly destroyed you," but of course she didn't say that; as a matter of fact she didn't say anything, she just gazed at Margaret with her large grey eyes open to their widest extent.

"Do you think it's a woman, Sarah?" Margaret asked with bated breath.

"Nonsense!" said Sarah.

"It was almost—almost as if he were trying to propitiate me," Margaret pointed out.

Well, it did look like that, but there was another idea beginning to move in Sarah's brain. She marshalled the facts at her command: Stephen had sat up very late, but he was not writing about Henry the Fourth (so Margaret said). What was he doing then? He was reading (he must have been reading since he wasn't writing, that was obvious) and he must have been reading something that enthralled him, something that he could not lay down. Sarah had been similarly enthralled not long ago. Her agile mind leaped very easily over the gap in her deductions and fastened itself firmly upon the hypothesis that Stephen had been reading *Disturber of the Peace,* by John Smith.

Supposing Stephen had been reading *Disturber of the Peace* last night, what effect would it have had upon him?

"Sarah—"

"Wait," she said quickly, "I'm thinking."

Margaret waited hopefully.

Sarah thought.—Supposing Stephen recognised himself as David Gaymer, it would have given him a bit of a shock, wouldn't it? David Gaymer was not a lovable character, he was selfish and irritable, he bullied his wife and domineered over his children. Sarah had thought when she read about David Gaymer,—This is a bit overdone. Stephen's horrid, but he's not quite so horrid as all that. But to-day's little talk with Margaret had shown her that David Gaymer was not a bit overdone, he was Stephen Bulmer down to the very last button on his waistcoat. David Gaymer wrote books, he was writing the *Life of Alva.* She remembered thinking at the time that Stephen should write a life of Alva in preference to *Henry the Fourth.* It seemed more suitable.

But let's follow this out—Sarah entreated herself— How would Stephen feel when he read about his prototype? He would be very angry at first. "I'm not like that," he would say, and then he would think about it and remember things.

And then after a bit he would read on, and find his wife getting alienated from him—Edith Gaymer was drawn very sympathetically in the book—and finally going off with another man, a man who could give her the love and sympathy she had so sadly lacked. And he would be torn between disgust for David Gaymer and sympathy for Stephen Bulmer. "Good heavens!" he would exclaim, "is Margaret really thinking of leaving me? What should I do without Margaret?" He would begin to think about Margaret, and what kind of a life she was having with him, and perhaps he would realise —for he was by no means a stupid man, only blinded by his selfishness and bad temper—that Margaret was having a pretty poor life of it with him, and that nobody could blame her very much if she *did* think of leaving him.

Stephen could not fail to see himself in David Gaymer, for there was no exaggeration about John Smith, nor did he beat about the bush. He simply described his characters and told his tale, and the characters were so real that they made the tale seem real too—even the fantastic part of the tale seemed probable. Of course Sarah was not in the book herself, but she was sure she would have recognised herself at once if she had been so honoured, because John Smith had the knack of breathing the very essence of the people he described into the pages of his book.

John Smith had held up the mirror to poor Stephen and had said, "Here you are, old chap! I hope you like

yourself. Those nasty marks from your nose to the corners of your mouth, and those others between your brows
are marks you put there yourself, you know. You can't
blame God for those." And poor Stephen had replied,
"Good Heavens, is that me?" (Or he would probably
have said, "Is that I?" for he was a pedantic and serious
soul) and he would gaze at Margaret—just as she had
described "in a queer way"—wondering if it could possibly be true that she was thinking of leaving him, and
he would make an effort to be less like David Gaymer.
And lastly he would fly up to town to tackle the publisher
and find out who this man was—this John Smith who
seemed to know more about himself and his wife than
he himself knew.

So that although Sarah had very little to go on it all
fitted beautifully. And, besides, she was quite sure that
she was right in her deductions, which was the main
thing, because if Sarah were quite sure she was right
about anything she always was—John said so too.

Margaret had waited patiently all this time, and now
she was to be rewarded for her patience.

"Now listen," Sarah said (quite needlessly, for of course
Margaret was all ears. Hadn't she been sitting there waiting for about five minutes merely to hear the pearls of
wisdom fall from Sarah's lips). "Now listen, Margaret.
I've thought it all out and I'm quite sure I'm right.
Stephen's not after a woman, and there is absolutely
nothing for you to worry about."

"D'you think he's lost a lot of money?" enquired Margaret. This reasonable but somewhat alarming idea had
occurred to her while she was waiting for Sarah to speak.

"No I don't," said Sarah firmly. "If he had lost a lot of money he would have behaved quite differently about it. Stephen was sitting up last night reading a novel."

"But he never reads novels," interpolated Margaret.

"He was reading a novel last night," Sarah told her. "It's a novel called *Disturber of the Peace,* and it has just come out. It really is a most extraordinary book. I will give it to you to read."

"I can get it from Stephen, he will give it to me to read," suggested Margaret.

"He will do nothing of the sort," replied Sarah. "Stephen will keep it away from you. He will hide it; he will burn it rather than let you have one peep at it."

Margaret's eyes bulged.

"No, there's nothing *like that* in it," Sarah said. "At least, I could see nothing wrong at all. Angela Pretty had hysterics over it, of course, and John had to tear round and administer sal volatile—but really it's quite harmless and very amusing."

"It sounds like it," said Margaret ironically.

"It is *really,*" Sarah assured her.

"Well, why hysterics?" enquired Margaret, not unreasonably.

"I don't quite know," said Sarah, wrinkling her brows, "I couldn't understand what John was driving at. He was furious about the book—said the man ought to be hanged and all that sort of thing—but he hasn't read it yet of course. He was just going by what *they* said. I'm going to make him read it himself."

"Why on earth did Angela have hysterics?"

"Well, it was partly because she didn't want to go to Samarkand," replied Sarah.

Margaret gazed at her in amazement.

"They go off to Samarkand in the book," Sarah explained patiently (Meg was really rather dense about the whole thing).

"You mean Miss King and Angela Pretty go to Samarkand in a book?"

"Yes—at least they start off at the end."

"Start off at the end," echoed Margaret stupidly.

"Start off to Samarkand at the end of the book," explained Sarah.

"And what do they do when they get there?"

"It doesn't say, it just says they are going, and they order riding breeches and things."

"But what has all that got to do with Stephen?" enquired Margaret after a short silence in which she had tried to make some sense of these extraordinary disclosures, and lamentably failed in the attempt.

"Nothing at all," replied Sarah promptly. "It was you who asked me all about Angela's hysterics and Samarkand and put me off the track. The thing that has to do with Stephen is that you are in the book too."

"Me!" cried Margaret in astonishment. "And do I go to Samarkand too?"

"No, of course not. What would you do at Samarkand?"

"What does anybody do there?"

"Well, you don't go there, anyhow," said Sarah, wishing that Margaret would be quiet and allow her to tell the story in her own way—and indeed they would have got on much quicker if she had.

"What do I do then?" said Margaret. She had never been in a book before, and she was rather thrilled about it all.

"You climb out of your bedroom window and elope with Harry Carter," Sarah told her.

Margaret was so dumbfounded that Sarah got her wish, she was able to continue without further interruption. "So now you see the whole thing. Stephen read the book last night and he's been thinking about it ever since and wondering if there is any truth in it, and now he's dashed off to London to find out who the author is, so that he can wring his neck or something."

"But what ever shall I say to Stephen?" exclaimed Margaret.

"If I were you I should pretend I hadn't read the book at all," said Sarah. "I know you haven't read it yet, but you had better stay to lunch and read it this afternoon. You had better just go on as usual and pretend you haven't heard anything about it. It will do Stephen no harm to keep on looking at you and wondering," said Sarah with fiendish satisfaction. "And you can sort of keep him guessing," she added.

"Keep him guessing?" asked Margaret.

"Yes, keep him guessing," said Sarah, and she went on to point out to her bewildered friend various ingenious ways in which she could keep her husband on tenterhooks.

But it was not until Sarah had put the book into

Margaret's hands, and settled her comfortably in the doctor's chair, and gone out with a basket full of flowers and oranges and calves' foot jelly for the Hobday child—who was ill again poor lamb—that Margaret began to understand what all the fuss was about.

She began to read *Disturber of the Peace* because Sarah said she was to read it, but as she went on and recognised all the people she knew, drawn just as they were, without one jot omitted or one tittle added, she became engrossed. And then Stephen appeared upon the scene, and it was just Stephen exactly—so much so that she blushed for his nakedness. For herself she almost wept, John Smith showed her herself as she had not realised she was—a woman hungry for tenderness, snatching at happiness and love, her last chance before she grew too old.

Margaret lunched with Sarah and spent the afternoon finishing the book, and as she put it down she said, "He knows everything about me, that man, except one thing, and that one thing is the strongest thing in my life. If it had not been for that one thing, I would have gone away and left Stephen long ago—just as Edith Gaymer did—but I couldn't leave the children—not for any man on earth—so I shall stay with him always, and grow old and ugly, without ever having known what it is to be loved."

She felt Sarah's arms round her, and Sarah's voice in her ear telling her not to cry.

"The children love you frightfully," Sarah whispered, "and Stephen will improve—I know he will. Look at how different he was this morning. You've been too lenient with him—too door-matty, Meg darling—take a firm line. It will be better for Stephen and better for everyone if you make him behave. I don't suppose he's happy being horrid—nobody is," said Sarah wisely.

CHAPTER X

"Feu de Joie"

*B*ARBARA BUNCLE waved her rake to Margaret Bulmer and continued to gather up the dead leaves and the prunings from her gooseberry bushes and apple trees and to pile them onto her bonfire. She had deposited the hundred pound note in her bank that morning, and it was necessary to celebrate the occasion in some way and to work off her excitement. What could be more fitting to celebrate the occasion than a bonfire? Great victories, King's Coronations and the birth of heirs have all been celebrated by bonfires, so why not the advent of peace and prosperity to Tanglewood Cottage?

The beauty of Barbara's bonfire lay in the fact that nobody knew it was a celebrating bonfire—nobody but herself. The gardener who worked occasionally in Tanglewood garden passed, and called out, "I see you are burning up your leaves, Miss." Burning up her leaves! What a way to speak of a bonfire.

Margaret Bulmer had shouted, "Lovely smell!" It was rather nice, thought Barbara, sniffing, but it was the flames she liked, the little red flames that licked round the twigs and shot up suddenly—she threw on some more twigs just to see the flames shoot up.

What fun it had been that morning at the bank!

Barbara had gone in soon after the bank had opened, and the young man with the fair hair and the supercilious expression (Mr. Black his name was, and he was one of Mrs. Dick's paying guests) had looked up from his desk and seen who it was and gone on writing for at least two minutes before he came to see what she wanted. No need to bother about that old frump, he had said to himself—or Barbara thought that he had—Barbara was sure that he knew her account was overdrawn, perhaps he had been told not to cash any more cheques for Miss Buncle. When he had quite finished what he was doing he lounged over to the counter and she produced the note.

"Ha, don't often see these chaps about!" he had remarked in his familiar way which Barbara detested.

"A little present from my uncle," said Barbara, quite casually, as if it were quite a usual occurrence to receive hundred pound notes from your uncle.

"Must be a rich man, your uncle," suggested Mr. Black, filling up forms—his manner had altered towards her, at least so Barbara imagined, he was much more respectful and attentive. It was the rich uncle in the background she supposed—

"Oh, he is, and so generous. He lives in Birmingham," said Barbara glibly. She was amazed at herself when she found what she had said—such dreadful lies, and they had tumbled out of her mouth without the slightest effort. It really was rather appalling She had intended to domicile her rich uncle in Australia as Mr. Abbott had humorously suggested, but it had suddenly struck her that perhaps the money in Australia was different from our money. It might have the name of an Australian bank inscribed upon it—or a Kangaroo or something. Barbara did not know, and she had no idea how to find out; so, all things considered, it seemed easier for the rich uncle to reside in Birmingham. Barbara had never been to Birmingham, and, to her, it seemed almost as far away from Silverstream as Australia, and therefore almost as safe.

She was thinking about all this, and piling leaves onto her bonfire, and the smoke was swirling round her, blackening her face and making her eyes pour with water, when suddenly a voice announced:

"Ooh—a bonfire!"

Barbara looked all round to discover where the voice came from, and finally found herself gazing into a pair of very blue eyes which were peering over the fence dividing her garden from that of old Mrs. Carter. The blue eyes, some fair curls, and a red tammy was all that was visible above the fence.

"I suppose—I suppose I couldn't come and help," said the voice plaintively, "I love bonfires."

"Do come and help," Barbara said. "There's a gap in the fence lower down the garden—"

The eyes disappeared instantly, and, a few moments later, there was a rustle of dry leaves dispersed by flying feet and a young girl appeared—a somewhat breathless young girl in grey tweeds, a slim willowy creature with a rose-leaf complexion and a small pretty mouth, rather a firm wilful mouth for such a fairy-like creature, Barbara decided.

"I'm Sally," said the girl, when she had recovered her breath.

Barbara remembered now. It was at that dreadful tea-party when Mrs. Featherstone Hogg had burst in like a bomb-shell and had thrown *Disturber of the Peace* onto Mrs. Carter's tea-table. They had been talking about Sally at the time. Sally was coming to live with Mrs. Carter because she required sunshine and milk.

"But I thought Sally was a child," said Barbara vaguely.

"You would," replied Sally darkly, "I mean if you heard Gran talking about me you would think I was about seven instead of seventeen. She treats me like an infant—tells me to change my stockings and wash my hands for lunch, and sends me up to bed at eight o'clock every night. *Me*, who has kept house for Daddy for two years—it's a bit steep, it really is."

"Steep?" enquired Barbara.

"A bit thick," Sally explained kindly, "absolutely the pink limit."

"Yes," said Barbara, somewhat bewildered.

"I knew you would think so," Sally told her. "The moment I saw you I said to myself *there's* a sensible person." She sat down on a convenient log and stirred the bonfire dreamily with an apple branch. "I said to myself there's a sensible person, I must speak to her or I'll go mad. You don't know how beastly it is to be treated like an imbecile and followed about all day long and stuffed with milk. You see I was mistress in Daddy's house and I did what I liked. We had a lovely time together. We had little dinners, and twice a week we went out to restaurants and then on to a play. And of course all the subalterns called just as if I were grown-up. We were at Malta before that —it was too marvellous. Have you ever been to Malta?"

"Never," replied Barbara sadly.

"You must, you simply must," said Sally, turning her face up to Barbara and almost dazzling that staid person with the bewildering beauty of her smile. "Everyone ought to go to Malta. There's the most heavenly bathing there, and dances every night, and darling little Snotties to dance with, and tennis parties—you *do* play tennis, I suppose."

"A little," replied Barbara, with truthful modesty.

"You'd love it," Sally told her, "you'd simply adore it. I'd like us to go together and then I could show you everything—don't you hate this dull hole?"

"Well—" said Barbara doubtfully.

"I knew it," Sally said eagerly, "I knew you were like me—pining to get away. Daddy's gone to India and left me here with Gran, and I simply can't bear it."

"It must be dull for you," Barbara admitted.

"It's simply foul," replied the remarkable girl, "I was yearning to go to India. I'd heard so much about it from everyone, and it seemed almost too good to be true when Daddy heard that he had been posted to Calcutta. It was all settled, and I was looking forward to it more than words can tell, and then my appendix went rotten."

"Dreadful!" said Barbara sympathetically.

"Ghastly—simply ghastly," Sally agreed. "They yanked it out of me of course, and I thought everything would be all right, and then the doctor—who was an absolute fiend—went and told Daddy that India was out of the question for me, and I must be fed up. I was fed up all right I can tell you. Fancy Daddy going off to India alone," Sally said tremulously.

"Dreadful!" said Barbara again, she hoped the girl was not going to cry. She need not have worried, Sally was made of sterner stuff.

"Have you ever had appendicitis?" enquired Sally more cheerfully.

"Never," replied Barbara.

"Well, don't," Sally advised her. "It's absolutely foul. It came on gradually with me, and I used to wake up at night and feel like David—'My reins chasten me in the night season', *you* know. It gave me a sort of friendly feeling for David. I wonder if he had a touch of appendicitis."

Barbara was feeling more and more bewildered, she was not used to this kind of conversation. She tried to fix her mind upon David and the facts known to her about him, so as to determine whether it could have been appendicitis he suffered from; but before she could do so Sally had abandoned the subject.

"Lovely bonfire!" Sally said, poking it so that the flames shot up with a roaring, crackling sound. "The French call it 'feu de joie'—I think that's an awfully good name for it, don't you? Is this a 'feu de joie' or is it just burning rubbish?"

"It's a 'feu de joie'," Barbara replied incautiously.

"Oh! That makes it ten times nicer," cried Sally. "Let's pile on more sticks until it's as high as the house. What's it for?"

"Well, it's for *me*," Barbara said lamely, "I can't tell you exactly—"

"A secret?"

Barbara nodded.

"How too marvellous!" breathed Sally. "Oh, I *do* think it was good of you to let me come and help you with it."

They worked away happily, piling more sticks onto the "feu de joie" so that the flames sank down for a minute and then leapt up higher than ever. It became so hot that they could not go near it. They poked at it with long sticks and laughed and the smoke poured into their lungs and made them cough; it was tremendous fun.

At last, worn out with their efforts, they retired to a short distance and sat down on a log to admire their handiwork.

"Gran would have a fit if she could see me sitting here," announced Sally placidly. She took a somewhat sticky paper bag out of her pocket and offered Barbara a toffee-ball. Barbara took one, she liked toffee and she was not foolishly fastidious.

"Perhaps you had better not sit here, then," Barbara pointed out, her utterance somewhat obstructed by the large ball of toffee.

"It's quite all right as long as she doesn't *see* me," replied Sally, "and she won't see me, because Mrs. Featherstone Hogg came in to see her and talk about that book, and Gran didn't want me to hear what they said so she told me to take a sharp walk. I hate sharp walks, don't you?"

"What book?" inquired Barbara, knowing quite well, but hoping that she was mistaken.

"*Disturber of the Peace,* of course. They all talk about it night and day. Have you read it? I had to creep down after Gran had gone to bed and pinch it out of the drawing-room. Gran said it was not suitable for young people."

Barbara chuckled; she couldn't help it, for when Sally quoted from "Gran" she put on the old lady's voice and manner so exactly that it almost seemed as if Mrs. Carter were sitting beside her on the log. She chuckled, but at the same time she was beset with fears—they were talking about her book night and day, were they?

"Something tickled you?" enquired Sally cheekily.

Barbara didn't answer this, she tried to make her voice sound stern as she pointed out the wickedness of reading books banned by your grandmother.

"Of course you have to say that," said Sally unrepentantly, "but you don't really think it's wicked. I had to read the book when they were all talking about it all the time, hadn't I? Besides Gran's such an old stickler, she thinks I ought to read *Little Women* and *The Fairchild Family*."

"You are under her care," said Barbara virtuously.

"Worse luck!" Sally agreed with a sigh. "But it's such rot, I've read whatever I liked for years. Daddy didn't mind what I read. I've read far worse things than *Disturber of the Peace*. There's nothing horrid about it at all. It's simply a *scream*. I had to stuff the bedclothes into my mouth when I came to the bits about Gran and Mrs. Featherstone Hogg."

"Did you think it was funny?" asked the author with interest.

"I should jolly well think it is," replied Sally, "but to me it's not just a funny book, it's something far better—"

"Is it?"

"It's a kind of—a kind of allegory," continued Sally gravely. "Here's this horrible little village, full of its own affairs and its own importance, all puffed up and smug and conventional and satisfied with itself, and then suddenly their eyes are opened and their shackles fall off and they act according to their real natures. They're not shams any more, they're real. It's simply marvellous," Sally said, turning a shining face upon the astonished author.

Barbara's heart warmed at this unsolicited praise. She had heard the child of her brain maligned and anathematized, she had been obliged to sit dumbly and hear it called filth; but now, here, at last was somebody who appreciated its worth. Barbara looked at Sally with affection and respect.

"He's wakened them all up," Sally was saying, "wakened them all up and made them see themselves as others see them. Of course that's what he meant to do. Have you read it?"

"Y—es," said Barbara.

"Perhaps you didn't read it as carefully as I did," Sally said consolingly. "I was so interested, you see, I seemed to get right inside the man's brain. I can see exactly what he meant when he wrote it—I know exactly what he felt— He's a marvellous man. I should like to marry John Smith," said Sally, nursing one knee and gazing at the bonfire with shining eyes.

"You—you would like to—to *marry* him?" echoed Barbara in amazement.

"Yes," replied Sally. "He's the sort of man I admire—

absolutely fearless. I'm sure he's tall and strong with shaggy sort of hair that keeps falling over his forehead until he tosses his head and shakes it back. He's not exactly good-looking of course, but he has a humorous mouth and nice eyes—piercing grey eyes that look straight through you. I can see him striding about the country with a drawn sword in his hand—*Disturber of the Peace* is a drawn sword—ready to attack all the dragons of modern life at a moment's notice, freeing poor little worms like Mr. Featnerstone Hogg from their shackles, and trampling on stupid conventions and shams. He doesn't care what people think of him, of course, he only cares to do good, to help the weak, and expose the humbugs—I wonder if I shall ever meet him," said Sally softly, almost reverently. "I'm afraid I shan't ever meet him, it would be too good to be true. I expect he has left Silverstream now and gone to some other horrid smug little place to waken it up and give it beans."

Barbara was absolutely dumb—she had no idea that she had written such a marvellous book, nor that its effects upon Silverstream were so far reaching. She was much too honest to credit herself with all those noble motives. She had written *Disturber of the Peace* to make a little money for herself, because she needed money very badly, but it was pleasant to think that more had gone into it than she had intended. If all that Sally said were true she was a public benefactor, and not—as she had been led to believe—a criminal of the deepest dye. As for John Smith, it was most extraordinary but he seemed quite real to Barbara; she could see him—just as Sally had described

—striding about the country, a modern Jack the Giant Killer, with his shaggy hair and piercing grey eyes.

"People like Gran and Mrs. Featherstone Hogg have no right to criticise a splendid man like that," Sally continued, "he's as far above their mouldy little minds as the stars. They don't understand him of course, but other people will. All over the country people are reading his book and leading better and nobler lives because of it."

Barbara felt she could go on listening to this sort of conversation for hours. What an extraordinary girl Sally was—a very clever girl indeed, with sense far beyond her tender years. Unfortunately time was flying and she felt bound to point out the fact to her companion. Mrs. Carter had lunch at one o'clock and punctuality was something of a fetish at The Firs.

Sally sprang up, "I wonder if Mrs. Hogg will still be there," she said, "I called her Mrs. Hogg this morning and she didn't like it a bit. I can't bear her, can you? I suppose you couldn't ask me to tea some day, could you?"

"I could," replied Barbara. "Would Mrs. Carter let you come?"

"Why not? You are quite respectable, aren't you?" enquired Sally in her direct manner.

"Oh yes—at least." It crossed Barbara's mind that perhaps she wasn't quite respectable now, by Mrs. Carter's standard. If Mrs. Carter knew that she was John Smith— but Mrs. Carter didn't know, so it was all right.

Sally had been watching her face, poised ready for flight.

"Aren't you?" she now demanded, with gleaming eyes.

Quite obviously she was hoping that her new friend was *not* quite all that Gran could desire, and therefore much more exciting to know.

"Of course I am, don't be silly," Barbara said, a tiny bit annoyed, though she couldn't have said why.

"All right—don't get ratty," Sally adjured her, "I suppose it was too much to hope for—"

And she fled.

. . . . .

This conversation with Sally Carter cheered Barbara on her way, and she needed cheering for it was a way strewn with boulders. Not only did the inhabitants of Silverstream discuss and vilify *Disturber of the Peace,* but people from all over the country wrote letters praising or blaming its author—curiously enough the praise was almost as disturbing as the blame—so entirely incomprehensible was it to the innocent and bewildered John Smith. Then there were the newspapers with their stupefying reviews. Mr. Abbott had advised Miss Buncle to contribute to a press cutting agency (she was lamentably ignorant in these matters), and Barbara, who was acquiring a habit of doing what Mr. Abbott told her, obediently contributed two guineas to one of these, hitherto unheard of, establishments.

A shower of criticism immediately descended. There was scarcely a single day when the postman failed to bring words of praise or blame to Tanglewood Cottage. Barbara read them all with care, and rejoiced or sorrowed according to the mede which was measured unto her. Sometimes she was completely puzzled by the critics' views upon her book and once or twice she was visited by the unworthy suspicion that the critic could not have studied *Disturber of the Peace* with the meticulous care it deserved before writing his considered opinion of it.

"This book is uneven," complained *The Morning Mail,* "the plot is good but the characterization is poor. There never were such people as those depicted in *Disturber of the Peace*. Major Waterfoot is a type of retired officer which never existed except in the vivid imagination of our younger novelist. We would recommend John Smith to study life at first hand before attempting to write about it."

"We can thoroughly recommend *Disturber of the Peace,* by John Smith, to anyone who is feeling blue," announced *The Evening Clarion*. "It is the funniest thing we have read for a long time. We hail a new writer to the ranks of Britain's humorists."

"Brilliant Satire," exclaimed *The Daily Post*. "Every page is a masterpiece of the most delicate ridicule. The characters are delineated with a sure hand. Mr. Smith is to be congratulated upon his first novel."

The Literary News was not so kind—"*Disturber of the Peace,* by John Smith (Abbott & Spicer 7s. 6d.)," it announced, "is one of those futile novels that behoves us to ask ourselves—as we lay it down with a sigh of relief—why it has ever been written. It is dull and prosy, the sentiment mawkish, the characters unconvincing. A dull Major living in a country village falls in love with his next door neighbour, who is a widow of independent means, but nothing happens until the god of love descends from Olympus to rouse him from his lethargy—why the god of love should take the trouble is a matter which the author fails to explain, and indeed it would be exceedingly difficult of explanation. There is a preposterous love scene in the lady's garden, the Major seduces her, and the book ends with the couple contemplating a honeymoon in Samarkand. There are some subsidiary characters and incidents dragged in to pad out the story, but this is the main theme and we do not feel that many of our readers will care to waste their time upon rubbish of this description."

"A Romantic Story of Love in a Village," said *The People's Illustrated* in capital letters. "Those of us who are weary of the so-called brilliant novel of modern life will enjoy the old world fragrance of Copperfield. There is nothing in *Disturber of the Peace* to bring a blush to the most modest cheek. The characters are drawn with a loving and discriminate hand. We seem to know them quite well ere we lay down the book—to know them and to love them as we know and love our friends. It is to be hoped that Mr. Smith will give us more novels from his pen of this same elevating type."

"Who is John Smith?" enquired Mr. Snooks who wrote the literary column for *The Weekly Guide*. "He seems to be a young man of singular discernment. There is no muddled thinking in his novel, every sentence is clear and concise and relevant to the purpose. Mr. Smith is somewhat scornful of love, he writes of love with his tongue in his cheek—the result is exceedingly funny. I can heartily recommend the book to those with a sense of humour."

"The last novel on our list is *Disturber of the Peace,* by John Smith (Abbott & Spicer 7s. 6d.)," said *The*

Morning Sun. "It is a type of novel we do not care to recommend to our readers, but no doubt it will gain large sales. It concerns itself chiefly with the description of characters under the influence of unbridled or perverted passions."

.   .   .   .   .

The writers of these criticisms would doubtless have been pleased if they could have seen John Smith poring over their words. Barbara tried in vain to arrive at some definite conclusion as to the merits of her book. But no sooner had one review plunged her into the depths of despair by saying that *Disturber of the Peace* was as dull as ditchwater, or perverted and immoral, and not fit for a respectable human being to read, than another cutting arrived, by the next post, informing all who cared to know that it was a charming book, clever, brilliant, elevating or supremely funny. It was certainly very puzzling. Meantime the sales went up by leaps and bounds and Mr. Abbott sent her congratulatory notes and urged her to start another book at once on the same lines.

CHAPTER XI

Colonel Weatherhead and the Bishop

COLONEL WEATHERHEAD was pulling up bishop-weed in his garden. He had a fearful tussle with the bishop every Autumn, for the bishop was entrenched in a thorn hedge at the bottom of the garden near the river, and however much of him Colonel Weatherhead managed to eradicate there was always enough root left embedded in the thickest part of the hedge to start him off again next year.

Colonel Weatherhead had a kind of sneaking admiration for the bishop—here was an enemy, worthy of his steel. The Colonel went for him tooth and nail, he dug and tore and burned the bishop, and the sweat poured off him in rivulets. Sometimes he stood up, and straightened his back, and felt himself round the waist, and wondered if that horrible two inches had diminished at all.

He was in the thick of the fight, and his hair was standing on end, and his face and hands were scratched with thorns, and one of his brace buttons had flown off in the struggle—in fact he was as filthy and as completely happy as a little boy making mud pies—when he heard a car drive up to his front door. He peered through the bushes and saw that it was Mrs. Featherstone Hogg's car, and there was Mrs. Featherstone Hogg herself, getting out of the car and going into his house.

The Colonel swore a regrettable oath, he did not like Mrs. Featherstone Hogg at the best of times, but even supposing he had liked her immensely she would have been unwelcome just now. Colonel Weatherhead was in no condition to appear before a lady. He would be in no condition to appear before a lady until he had soaked himself in an extremely hot bath and changed all his clothes.

The Colonel now perceived to his horror that Simmons was coming down the garden to find him—Simmons was the Colonel's soldier servant, an excellent creature in his way, and thoroughly conscientious, but somewhat lacking in initiative—Colonel Weatherhead made a rapid reconnaissance of his position and sprinted for the toolshed. It was a dark musty place (as toolsheds so often are) filled with worn-out tools, and a wheelbarrow and a lawnmower, and festooned with spider's webs; but the Colonel was already as dirty as any man could be, so there was no need to be fastidious. He crawled underneath the wheelbarrow and pulled a piece of sacking over his legs. He was concerned to find that he was breathing heavily, it was partly the short sprint and partly the excitement, but it showed he was out of training. I must shorten the tobacco ration, he thought, regretfully.

Simmons looked all round the garden faithfully, he even glanced into the toolshed, although it was unlikely that Colonel Weatherhead would be there, then he returned to the house and informed Mrs. Featherstone Hogg that the Colonel seemed to have gone out.

"What do you mean?" enquired that lady haughtily. "You said Colonel Weatherhead was in the garden."

"I thought he was, ma'am," replied Simmons.

"Either the Colonel is out, or else he is in," said Mrs. Featherstone Hogg. "What do you mean by saying he seems to have gone out?"

"Well, I can't find him, ma'am," Simmons returned, scratching his ear in perplexity, "and yet I'd take my affy davvy he's somewhere about, for he wasn't dressed to go out, so to speak."

"It's most annoying," Mrs. Featherstone Hogg said. "I suppose it is no use waiting for the Colonel—you don't know when he will be in?"

"No ma'am, I don't—and that's the truth. I don't know where he's gone, and I don't know when he'll be back."

Mrs. Featherstone Hogg looked at him with disapproval, then she produced a brown paper parcel and laid it on the table. "You will give this parcel to Colonel Weatherhead directly he comes in," she informed Simmons, "and tell him that I came down here specially to see him—you understand?"

Simmons replied that he did.

"It is very *important*," said Mrs. Featherstone Hogg.

Colonel Weatherhead waited until he heard the car drive off before he emerged from his lair. He was even dirtier than he had been, there were spider's webs in his hair, and his face was streaked with soil, and he had torn a jagged rent in his trousers with a nail. His language might have set fire to the toolshed if it had not been so damp—

Should he have another go at the bishop, or should he

return to the house and bathe? That was the question. He consulted his watch and found that there was half an hour before tea. He took up the fork and hesitated— bath or bishop? A spider chose the moment to crawl over the Colonel's ear.

"Ugh, damn and blast!" he cried, rubbing his ear with a thoroughly grimy hand, and decided for a bath. The decision had been made for him by a spider (not for the first time had this intelligent insect helped a gallant soldier to make an important decision at a critical moment—it will be remembered that Robert the Bruce was similarly guided). Robert Weatherhead put the fork into the toolshed and went up to the house.

Simmons was waiting for him when he emerged from the bath-room clean and pink as a newly-washed baby.

"Mrs. Featherstone 'Ogg was here, sir, and I was to say she came down special to see you, sir, and this parcel's very important," he recited glibly.

The Colonel slapped on his braces and grunted.

"I looked everywhere for you, sir."

The Colonel grunted again.

Simmons laid the parcel on the dressing-table with reverent care and departed to the kitchen. He had shifted the responsibility of the parcel, his conscience was clear.

"I wonder where the old codger *was*," he said to his wife as he sat down to his tea, and spread his bread with a liberal helping of butter and stretched out his arm for the jam.

" 'Iding," suggested Mrs. Simmons promptly.

"But I looked all over the place—I looked in the tool-shed even—"

"More fool you!" retorted his better half scornfully, "if 'e 'ad bin in the toolshed it would 'ave meant 'e didn't want to be found. What call 'ad you to be 'unting for the pore gentleman in the toolshed? None. If 'e didn't want to be found it was yore place not to find 'im—see?"

Simmons saw. "You *are* a one!" he said in awed tones.

Colonel Weatherhead glanced at the mysterious parcel as he put on his collar and struggled with his stud—it looked like a book. He put out one hand and felt it—yes, it was a book, he could feel the hard edges of the cover through the brown paper. Why had Mrs. Featherstone Hogg sent him a book? What kind of a book would it be? Colonel Weatherhead was pretty certain that Mrs. Featherstone Hogg's taste in literature was different from his—it would be one of those high-brow books, deadly dull. He left it on the dressing-table and went downstairs to have his tea. There was a novel of Buchan's waiting for him to read, it had just come from the library—much more his style.

The Colonel drank his tea and read his Buchan, he was very comfortable after his exercise and his bath. He ate two crumpets, they were fattening, of course, but he felt entitled to them after his strenuous work.

At seven o'clock the telephone bell rang, and Simmons came to report that Mrs. Featherstone Hogg was on the line and wished to speak to him. Colonel Weatherhead lifted the receiver and heard a voice say—

"Have you read it?"

"Read what?"

"The book I left for you, of course."

"Oh, yes. No, I haven't read it yet. Been awfully busy, you know."

"Read it," said the voice that purported to be the voice of Mrs. Featherstone Hogg but did not sound like hers. "Read it immediately."

"Yes, yes," agreed the Colonel.

"I'm going to London on important business, but I shall be home on Saturday. I want to hear exactly what you think of it."

"Yes, yes. All right, my dear lady," soothed Colonel Weatherhead to the excited voice at the other end of the telephone, so unlike the usual languid, die-away tones of Mrs. Featherstone Hogg.

Something must have stung the old girl properly, he thought, as he returned to John Buchan and his comfortable fire.

That was Wednesday, it was not until Friday morning that he undid the wrappings of the book sent to him by Mrs. Featherstone Hogg, and looked at it curiously. He was sufficiently in awe of Mrs. Featherstone Hogg to feel that it would be wise to have read the book before she returned from London (or at any rate glance through the thing). She would probably ring him up and ask him if he had done so, it was too much to hope that she would have forgotten all about it. Most people in Silverstream did what Mrs. Featherstone Hogg told them to do, it was easier in the long run, they found.

On first inspection the book seemed quite an ordinary sort of novel—not at all the high-brow stuff that he had expected. He started on it about eleven o'clock on Friday morning, for it was raining hard, and much too wet to go out and dig; besides he was somewhat stiff after a last struggle with the bishop which had absorbed the major part of Thursday.

Disturber of the Peace amused him—"Damned good," he commented as he read the description of Major Waterfoot, "not unlike that feller in the Dragoons." At one o'clock he laid it on the table, open and face downwards to keep his place, and went in to his solitary lunch. At one-thirty he was back in his chair, reading.

The rain fell steadily all afternoon and the Colonel read on. He chuckled once or twice and decided that the people were very real, it might almost be Silverstream. Simmons brought in his tea, and he continued to read.

Colonel Weatherhead finished the book about seven o'clock and sat and thought about it for a bit. It was an amusing and interesting book—he liked it—but he couldn't see, for the life of him, why Mrs. Featherstone Hogg had been so excited about it. He would never have supposed that it was her style at all. The people in the book appealed to him, they were real live people, just the sort of people you meet every day. Copperfield was a typical English village, and the people were typical English people. They were quite contented with their lot, they went on day after day doing the same things, and saying the same things—a bit futile, wasn't it? They never got anywhere, nothing ever happened to them except that they grew old. And then suddenly that Golden Boy came along with his pipes and stirred them all up.—Fancy if a Golden Boy came to Silverstream and stirred us all up! Colonel Weatherhead thought. He reviewed his own life, it was pretty futile, pretty empty and lonely. It would become even more so as time went on and he got older and couldn't do all the things he liked doing, such as walking, and digging, and fighting with the bishop. Gradually all these things would desert him and he would be nothing but an old crusty crock. It was a horrible thought. He poked the fire fiercely, and went up to dress for his solitary dinner.

The evening stretched before him like a desert. Damn that book, he thought, it's upset me. It's upset me frightfully. Something queer about that book to upset me like this—

As he sipped his coffee he noticed that the rain was no longer beating against the windows. He pulled aside the blind and looked out, it was fine. The moon sailed like a silver crescent in a cloudless sky, the stars were brilliant.

"I shall go out, Simmons," said the Colonel. "Bring my galoshes, will you?"

Simmons brought his galoshes and he went out. The air was very sweet after the rain. The moon silvered the leaves of the evergreens, the bushes dripped heavily, the hedge was a mass of diamonds. The moon turned the flooded paths to silvery streams.

"Dashed pretty!" said Colonel Weatherhead, it made him feel quite poetical. But all the same it was a sad eerie sort of scene, not the sort of scene to cheer you up when you were feeling a bit blue, not the sort of scene to be out in all by yourself. The gorgeous moonlight reminded the Colonel of that love scene he had just been reading about, when Major Waterfoot had proposed in such a dashing manner to the pretty Mrs. Mildmay. He had thought it "dashed good" at the time, it had made him feel quite young and ardent—that's the way to propose to a woman, by Jove it is!—he had thought. That fellow knows what he is writing about. But, unfortunately, thinking of it now, made the Colonel feel even lonelier than before.

He splashed along the drive in his galoshes and went through the gates onto the road, it would be cleaner on the road. Mrs. Bold's small house was just opposite, he could see the lighted windows of her drawing-room through the—now almost bare—branches of the trees. The pink curtains which were drawn across the windows gave it a particularly cosy appearance.

"I haven't seen her for days," he said to himself, hesitating before the gate of Cosy Neuk. "Hope she's not ill or anything. Nice sensible little woman—pretty too—perhaps it would be neighbourly to enquire."

He pushed the gate open and went in.

Mrs. Bold was sitting on a sofa by the fire making herself a "nightie" of peach coloured crêpe de chine. She huddled it into her work basket as the Colonel was announced and looked up, a trifle flustered.

"Just looked in to see how you were getting on," he apologised.

"How nice of you! I was feeling so lonely," said Mrs. Bold smiling at him pathetically.

By Jove, *she* was lonely *too,* thought Colonel Weatherhead—must be dashed lonely for a woman living by herself, and she was always so bright and cheery. Plucky little creature! Pretty little creature! He was emboldened to pat the hand which she held out to him—Mrs. Bold made no objection.

"Well," he said, "it *is* lonely living alone—nobody to talk to or anything." He sat down beside her on the sofa and told her all about how lonely he was, living in The Bridge House all by himself. Mrs. Bold listened and sympathised.

It was very cosy and comfortable in Mrs. Bold's drawing-room. The fire burned brightly, Colonel Weatherhead noticed that it was composed of coal and logs—an ideal fire. He said so to his hostess. They talked about fires and found that their tastes tallied exactly—it was astonishing.

Colonel Weatherhead began to think he had been a fool. He had known Mrs. Bold for four years—she had lived opposite his gate for that period—and, although he had always liked and admired the little woman in a vague way, he had never, until this moment, realised how charming she was, how sensible and intelligent, how sympathetic.

He glanced at her sideways, her eyes were fixed upon the fire which irradiated her small round face with rosy light—how pretty she was! Her hair was pretty too, it was brown with reddish glints in it, and it curled prettily round her forehead and at the back of her neck. She was talking about the Coal People, and telling Colonel Weatherhead what trouble she had with them. She had ordered two tons that morning, and the men had insisted on bringing the heavy carts into the garden instead of carrying it in bag by bag as they usually did. The consequence was they had broken a drain pipe which had been put too near the surface of the drive. She had known this would happen,—it had happened before when she moved into the house and the furniture van had driven in—but the coal-man wouldn't listen to her and now she would have to send for a plumber. Colonel Weatherhead had no idea—she told him—how dreadfully these sort of people imposed on a lone woman.

"Don't be one any more, Dorothea," said Colonel Weatherhead earnestly.

This fell far short of the dashing manner in which Major Waterfoot had proposed to Mrs. Mildmay, but it was quite as effective. Dorothea was in his arms and he was kissing her before he knew where he was—it was a delightful sensation.

The Colonel did not go home until it was quite late, the moon was still shining, but it did not make him feel sad, in fact it made him feel somewhat light headed. Simmons and his wife had gone to bed long ago of course. The Colonel let himself into his silent house and went to bed also—he had all sorts of strange unusual feelings. Presently he went to sleep and dreamed about Dorothea.

CHAPTER XII

Mrs. Featherstone Hogg

MRS. FEATHERSTONE HOGG did not enjoy her two days in London. She had not intended to go to London herself just now, it was not the right time of year for London. Christmas was coming on and the hotel was crowded, she could not get a room to suit her tastes. The streets were wet and draughty, the shops were stuffy and overheated, there was "flu" about—and Mrs. Featherstone Hogg was terrified of "flu"—but in spite of all these horrors—which she had known about before ever she started—she was obliged to go to London because of Edwin's stupidity. Edwin's visit to the lawyer had been a complete failure, he had returned to Silverstream with the information that Mr. Spark was of the opinion that they had no case for a libel action against Abbott and Spicer. It was always unsatisfactory to bring up a case of libel based upon a novel. It was so unsatisfactory that it was scarcely ever attempted. Nothing would be gained by it.

Edwin appeared to think that he had done all that was necessary in consulting Mr. Spark. Mrs. Featherstone Hogg did not share his views, and she told him so all the way up to London in the car.

"Do you mean to tell me that you will allow any low

down scribbler to say what he likes about me without moving a finger to have him punished?" she enquired.

"Well, I asked Spark," Edwin pointed out.

"You asked Spark," repeated Mrs. Featherstone Hogg, scornfully.

"Yes, I asked Spark, and he said it was no use."

"So you decided to do nothing about it," declared the lady, her eyes flashing dangerously. "It's nothing to you, I suppose, if I am insulted, ridiculed, held up to scorn? Have you no pride, Edwin? Can you sit at your ease and have it bruited abroad that I was in the chorus when you married me?"

"But you were, Agatha," Mr. Featherstone Hogg pointed out with amazing indiscretion.

"You liar!" screamed Agatha. "I had a speaking part."

"You said, 'Girls, girls, what a wonderful time we are having!'" said Mr. Featherstone Hogg reminiscently. "And then you all danced. You were third from the end in the front row."

"Well, and what of that? It's nothing against a girl if she has to earn her own living, is it?"

"Nothing," replied Mr. Featherstone Hogg promptly. "Nothing in my opinion—it was you who—"

"Stop it now," cried his better-half holding her ears tightly.

"I was only going to say it was you who seemed ashamed of it," said Mr. Featherstone Hogg mildly. "I'm not, and never was."

The interview with Mr. Spark took place that afternoon. It was a very unsatisfactory interview. Mr. Spark merely reiterated the arguments which he had used to

Mr. Featherstone Hogg; he hadn't even read the book
which Mrs. Featherstone Hogg had sent him to read; he
did not see any object in reading the book; he thought
the matter was closed. Mrs. Featherstone Hogg disabused
his mind of this idea. She commanded him to read *Disturber of the Peace* and made an appointment with him
for the following day.

Mr. Spark read the book and enjoyed it—especially the
bits about Mrs. Featherstone Hogg—but he was even less
anxious to take the case to court after he had read it. He
visualised the scene in court—everyone giggling, the
judge making witticisms—what barrister would take
such a case? He imagined the roars of laughter as the
passages objected to by his client were read aloud. Mrs.
Featherstone Hogg had marked the offending passages in
red ink so that there should be no mistake about it.

When the Featherstone Hoggs appeared on the following day at the appointed hour Mr. Spark had decided on
his line—

"My dear Mrs. Featherstone Hogg," he said, rising and
offering her a chair, "I have been reading the novel
(quite a second-rate affair and not worthy of your notice,
I assure you), and the character which you object to is
not you at all. You have been too sensitive altogether."

"It is Mrs. Horsley Downs."

"I know, I know. You marked it for me. It bears—I
admit—some small resemblance to you; but that is merely
a coincidence. Fundamentally you are totally unlike Mrs.
Horsley Downs—totally unlike. Of course it is quite natural that anyone with your sensitive nature should be hurt
by—by the mere suggestion that a character in a novel of

this description should be based upon your unusual personality, but believe me you are labouring under a misconception, believe me the resemblances are mere chance resemblances, the differences are fundamental. I would even go so far as to say—"

"Nonsense," said Mrs. Featherstone Hogg, unmoved by this peroration. "The thing is a libel. It's not only a libel upon me, it's a libel upon the whole of Silverstream. I've got the whole of Silverstream behind me—they'll all bring actions—"

"I *very* much doubt it," said Mr. Spark. "The case would serve no good purpose and would bring a great deal of unpleasant ridicule upon the plaintiffs."

At this stage in the proceedings, Mrs. Featherstone Hogg completely lost her temper. (In her defence be it said that she had been having a very trying time for the last ten days. *Disturber of the Peace* had disturbed her peace most thoroughly. The foundations of her social position in Silverstream were shaking, and her social position in Silverstream was of supreme importance to Mrs. Featherstone Hogg.) She raged and stormed at Mr. Spark and Edwin, she pointed out that the book was a disgusting book, it had ridiculed her, she wanted an abject apology and large damages. She explained, somewhat incoherently, that the character of Mrs. Horsley Downs was a horrible character and not in the least like her, but that it was obviously intended for her, because it was exactly like her, and that therefore it was a libel and as such ought to be punished to the utmost rigour of the law. She said the same thing a dozen times in different words, but always loudly, until Mr. Spark thought his

head would burst. Her language became more pictur-
esque and less polite every moment. Mr. Spark began to
wonder whether she really had been in the chorus when
Mr. Featherstone Hogg had been so misled as to marry
her and elevate her to a higher sphere of life.

When, at last, she paused for breath, Mr. Spark merely
shook his head and said that it was no use.

"You mean you refuse to help us?" asked Mrs. Featherstone Hogg, incredulously.

"I do," replied Mr. Spark with spirit. The Featherstone Hoggs were wealthy clients, and he could ill afford
to lose them, but there were limits to his endurance, and
he had reached the limits now.

"We shall go elsewhere then," announced Mrs. Featherstone Hogg, rising, and gathering up her sables with the
air of a tragedy queen.

Mr. Featherstone Hogg had contributed absolutely
nothing to the conversation—if conversation it could be
called. He had remained in the background twiddling his
thumbs and wishing from the bottom of his heart that he
had stayed at home. But now that the interview was at
an end and Agatha had said all that she wanted to say he
leant forward a little and cleared his throat.

"Did you speak, Edwin?" enquired his wife, turning
upon him with a quelling glance.

"No, but I'm going to," replied the worm, turning at
last. He too had read *Disturber of the Peace* and the
seeds of rebellion had been planted in his heart by that
amazing publication. The seeds had taken some time to
germinate, for Edwin's heart was poor soil in which to
grow rebellion, but they were beginning to grow now.

"I intend to take Mr. Spark's advice," said Mr. Featherstone Hogg, blinking a little, nervously.

"*You* intend to."

"Yes, Agatha. I intend to take Mr. Spark's advice. I have no money to throw away upon a hopeless lawsuit. I have no wish to look ridiculous—"

"You look ridiculous already," snapped Agatha.

Mr. Featherstone Hogg took no notice of this unladylike remark. He found his hat and gloves and shook hands with Mr. Spark.

"I may be calling upon you in a few days to make some alterations in my Will," said Mr. Featherstone Hogg in very distinct and somewhat significant tones.

"Any time that suits you," the lawyer replied effusively.

"I may come—or again I may not. It all depends upon circumstances," said Mr. Featherstone Hogg.

"Just as you please—my time is at your disposal," said Mr. Spark. "You might like to have a look over your Will with me. Perhaps there are some minor points you would like to revise."

"It is a major alteration I have in mind," said Mr. Featherstone Hogg firmly.

Mr. Spark accompanied the couple to the door with admirable courtesy. He stood upon the step, bowing until the Daimler had borne them away. Then he went back to his sanctum, and shut the door carefully, and laughed and laughed and laughed.

CHAPTER XIII

Colonel Weatherhead and Mrs. Bold

*T*HE first thing that Mrs. Featherstone Hogg did on her return to Silverstream was to ring up Colonel Weatherhead. Simmons answered the telephone and informed her that the Colonel was out.

"When will he be back?" enquired Mrs. Featherstone Hogg.

"I don't know at all, ma'am."

"Where has he gone? Has he gone to London?"

"Oh no, ma'am—I think he's over at Mrs. Bold's."

Mrs. Featherstone Hogg rang off. It was most annoying, the man was never in when she wanted him. She supposed that Colonel Weatherhead had gone to talk it all over with Dorothea Bold. It seemed obvious, but, wasn't it a trifle—well—indelicate? In *Disturber of the Peace* Major Waterfoot had proposed to Mrs. Mildmay—some people said he had seduced her—surely that put their prototypes in a very awkward position. Most people would have wanted to avoid each other, at any rate, until the first strangeness of the position wore off. Still, some people were queer, not everybody had such sensitive feelings about matters of this kind as *she* had, and anyhow it was their own affair, if they liked to talk it over with each other it did not affect Mrs. Featherstone Hogg. She decided to go down to Dorothea's and meet the Colonel there, they could all talk it over together and decide what was to be done.

She ordered the car to come round directly after lunch. It had just brought her down from London and the chauffeur had started to clean it, but that did not disturb Mrs. Featherstone Hogg in the least. Cars were there to be used; chauffeurs were there to drive you when and where you wanted to be driven. It had started to rain and Mrs. Featherstone Hogg's chauffeur was not very pleased about it.

It will be seen that Mrs. Featherstone Hogg had by no means abandoned her campaign against John Smith. The action for libel was definitely off, Edwin had been most unreasonable about the whole thing. He had told her— as they drove away from Mr. Spark's door—that he did not wish to hear another word upon the subject, and she had bowed to his decision. She was obliged to bow to Edwin's decision because he had been so very queer about his Will. As it stood the Will suited Agatha exactly—it left her everything without any restriction whatever— why alter it then?

Agatha had no wish to lose Edwin, he was, as a rule, quite docile, and very little trouble, he never interfered with her, and he gave her a generous allowance; but we must all die sometime, and Edwin was twenty years older than Agatha, and suffered from a weak heart. It was only reasonable to suppose that he would pass on to a better land before she did. Agatha felt that she could bear the loss more courageously if she had all Edwin's money to comfort her in her bereavement—every penny of it with out any stupid restrictions about re-marriage, or anything else—

Mrs. Featherstone Hogg thought all this over very carefully and decided that she would say no more about the libel action, it was safer not to. Edwin was not *likely* to do anything very drastic, but he might—he had been quite unlike his usual self ever since the somewhat stormy interview with Mr. Spark. The libel action must go, but that was no reason why John Smith should get off scot-free. Something else must be thought of, somehow or other the mystery of the book's authorship must be solved and the man punished.

Before going down in the car to see Dorothea Bold, she rang up Mr. Bulmer on the telephone and they had a long conversation about *Disturber of the Peace*. Mr. Bulmer told her that he was alone in the house, he had sent Margaret and the children to her people in Devonshire for a long visit. It seemed wiser, said Mr. Bulmer. Mrs. Featherstone Hogg praised his forethought. Neither of them mentioned why it was wiser to banish Margaret from Silverstream at the moment, but both knew that it was because Mr. Bulmer did not want his wife to read *Disturber of the Peace,* nor to hear it discussed by the inhabitants of Silverstream. Mrs. Featherstone Hogg wished that she could have banished Edwin before he had been contaminated by the book. She heaved a sigh.

"What are you doing about it?" enquired Mr. Bulmer. "Are you going to sue them for libel?"

Mrs. Featherstone Hogg replied that it was all off— the laws of England were in such a decadent condition —they must take the law into their own hands. Did Mr.

Bulmer think it would be a good plan to hold a Meeting in Mrs. Featherstone Hogg's drawing-room and invite all the people who were annoyed about *Disturber of the Peace?*

Mr. Bulmer thought the plan sound.

Surely between them they would elucidate the mystery of John Smith—suggested Mrs. Featherstone Hogg—a clue here and another there, put together they would discover John Smith.

Mr. Bulmer thought they might.

Mrs. Featherstone Hogg said she would let him know what day—she thought perhaps Thursday—it would give them time to collect everybody. Besides it was the half-day in Silverstream so Mrs. Goldsmith could come too, she had heard that Mrs. Goldsmith was annoyed about *Disturber of the Peace.*

By this time Mr. Bulmer was tired of the conversation, he replied briefly that Thursday afternoon would suit him, and rang off.

Mrs. Featherstone Hogg got into her car which had been waiting at the door for twenty minutes—

"Mrs. Bold's house," she said laconically.

She was pleased with the idea of the Meeting—it was an inspiration. It had come to her quite suddenly when she was speaking to Mr. Bulmer (great inspirations often come quite suddenly and unexpectedly to their fortunate recipients). Surely the combined brains of Silverstream would discover the identity of John Smith. It had become an absolute obsession to Mrs. Featherstone Hogg, the thing had got on her nerves, she felt she could not rest until she had found him. Once they knew who it was they could decide what was to be done, everything depended upon who the man was. Whether it was the sort of man who could be terrorized, ostracized, or horse-whipped. At the very least he could be made to apologise and hounded out of Silverstream. In this case the punishment must be made to fit the criminal. Mrs. Featherstone Hogg decided that Colonel Weatherhead would be the best person to wield the horse-whip should the horse-whip be necessary. She was a little doubtful as to what horse-whipping really was, but Colonel Weatherhead would know.

Mrs. Featherstone Hogg had now reached her destination. The Daimler could not drive into Cosy Neuk because the drive was up. There was a large hole right in the very middle of Dorothea's drive and several men in overalls were standing round, smoking clay pipes and talking about it. One man was in the hole, up to his armpits, he was the only one who was not smoking and talking; he was merely leaning against the edge of the hole listening to the others. Two pick-axes and several large shovels were lying about, or propped against the gate, it had started to rain again, and there was a very disgusting smell—

Mrs. Featherstone Hogg took out her handkerchief and sniffed it delicately, it was scented with "Rose D'Amour," and it put up a fairly effective barrage against the other and much less pleasant odour, which was coming from the hole in Dorothea's drive.

Mrs. Featherstone Hogg looked out at the rain, and decided to send a message to Dorothea by her chauffeur. It was no use plodding through the rain and mud and ruining her shoes unless Dorothea was at home and could see her. She was explaining all this to the chauffeur when suddenly the men standing about the hole were galvanised into activity. They seized pick-axes and spades and tore fiercely at the drive. The man in the hole stopped listening—there was nothing to listen to now of course—and began to throw up spade-fuls of mud from the depths of the hole.

Mrs. Featherstone Hogg wondered what had happened to induce such sudden industry, and then she saw that Colonel Weatherhead had emerged from the house and was coming down the drive. He was wearing a very dirty Burberry and a tweed cap. He stopped and spoke to the foreman and peered into the hole. Mrs. Featherstone Hogg could not hear what he was saying but it looked as if he were giving instructions as to what was to be done. What business was it of Colonel Weatherhead's? It was not his drive. The faulty drain (there was unfortunately no doubt that it was a faulty drain) was not his either—it was Dorothea's. Anyone would have thought that Dorothea might look after her own drains.

Colonel Weatherhead finished talking to the foreman and looked up and saw the car. Mrs. Featherstone Hogg beckoned to him through the window. He was not at all pleased when he saw who it was, but there was no escape this time—no handy tool-shed to hide in. The Colonel walked over to the car and greeted its occupant with a singular lack of enthusiasm.

"Have you read the book?" asked Mrs. Featherstone Hogg eagerly. "Come into the car for a minute or two—it's so cold with the door open."

"I'm very wet," objected the Colonel.

"Never mind that. Come in. I want to speak to you."

Colonel Weatherhead got in reluctantly, and the door was shut.

"Well, have you read it?" demanded Mrs. Featherstone Hogg. "What do you think of it?"

"Charming," replied the Colonel. "Most amusing book I've read for a long time."

"Charming? Amusing?"

"So true to life," added the Colonel. "That soldier feller —Rivers or something—was the dead spit of a feller I used to know in India—ha, ha—couldn't help laughing when I read it. Haven't laughed so much over a book for years."

"But it's *you*," cried Mrs. Featherstone Hogg in amazement. "Can't you see that it is yourself, libelled, held up to ridicule; it's a caricature of *you*."

"Me?"

"Yes, of course." (Good Heavens, how dense the man was!)

"But why should it be me?" enquired Colonel Weatherhead. "I mean I don't know the feller who wrote it—"

"You may not know who he is, but he knows you all right—can't you see that the book is all about Silverstream —the whole thing is a wicked caricature of Silverstream —an outrageous attack on innocent people."

"Nonsense," said the Colonel.

"Didn't you *see* it?" demanded the lady irately.

"No, I didn't. Who *are* the people anyway? Who's that

Mrs. Thingumbob—the woman that the soldier feller gets engaged to?"

"Dorothea Bold, of course," replied Mrs. Featherstone Hogg, scornfully.

Colonel Weatherhead was silent.

"It's the frightful wickedness of it," said Mrs. Featherstone Hogg. "It's the frightful wickedness of it, that—that makes me so angry. Here we are all living together like a—like a happy family" (this was a good comparison, she thought, she must make a note of it for her speech at the Meeting)—"and then that horrible man comes along and spoils everything. Nothing will ever be the same again," she added pathetically, with her mind on Edwin and his rebellion—Edwin who had always been so mild and reasonable but was now asserting himself and making strange and sinister threats about Wills.

Colonel Weatherhead was still silent, he was not a quick thinker, he was wondering whether it could possibly be true. If so it was very queer—very queer indeed. He had done exactly what the book said (or at any rate as near as made no odds). What would Dorothea say when she heard about it? How would it affect his new relationship with that charming and altogether delightful person? Dreadful if she thought that he had proposed to her because he had read it in a book. It would be difficult to explain that the book had nothing to do with it, because, in a way, the book had everything to do with it. Dorothea might be annoyed. It would make them look slightly ridiculous in Silverstream if their union had been foretold in a book. People would say they had lived opposite to each other for four years and couldn't make up

their minds to marry each other until they read it in a
novel. Not a nice thing for all Silverstream to be saying—
not nice at all.

"The man must be found," Mrs. Featherstone Hogg
was saying, she had said a lot more—all about herself
and Edwin, and how the character of Mrs. Horsley
Downs was not in the least like her, and that she didn't
see how a man she didn't know could possibly have
found out all that about her private affairs, and that
obviously he didn't know anything about her at all, or he
could never have written such an outrageous libel—but
Colonel Weatherhead had not been listening. He came to
the surface again just in time to hear her saying that the
man must be found.

"What man?" asked the Colonel.

"John Smith, of course—only his name isn't John
Smith."

"Why?"

"Because he must be somebody in Silverstream, somebody who knows us all—otherwise he couldn't have written about us in his book."

"Oh I see—well I expect it's that Bulmer man. He
writes books, it must be him."

"I ask you, would he be likely to make his wife run
away with Harry Carter?" said Mrs. Featherstone Hogg
impatiently. "Would any man be likely to do such a
thing?"

"Run away with Harry Carter!" echoed the Colonel.

"Would he be likely to make her do that?" repeated
Mrs. Featherstone Hogg, getting more and more enraged
at the Colonel's stupidity.

"I've often wondered why she didn't run away with somebody," he said vaguely, "nice little woman, far too nice for a cantankerous beast like Bulmer—"

"Well, what do you think ought to be done?" she asked trying to bring him back to the point, they would never get on at this rate, and John Smith *must* be found.

"Done?" asked the Colonel.

"Yes, do you think he ought to be horse-whipped?"

"Well, I don't really blame Carter, y'know. She must have been dashed unhappy with that sour-faced husband of hers. It's not like going off with the wife of a brother-officer—not quite so rotten—besides Carter's gone to India with the Fiftieth. I suppose he's taken her with him—"

"What *are* you talking about?" cried Mrs. Featherstone Hogg. "She hasn't run away with him yet—"

"Send Bulmer an anonymous letter, then," suggested Colonel Weatherhead with sudden brilliant inspiration. "That'll put a stopper on it."

"She's not going to run away—at least so far as I know —Mr. Bulmer's sent her to Devonshire to spend Christmas with her people—"

"She'll enjoy that."

"She may or she may not—that's scarcely the point. We're not talking about the Bulmers at all."

"Oh—I thought we were," said the bewildered Colonel. "I thought you said Mrs. Bulmer had run away with Harry Carter."

"It's only in the book—it's all in the book—didn't you read it?" asked Mrs. Featherstone Hogg angrily. She felt she would like to shake the man, he was so hopelessly dense. She was not far off shaking him if the truth were told.

"Good Lord!" said Colonel Weatherhead. He tried to remember the book in detail, but Dorothea had swamped his mind and the book—read through rapidly—had faded into an indistinct blur. He could remember quite distinctly his own reaction to it, and the love scene in Mrs. Mildmay's garden, but not much else.

"Don't you think John Smith ought to be horse-whipped?" said Mrs. Featherstone Hogg, savagely.

"What's the feller done?"

"He wrote it—he's the author of it," said Mrs. Featherstone Hogg, trying very hard not to lose her temper completely. It was so important to keep on friendly terms with Colonel Weatherhead, because he was the only man who could possibly be visualised horse-whipping John Smith. And John Smith must be horse-whipped, she was convinced of that now. He had caused such a lot of trouble and worry. If it had not been for John Smith, Mrs. Featherstone Hogg would have been sitting at home over a nice fire reading or sewing comfortably, instead of boxed up in a draughty car, with the rain pattering on the roof, trying to talk to an imbecile. John Smith must certainly be horse-whipped and the Colonel was the man to do it, therefore the Colonel must be won over; his stupidity must be tolerated with superhuman patience, he must be wheedled, flattered, cajoled, infuriated, and so roused to action.

"Listen to me," said Mrs. Featherstone Hogg, laying her hand upon the Colonel's arm, "you had better read the book again, carefully, and then we can talk it all over quietly together, and decide what is to be done. I am having a Meeting at my house on Thursday. Thursday at half-past three and tea afterwards. Tell Dorothea I shall expect her too. I will go round in the car and invite everybody in Silverstream—everybody must come."

"All right," said the Colonel. He realised that the interview was over and he was glad. He wanted to get away and arrange his thoughts. He did not care a bit whether Mrs. Featherstone Hogg found John Smith, nor whether that gentleman received the punishment she so vehemently desired to mete out to him: he only cared for the possible effects which these extraordinary disclosures might have upon Dorothea and himself. Besides it was bad for his rheumatism to sit in a cold car with wet shoes on, and the legs of his trousers all damp and clammy from the drips off his waterproof—

He said "Good-bye" to Mrs. Featherstone Hogg, stepped out of the car with alacrity, and went home to have a bath and change his clothes. Dorothea was coming to dinner with him.

    .   .   .   .   .

So far nobody knew of their engagement. They had decided to keep it a secret, but they would not be able to keep it a secret for long. The servants would soon guess what was afoot, and, in a few days, the news would be all over Silverstream. And now the whole thing was complicated by that book, if what Mrs. Featherstone Hogg said was true. Colonel Weatherhead thought about it in his bath and all the time he was dressing.

He came down to find that Dorothea had arrived and

was standing on tiptoe in front of the drawing-room mantelpiece arranging her hair in the mirror. There was something very sweet and feminine about her as she patted the curls into shape. He crept in very quietly and kissed her on the tip of her ear—it was very neatly done, Major Waterfoot himself could not have done it better—

Dorothea screamed, and blushed, and told him he was a wicked man—positively wicked. "Supposing Simmons had seen you," she pointed out, "what *would* he have thought?"

"Simmons never thinks," replied Colonel Weatherhead. "He leaves all the thinking to his wife. Jolly good idea, too," added the Colonel chuckling.

"Now, now!" threatened Dorothea.

They were very circumspect during dinner, and Simmons saw nothing that he shouldn't have seen. They discussed Dorothea's drains, and from thence wandered on by some strange bypath to chrysanthemums. Dorothea's were all frosted, but the Colonel had a few which he had protected from the night-frosts with elaborately rigged sacking.

"Mrs. Carter still has some," Dorothea said. "I was having tea with her the other day and such a queer thing happened. Mrs. Featherstone Hogg burst in; she was in a frightful rage about a book—she practically threw it at us and said it was filth and that it was all about *us*."

"Did you read it?" enquired the Colonel anxiously.

"No. She left it for Mrs. Carter to read, but I must get hold of it. I shall ask for it at the library."

"Don't," said Colonel Weatherhead, taking her hand, which lay conveniently near him on the table. "Don't read it, Dorothea. Why should you waste your time and —soil your beautiful mind reading filth?"

They gazed into each other's eyes adoringly, then, with a sigh Dorothea withdrew her hand—Simmons was coming in with the pudding.

"I rather wondered what the book said about me," said Dorothea, returning to the subject which intrigued her somewhat. "You wouldn't think there was much material for a book in a place like Silverstream. Mrs. Featherstone Hogg was really very queer about it, she told Mrs. Carter that she wore a wig—that Mrs. Carter wore a wig, I mean —I've always thought her hair looked too good to be true. Mrs. Carter didn't like it."

Colonel Weatherhead was trying to make up his mind whether to make a clean breast of the whole thing, or whether to pretend that he knew nothing about it. His inclinations veered to the latter course—it was much the easier—but he was rather afraid that Dorothea might hear Mrs. Featherstone Hogg's account of it and realise that he had not been quite open with her. That would be disastrous. There was a third course open to him, the course of telling Dorothea a little, and making light of it. This course was fraught with difficulties, but, on the whole, it seemed best.

"Mrs. Featherstone Hogg is absolutely crazy about that wretched book," said Colonel Weatherhead, trying to laugh convincingly. "She came down here this afternoon and made me sit in her car with her, and she talked at me until I didn't know whether I was standing on my head or my heels. What an awful woman she is!"

"Did you read the book?" enquired Dorothea.

"I glanced through it," replied the Colonel casually. "She sent it to me, and then kept on ringing me up and asking me what I thought of it. I saw nothing very much in it—quite an ordinary novel, I thought."

"*Am* I in it?"

"There was nobody the least like you in the book. Nobody half so pretty, and charming, and sweet, and dainty," said the Colonel gallantly (Simmons had brought their coffee and departed for good, so it was quite safe).

Dorothea laughed roguishly.

The Colonel leaned over and kissed her hand.

They smiled into each other's eyes.

"We've wasted years," said Colonel Weatherhead, with a sigh. "Years, and years, and years. One, two, three, four," he added, telling them over on Dorothea's fingers.

Dorothea did not know the correct answer to this. Privately she thought that Robert was right, but it was his fault that the years had been wasted—not hers—so she said nothing.

The Colonel was not talking at random when he said they had wasted years, he had an idea at the back of his mind, but he didn't know how to broach it to his beloved. He could not see how to go on. Perhaps it would be better to approach the subject from a different angle.

"Those drains of yours have a horrible smell," he said thoughtfully.

Dorothea withdrew her hand (it will be remembered that he had been counting her fingers) she was a little hurt at the aspersion on her drains, it was a frightful come-down from wasted years to drains.

"Everybody's drains smell when they're blocked," said Dorothea shortly.

"I know, I know," he said hastily. "But what I mean is it's not healthy for you—it would be dreadful if you got ill or anything. I've been thinking it over carefully while we've been talking. Your drains are blocked; the weather is ghastly (it does nothing but rain); and I've finished with my bishop, for this year—I hope I've finished the brute for good, but I can't be certain of that, of course, until next Spring—there's nothing to keep us here as far as I can see, absolutely nothing."

"Nothing to keep us here?" enquired Dorothea who was considerably puzzled by the connection between the weather and her drains and the Colonel's bishop. Who was the Colonel's bishop? Was he some troublesome relative who required consideration—an older brother perhaps, or possibly an uncle. She had never heard Robert say that he had a brother who was a Bishop.

"Dorothea," said the Colonel, who had beaten about the bush to no purpose and was tired of the game, "Dorothea, I want to marry you."

Dorothea was surprised. She had already promised to marry Colonel Weatherhead (or Robert as she now called him). She had thought—with good reason—that the matter was decided.

"I know you do, Robert," she said feebly.

"But I want to marry you now, at once," he told her urgently. "Don't you see how everything points to our getting married immediately? The weather, my Bishop, your drains, *everything*. We'll go up to town on Monday and get married quietly, without any fuss, and go off to

Monte Carlo for Christmas. Say you will, Dorothea darling."

"Robert!" she exclaimed in amazement.

"Why not?" he enquired in wheedling tones. "There's nothing to stop us, and everything to—to—you know what I mean, I can't think of the word—it's absolutely the hand of Providence pointing. The weather is as foul as your drains, and my bishop is done for—"

"Who is your bishop?" interrupted Dorothea somewhat irritably for such a good-natured woman. "*Who on earth is your bishop?* You've been talking about him for ages, and I don't see what he has got to do with our getting married—"

Colonel Weatherhead roared with laughter.

"Good Heavens! I thought everyone in Silverstream had heard about my bishop—I can't be such a garrulous old bore after all—have I never told you about my struggles with the brute every autumn?"

"Never," said Dorothea primly, "and I really do not think you should speak of a bishop in that way, Robert dear. He may be very trying at times—I am sure he is—but after all we must remember that he is consecrated—consecrated with oil," said Dorothea vaguely, "and therefore—"

"It's a weed," gasped the Colonel between his spasms of laughter. "Bishop—weed—it grows in my hedge—it has roots like an octopus—"

Dorothea did not join in his mirth. How was she to know that it was a weed he was talking about? She saw nothing very funny in the misunderstanding.

Colonel Weatherhead took out a large white silk handkerchief and mopped his eyes. When the film of moisture was removed he was horrified to find that his lady-love was offended. She was sitting up very straight in her chair gazing before her at the picture of the Colonel's grandfather, in oils, which hung upon the dining-room wall.

"Never mind the stupid old weed," he said hastily. "It's just one of my silly jokes—damn silly joke, I know. Somehow I always enjoy my fight with the bishop-weed. It's the only fight I'm fit for now, and the old soldier enjoys a fight. Let's go into the drawing-room, shall we?"

Dorothea was immediately appeased. They went into the drawing-room arm in arm. Simmons had built up the fire to an alarming height—he had been brought up in the Army, of course, where coal is free—Dorothea thought it was rather extravagant but it was certainly very cosy on a cold night. They toasted their toes and talked about themselves and were very happy.

The Colonel walked home with his guest. It was still raining and everything was dripping wet—they nearly fell into the hole in Dorothea's drive which had escaped their memory for the time being.

"What about Monday?" whispered the Colonel.

"Not *Monday*," she pleaded.

"Why not Monday? What's the matter with Monday?" he demanded boldly.

"Too soon. How can I get my clothes ready?"

"We'll stop in Paris and get clothes," he told her with diabolical cunning. "Listen, Dorothea. We don't want a lot of fuss and bother in Silverstream. Let's give them the slip. Just vanish quietly and tell them nothing about it until it's all over. We'll send them postcards from Paris or Monte, then they'll have time to talk themselves out before we get home. What do you say?"

Dorothea wanted fuss as little as he did. She could almost hear the gossips saying, "Well, it's taken her four years. I wonder how she managed to hook him in the end. He must be in his dotage, I suppose." That is what they would *all* say when they heard of her engagement, and she would know they were thinking it when they offered her their congratulations.

"Well," she said, wavering.

"You will!" he jubilated. "Hurrah!"

He really was quite like a boy, and it was much more exciting, being engaged to him than she had expected. Fancy his planning all that about Monte Carlo for Christmas—you would never think him capable of such a dashing idea. It was rather a nice idea too, it would be lovely to get away from Silverstream for a bit and bask in the sun. Robert was really a dear, she loved him. She had wanted him for years and she had almost despaired. He had always been friendly and neighbourly, ready to help and advise her in any emergency that required male help and advice—when her tree fell, for instance, it was Colonel Weatherhead who arranged with the man to come and cut it up for her—but he had never shown the slightest signs of wanting to marry her until last night. What had suddenly wakened him up? Dorothea wondered, as she shut and bolted the front door and went slowly and thoughtfully up the stairs to bed.

She lighted the gas fire in her bedroom and thought about it all, sitting in a low chair and warming her knees the while. There was nobody to consult about her marriage, she was independent, her money was her own. She had two sisters, both married. One lived in London and the other in a country parsonage. They would be surprised, of course,—perhaps even rather amused for they were both younger than herself and both very much married matrons—but they would be quite nice about it, she knew. I can stay with Alice while Robert arranges about the wedding, she thought. Alice was always quite pleased to give her house-room for a few days when she wanted it.

Dorothea had decided to humour Robert's boyish whim, there was no reason against it. I wonder how old he is—she thought—perhaps nearly sixty, but he doesn't look it, and anyhow it doesn't matter. I'm not as young as I was, and Robert's a dear. The drawing-room at The Bridge House is rather dull—she thought—but I could brighten it up with some of my own things. Perhaps Robert would throw out a bow-window in the drawing-room, that would make a lot of difference.

After a little she got up and began to pull out drawers and burrow into tissue paper. I shan't take much—she thought—it will be fun getting things in Paris—pretty things. Fancy him suggesting that!

Dorothea paused for a moment with a silk scarf in her hands. It almost looked as if—as if he knew a good deal about women. He was so glib about it. Had he taken other women to Paris to choose clothes? Well I can't help that—she told herself sharply—what does it matter anyhow? Get on with the job, Dorothea.

She got on with it.

CHAPTER XIV

Sunday and Monday

*T*HE next day was Sunday. The newly engaged
couple had decided to go to Church separately, to
sit in their separate pews and to behave as if nothing had happened. It was rather fun to deceive Silverstream, and Silverstream would be all the more surprised
when it received its postcards from Paris.

Dorothea tripped along sedately—it was a lovely morning, the clouds had all vanished and the sun was shining
brightly through the bare trees—she did not know
whether Robert was ahead of her, or behind. (Her clocks
were all different, clocks are one of those mysterious
things that never go so well in a woman's house, clocks
need a man to keep them in proper subjection.) First she
thought that Robert must be ahead of her, and hurried
on, and then she was sure he was behind her, and
dawdled.

Barbara Buncle was just coming out of her gate when
Dorothea passed, they walked along together talking
about the sunshine and how nice and warm it was for
December. Dorothea liked Barbara, she felt sorry that
Barbara's clothes were so appalling. Probably Barbara
was very badly off, but even so she might have done
better than that. The truth was she looked less peculiar
in her everyday garments because they were tweeds and

jerseys—you couldn't go far wrong with tweeds and jerseys. On Sundays poor Barbara looked a perfect sight, her hat was frightful.

"Why don't you get a new hat, Barbara?" she said suddenly.

"Well, I did think of it, but this one is still quite good," replied Barbara.

"Give it to Dorcas and buy another," suggested Dorothea, daringly.

"Perhaps I will," said Barbara, and why shouldn't I? she thought—why shouldn't I have some nice clothes now that I can afford it? The only bother is I never seem to be able to get nice ones. I always feel an absolute guy in new clothes. How nice Dorothea looks!

"How nice you look, Dorothea!" she said.

"Do I?"

"Yes. You always look nice, of course, but to-day you look even nicer than usual."

"You *lamb!*" said Dorothea.

Colonel Weatherhead passed them, and bowed gravely.

"A pleasant morning after the rain, Mrs. Bold," he remarked as he went by.

Dorothea laughed inwardly—he *was* a naughty boy! Barbara collected the phrase for her new novel. "A pleasant morning after the rain," was exactly what Major Waterfoot would have said. Not to Mrs. Mildmay, of course, for they were married now and it was not a remark that a man was likely to make to his wife, but Major Waterfoot could say it to somebody else—it was too good to waste.

The new novel had sarted, and it was proving uphill

work. Inspiration had not visited Barbara, she was toiling
at it nobly, if somewhat hopelessly. It will never be as
good as *Disturber of the Peace,* she thought.

The three people with their secret thoughts—so secret
and so diverse—entered St. Monica's together. Mrs.
Carter and Sally were close behind. Mrs. Greensleeves
·vas already in her pew. Miss King and Angela Pretty
were hurrying across the field-path followed by Mrs.
Goldsmith and her family. The Bulmers were there, and
the Snowdons, and the Featherstone Hoggs, even the
two young men from Mrs. Dick's had come to church
this morning. The sunshine after the rain had lured them
all out. Of all our Silverstream friends only the Walkers
were absent. The doctor scarcely ever went to church,
and Sarah had stayed at home because the twins had a
feverish cold.

Mrs. Carter sat in the same pew as Barbara Buncle.
Usually they sat one at either end of the pew with four
vacant seats between them, but to-day Sally was there
to fill the vacancy. Barbara could not help noticing that
Sally was a little restless during the service, she seemed
doubtful when to stand up, and when to kneel down.
She fluttered the leaves of her prayer-book in the vain
endeavour to find her place. Sally doesn't go to church
often—Barbara decided.

During the sermon a small piece of paper was pushed
into Barbara's hand. "I'm coming to tea with you to-
day" was written on it. Barbara looked at her, and nodded and smiled, she felt pleased and excited at the idea
of Sally coming to tea—it was nice that Sally wanted
to come. Perhaps Sally would talk about *Disturber of*

the Peace, she liked hearing Sally talk about it. Mrs. Featherstone Hogg was having a Meeting at her house on Thursday to talk about it, and she had asked Barbara to go. "There will be tea afterwards," Mrs. Featherstone Hogg had said. Barbara did not want to go to the meeting and hear them discussing *Disturber of the Peace.* She knew exactly what they would say about it. The tea was no inducement to those who knew Mrs. Featherstone Hogg's teas. Barbara had endured many teas at The Riggs, so she knew exactly what to expect—shallow cups with grey-looking luke-warm liquid and a sandwich containing banana paste or gentleman's relish, you didn't know which it was going to be until you bit into it. Still, it would look funny if I didn't go—Barbara thought.

She tried to fix her mind on the sermon. It was all about loving your neighbour, and how you must seek out the good in people and only see the good. Mr. Hathaway said that was the way to make people good—by refusing to see the evil. Barbara wondered if this were true, and, if so, how deep it went. If you refused to see the evil in a murderer, did that cure him? Doubtful. Mr. Hathaway had passed on to the subject of money. Money was the root of all evil. St. Francis had no money, he had nothing, and he was superlatively good. People had too much money nowadays—Mr. Hathaway said— our lives should be simplified, a man needed very little in this world, it was in the next world that a man should lay up treasure. "Sell all that thou hast, and give to the poor," said Mr. Hathaway. "And now—"

Barbara stood up, wondering whether Mr. Hathaway

had done that, it was said in the village that he had lots of money.

Vivian Greensleeves did not listen much to the sermon, she had other things to think of. She had made considerable progress with the Vicar since that first luncheon party and the supper that followed. He bored her frightfully but that could not be helped, the main thing was that he had money. Vivian needed money more and more. The shops in Silverstream were beginning to get impatient. Her dressmaker in London had sent her a lawyer's letter demanding instant payment of her account. It was all so unjust—thought Vivian—if she had had money she would have paid her bills gladly, but she couldn't give the wretches money when she had none to give them. Ernest Hathaway was her only hope, she must just make the best of him, and once they were married she need not listen to his dull and stupid dissertations any more.

After the service Vivian waited for the Vicar in the church-yard and they walked up the hill together. Ernest Hathaway had drifted into the habit of lunching with Vivian on Sundays. It was now an understood thing that she should wait for him after Matins and that they should walk up the hill to Mon Repos together.

To-day they talked about some books which Mr. Hathaway had lent Mrs. Greensleeves to read. They were incredibly dull books, but Vivian had actually read them —or partially read them—so as to have some intelligent questions all ready to ask him when they met. She had decided that her campaign must be speeded up—Mr. Hathaway admired her, and liked her, she knew. It was almost time he proposed. To-day she would ask him to call her Vivian. He would be quite pleased to call her Vivian, she thought, and she was right. Ernest was quite ready to call her Vivian—he asked her to call him Ernest, and discoursed for some minutes about the religious significance of Christian names. Vivian didn't care a jot for their religious significance but she listened meekly. After all, whatever significance he attached to her Christian name it was a step in the right direction to call her by it.

Ernest called her by it several times with a great deal of pleasure. He was very proud of this sheep which he had shepherded so energetically into the fold. He thought she was beautiful, and, now that she had repented of her sins and remedied her omissions, she was also good. What more could any man want than a good and beautiful wife?

．　　．　　．　　．　　．

Sally arrived at Tanglewood Cottage for tea as arranged. Barbara had nothing to give her for tea, she had not expected a guest, and, being Sunday, she could not rush out and buy buns from Mrs. Goldsmith as she would most certainly have done had the day been an ordinary day. But there was a nice fire and they made hot buttered toast and scorched their faces and were thoroughly happy.

"I've been thinking of getting a new hat," said Barbara suddenly.

Sally pricked up her ears. "How exciting!" she exclaimed, and, visualising the hat which had sat next to her in church that morning, she added fervently, "yes, you really should."

"I'm so bad at choosing hats," sighed Barbara. "That's the worst of it. I never seem to get one that really suits me, and Miss Bonnar has such a poor selection."

"My dear—you would never buy a hat at Miss Bonnar's!" cried the horror-stricken Sally.

"But I always go to Miss Bonnar—"

"Nonsense, you must go to town of course. Go to Virginia's."

"Where's that?" enquired Barbara with interest.

"She's a friend of mine," Sally confided. "She has a little shop for hats and frocks in Kensington High Street. I'll write a note to her, if you like, and tell her not to rook you."

"Will you really?"

"Rather. It will be doing her a good turn too. And really she's a frightfully decent sort, and frightfully clever at knowing exactly what will suit you."

"I'll go to-morrow," Barbara said dashingly. "And I'll get some really nice clothes as well as a hat." Why shouldn't she? The hundred pounds in the bank seemed every reason why she should.

"Have your hair waved first," advised Sally as she went away, regretfully, at seven o'clock. "But don't let them cut it off whatever you do, it wouldn't suit you at all, but they're sure to want to do it." She came back from the gate to add, "Give my love to Virginia, and tell her I'm miserable."

Thus it fell out that Barbara and Dorothea Bold were both passengers in the 10.30 train to London on Monday morning. (Colonel Weatherhead had gone up by the 8.15

to transact some important business and to make enquiries about a Special Licence.)

Barbara hailed Dorothea cheerfully and they selected an empty third class carriage and bestowed themselves therein.

"I'm going to stay with Alice for a day or two," said Dorothea truthfully—it seemed better to forestall any questions with an appearance of absolute frankness.

"How nice!" said Barbara. "I'm only going up for the day. I'm going to have my hair waved, I think."

"Oh do," cried Dorothea. "Go to my woman—she's simply marvellous."

Barbara noted the address and thought how nice people were. It was all being made so easy for her. First Sally and now Dorothea had flown to her rescue. They talked in a friendly desultory sort of fashion all the way to town and parted at the station—Dorothea to go off to her sister's, in a taxi, with her luggage, and Barbara to board a bus which her friend assured her would land her quite near the marvellous woman who would transform her lank locks into ravishing waves.

The ravishing waves took some time to materialise. It was an amazing experience, Barbara decided, and she was not quite sure that she liked the result. Her old hat certainly looked most peculiar perched on the top of her undulating coiffure. However, she paid her money without a murmur and marched out of the shop—she was nearly sure that the girl at the desk was giggling at her appearance.

She lunched frugally at a Corner Shop and then set out to look for Virginia. "A little yellow shop," Sally had said, "with one small hat in the window and the name above the door in black letters." It was difficult to find, because it was really so very small and unassuming, but Barbara found it at last wedged in between a huge drapery establishment and a flourishing flower shop. She pushed the door open and went in.

The little shop was empty save for a few fragile-looking gilt chairs and long mirrors which showed Barbara her own form at several distressing angles. No wonder that girl laughed, thought Barbara disconsolately, I look an absolute freak with my hair like this. I wonder if there's anything on earth that would straighten out a permanent wave. I don't suppose there *is* anything short of cutting it all off at the roots.

These desperate reflections were cut short by the appearance of a young woman gowned in black, with a supercilious expression who offered Barbara a gilt chair and enquired what she could do for "Moddam". Barbara was too terrified to speak, she merely handed over the letter from Sally and awaited the result.

"Oh I see," said the young woman in patronising tones. "A letter for Moddam. Kindly wait for a few moments until I find out if she is disengaged."

Barbara had not long to wait, she only just had time to seize her hat in both hands and pull it down on to her hair before Virginia herself appeared with Sally's letter in her hand. She was rather like Sally—Barbara thought—only taller, and dark instead of fair.

"How nice of Sally to send you to me," she said in a friendly manner. "Do come in here, won't you?"

Barbara was quite ready to go anywhere, she found

herself being ushered into a large room at the back of the shop—a large square room hung with coats and hats and frocks of every shape and hue.

"Now we can talk," said Virginia. "Tell me all about Sally. She says she's miserable, is she?"

"She says she is," said Barbara, blinking a little. "But I really don't think she is *very*."

"Because if she is, something will have to be done about it," said Virginia firmly. "We can't have Sally being miserable, you know. I wanted her to come in with me when Colonel Carter went to India without her, but the doctor said she would be better in the country."

"Milk and sunshine," suggested Barbara.

"Yes, that was the idea," replied Virginia. "But milk and sunshine are no good if you're miserable. You must let me know if you think she'd be better here. You live near her, don't you?"

"Next door," Barbara said.

"Sally's a dear isn't she?"

They discussed Sally for several minutes.

"And now," said Virginia at last, "you want some things, don't you? Sally says I'm to choose for you. Take off your hat."

Barbara removed it thankfully, once more it had slid up and perched on the top of her head.

Virginia stared at her with narrowed eyes. "Bottle green with your nice complexion," she decided, "or that new shade of wine—let's see—" she dived into various cupboards.

They spent three crowded hours together in the large square room. Virginia was most exacting, she flung dresses on to Barbara and tore them off again. "It's not your style at all," she told Barbara when the latter expressed a preference for a brown crêpe de chine with a straight bodice and flared skirt. "Sally would kill me if I let you have it. Just wait a moment till I find what I am looking for," and she burrowed into the cupboard again.

Barbara tried on coats and jumpers and frocks and hats until her newly-waved hair was like a wind blown hay-stack.

"I'm so sorry about your hair," Virginia said. "It's awful of me to rumple you up like this, but we *must* get the right thing. You must wet it and set it in waves when you go to bed—I'll give you a net."

When at last Barbara emerged from the shop she felt somewhat dizzy, and tremendously excited—she had never known until now that clothes could be exciting. There were a few alterations to be made, but Virginia had promised to send off the things on Thursday. She would get them on Friday morning. Barbara had spent nearly fifty pounds but she had got her money's worth and she knew it. There was a bottle-green coat with a fur collar and a hat to match, and a jumper suit to go with it; and there were two "little frocks" and an evening gown—and there were slips and stockings and shoes to match.

CHAPTER XV

More About Monday

*B*ARBARA little knew that, while she was enjoying
herself in London and buying a complete set of
new clothes under the expert advice of Virginia,
Disturber of the Peace was having a busy day in Silverstream, but such indeed was the case. It was spreading
rapidly like the desperate disease to which Miss King
had compared it. Mrs. Featherstone Hogg was its most
valuable publicity agent, she went round in her car dis-
tributing invitations to her Drawing-room Meeting and
copies of *Disturber of the Peace* to all those who had
not read it. She did not realise that John Smith obtained
royalties upon every copy of this book that was sold, or
she would have confined her expenditure upon the book
to narrower limits. It would have distressed her exceedingly to think that she was putting money into the pocket
of the detestable John Smith.

Mrs. Featherstone Hogg's Drawing-Room Meeting
was to be representative. It was not to be confined to any
one class of person. She would throw open her drawing-
room to everyone in Silverstream who was mentioned in
Disturber of the Peace,—it was a noble gesture.

She asked Mrs. Goldsmith, and one of her daughters,
and she asked Mrs. Dick and two of her paying guests,

and she asked the military people who were merely mentioned in passing. She even asked the old grave-digger from St. Monica's who had been terrified (so said *Disturber of the Peace*) by the sight of Mrs. Nevis (or Snowdon) arising from her grave to attend the dinner-party given by her family. Unfortunately Mr. Durnet was frightfully hard of hearing, and they could not make him understand what it was all about, but his daughter promised to have him all ready and send him up to The Riggs on Thursday at three-thirty.

The Snowdons had received their invitation on Sunday and had spent Sunday evening reading *Disturber of the Peace*. Nobody knows what they said about it in the privacy of their home—they said very little outside—but Miss Isabella, who was of a nervous temperament, awoke screaming in the middle of the night and declared—when her adoring relatives appeared in her bedroom in déshabillé—that her mother had come back from the dead.

"That's impossible, Isabella," said Mr. Snowdon with unwonted sternness.

"It may be impossible but it is true all the same," said Isabella tearfully, "She was standing there at the end of my bed, just where you are standing. And she called me 'Izzy'. You know how I hated it when she called me Izzy."

The cook had now appeared upon the scene with her hair in curl-papers and her eyes staring out of her head.

"It's gall-stones, that's what it is," she announced, "my married sister was taken just the same and she had four. They gave them to her at the hospital in a bag."

It was some time before Miss Olivia could persuade her that Miss Isabella was in no pain, and induce her to return to bed. Meanwhile Mr. Snowdon was endeavouring, without much success, to soothe his younger daughter, by assuring her that she had been the victim of a nightmare.

"But I saw her distinctly," Isabella declared, "I was awake at the time. I know I was."

"You couldn't have been."

"I was, I was," cried Isabella hysterically.

Peace was ultimately restored by the administration of two aspirin tablets, and Mr. Snowdon and Olivia covered the sufferer with her disarranged bed-clothes and tiptoed softly from the room. They discussed the whole matter in whispers on the landing. Olivia thought that Dr. Walker should be summoned, but her father disagreed. It was inadvisable to reveal family secrets to outsiders if it could be avoided. They must think of other means of laying the spectre which had disturbed dear Isabella's rest.

"What other means?" demanded Olivia, in an urgent whisper. "You know how sensitive the poor darling is. Once she got an idea like that into her head—"

Mr. Snowdon shivered—not entirely because he was cold—he was remembering other occasions when ideas became fixed in dear Isabella's head and produced nightmares. He felt he was too old now to go through all that sort of thing again. When you grew older you required refreshing sleep during the night if you were to be any use at your office during the day.

"What about Chemical Food?" he suggested.

Olivia was afraid that Chemical Food would be inadequate.

Mr. Snowdon sighed and agreed that Olivia might be right, they must think of something else.

They went back to bed.

.　　　.　　　.　　　.

Mrs. Greensleeves was another to whom *Disturber of the Peace* brought unrest. She met Mrs. Featherstone Hogg in the butcher's on Monday morning.

"I was just coming to see you," said Mrs. Featherstone Hogg, with unwonted friendliness—hitherto she had treated Vivian with contempt and had scarcely deigned to see her when they met—"I want you to come to my Drawing-room Meeting on Thursday afternoon. You will come, won't you?"

"What's it about?" asked Vivian suspiciously. "Is it Foreign Missions or something?"

"It's about *Disturber of the Peace*," replied Mrs. Featherstone Hogg.

"*Disturber of the Peace*," echoed Vivian, "what on earth is that?"

Mrs. Featherstone Hogg was amazed. "Do you mean to say you haven't read that dreadful book?" she demanded incredulously. "I thought everyone knew about it. You must read it at once, it's the wickedest book that has ever been written."

She had no time to say any more, for she was late for lunch already, but she had said quite enough to arouse Vivian's interest to boiling point. Vivian went into Miss Renton's there and then, and bought a copy of the book to take home with her. Miss Renton was doing a tremendous trade in John Smith's novel, she had had to order a special consignment of copies from London and even these were nearly exhausted. Everybody in Silverstream wanted to read *Disturber of the Peace,* and everybody wanted to read it at once. The library copy was booked for weeks ahead by those who were too poor or too thrifty to pay seven and sixpence for a copy of their own.

Vivian put the copy of *Disturber of the Peace* under her arm and walked home quickly. It had started to rain again—she put up her umbrella and nearly bumped into Dr. Walker, who was hastening home also.

"Isn't this weather awful?" Vivian said crossly.

Dr. Walker agreed with her. His car was being decarbonised and he had had a busy morning. The afternoon would probably be worse. People usually chose the moment when the doctor's car was out of action to hack their fingers to the bone, or scald their children with boiling tea, or fall downstairs. He had no time to stop and talk with Mrs. Greensleeves.

Vivian thought the doctor was curt, she went home in the rain with her book, and started to read it with avidity. ("The wickedest book that has ever been written" was sufficient recommendation to whet the appetite of the most jaded novel-reader.) At first it seemed quite an innocent sort of book, but after a little she recognised its peculiarity, and when she was half way through she recognised the libellous portrait of herself. She was so enraged by the impudence of the thing that she hurled the book across the room. "No wonder Mrs. Featherstone Hogg said it was wicked," she announced fiercely. And then of course she had to get up and fish it out from under the piano and finish it, and the end was a hundred times more wicked than the beginning.

Vivian flew into the most fearful rage, she stormed about all over the house like a lunatic—even Milly Spikes, who was no stranger to her mistress's temper, was alarmed by the violence of her rage and retired to the scullery in company with the cat until it should have spent itself somewhat—

The idea of this man (who was he? John Smith) writing about her private affairs in a horrible twopenny-halfpenny novel! And writing about her private affairs in such a way too! As if she—Vivian—would have anything to do with that horrible man who lodged with Mrs. Dick as a paying guest. She had been kind to him, of course, at one time, when she was bored to tears by the dullness of Silverstream—you must have somebody to talk to, and Mr. Fortnum was the best that Silverstream could provide. But she had soon found out that nothing was to be gained from Mr. Fortnum's friendship—he had sold his car for one thing so he couldn't even take her for an occasional run—and she had choked him off fairly easily. So it was all the more maddening to have the whole affair raked up like this. Supposing Ernest read the book and recognised the portrait? He was coming along so nicely now, Vivian thought her financial troubles were practically settled.

Oh how maddening it all was! How utterly maddening! How dare that horrible man write such lies about her—such disgusting lies!

Vivian wept tears of sheer rage.

It was in the midst of this storm that Ernest Hathaway walked in, heralded by Milly. Vivian had quite forgotten that she had asked him to supper.

The sight of Ernest pulled Vivian together as nothing else could have done, she hid the book under a convenient cushion and looked up at him with dewy eyes.

"Oh, Ernest, I'm so miserable," she sobbed, changing the tears of rage to tears of woe at a moment's notice.

Ernest was aghast to find his beautiful penitent in tears, he sat down on the sofa and tried to comfort her, soon she was weeping softly in his arms. She continued to weep for several minutes while she tried to find some plausible and pathetic story to account for her tears. Then she stopped weeping and told it to him.

She was lonely, she said, terribly lonely and somebody had been unkind to her because she had nobody to protect her. It was a much longer story than that of course and complicated by sobs, and assurances that she was not going to burden Ernest with her small troubles, but that was the gist of it. The person who had been unkind to her dwelt in London, she would not reveal his name under any persuasion whatever, it was her own fault for not seeing that he was a horrid sort of man from the very beginning—

Ernest listened and sympathised and eventually when Vivian had almost given up hope, he asked her to marry him.

.   .   .   .   .

We must now return to Dr. Walker who had nearly collided with Vivian Greensleeves in the High Street. It will be remembered that he was hastening home to lunch after a busy morning. He was frightfully late for lunch, of course, and Sarah had had hers, and gone out, but she had left a message for Dr. John on the telephone block. Sometimes these messages left by Sarah for her husband's perusal were slightly unofficial, but they were always perfectly clear. She did not allow her sense of humour to interfere with business; she only used it as a sauce to make the boiled fish more interesting—so to speak. Sarah loved a joke. Why not indulge herself since it did nobody any harm and did John good? John took life so awfully seriously, it was good for him to be shaken up a little now and then. To-day she had written, "Please go and look at Angela's Pretty chest."

Dr. John smiled as he tore off the leaf and put it carefully away in his notebook. He kept every letter and every scrap of paper that Sarah had ever written to him. He was—he knew it himself—quite foolishly sentimental about Sarah. When he had put the leaflet safely away his brow clouded over, and he slipped his stethoscope into his pocket and went in next door.

Angela's chest lay heavily upon the doctor's mind. There was nothing definite about it (it was one of those doubtful borderline cases which are really more anxiety to their medical man than a definite disease. Last year he had had a specialist down from town to look at Angela, and Angela had been ill for a week with sheer fright, and the specialist had said, "There's nothing definite, nothing at all yet, but keep an eye on her." So helpful after all the fuss; and every cold that Angela took, settled firmly on her chest).

To-day Dr. John was full of jokes with Angela. He

pretended to upset the tumbler and caught it in the air, and he teased her about her new bed-jacket, and told her all about the latest mischief perpetrated by the twins. He was so cheerful that he left Angela feeling much better, and much happier about herself; feeling, indeed, that it had been quite an unnecessary expense to send for him at all.

But as he went downstairs, the clouds gathered once more upon the doctor's brow, and he went into the drawing-room, where Ellen King was writing, and shut the door behind him.

"Well John?" she said, rather breathlessly.

"I don't like these continual colds," he said. "I don't like them, Ellen."

These two were old friends, they had always lived next door to each other (for Dr. John's father had been Silverstream's doctor before Dr. John was born). Ellen and John had played together as children, and together had climbed every climbable tree in the two adjoining gardens. Dr. John had a great respect for Ellen King, and a great compassion, she was such a lonely sort of creature and ridden by a curious temperament. Her excellent brain had never been developed and turned to use. Ellen would have made a good doctor or lawyer (the stuff was there), but her father had abhorred clever women and had denied her the opportunity of a decent education.

"What do you mean, exactly?" she asked him anxiously.

"I don't mean anything very much," Dr. John told her. "In fact I mean exactly what I say—I don't like these continual colds that Angela gets. Could you possibly go away?"

"Go away? You mean to Bournemouth or somewhere?"

"Bournemouth? No. I mean to Egypt. It is warm and dry there. Just for the rest of the winter, of course."

"I suppose we could if it is necessary—I mean of course we could if it is necessary," she amended in sudden alarm.

"I wouldn't like to say it is necessary, but it is advisable," he replied, choosing his words carefully.

Miss King knew that he was wondering whether they could afford it, and she answered him as if he had put the question.

"We have got a little, put away for a rainy day," she said, smiling a trifle wanly.

"It's raining all right," he replied pointing to the window.

"But not very hard?" she asked him.

"No," he said. "Just a shower, Ellen, just a shower. But we want to get Angela off to some place where she will get sunshine and dry air to breathe. Wait and go after the New Year. I'll look in to-morrow when you've thought it over, and we can arrange for the whole thing."

"John!" she said suddenly. "Shall I let Angela go alone? I could take up some sort of work—no, don't say anything yet—I believe I'm bad for Angela, John. I have begun to think she would be better without me. She depends upon me too much. Sometimes I think she is beginning to lose her identity altogether—"

"What on earth are you talking about?" said Dr. John

furiously, taking a few strides across the floor and back again to his usual station in front of the fire. "What on earth are you talking about, Ellen? I thought you had more sense. Angela would depend upon anybody who happened to be there to depend upon. It's her nature to—to lean—Angela is weak in body, and soul, and mind."

"I know," said Ellen, "I know all that, John, but I love her just the same. I love her too much. I fuss over her too much—I agonise over her—"

"Look here, we all agonise over people we love. But we mustn't fuss—that's the important thing. It's difficult not to fuss, but we mustn't do it, Ellen. I don't think you do fuss over Angela. I think you're very sensible with her."

"I've begun to doubt it," Ellen replied. "You don't know how she depends upon me for everything. She can't even decide what to wear without asking me what I think. That's bad, isn't it, John?"

"It's the woman's nature," he said impatiently. "You've done such a lot for her, you've been wonderful to her, Ellen. Believe me it's not your fault that she's weak and vacillating—you're not bad for her, it's absurd and ridiculous to think so. As for her going to Egypt by herself, the thing's simply unthinkable, I couldn't countenance it for a moment. I'd rather she stayed here, infinitely rather. You must go and look after her, she needs you. For pity's sake don't go and get a lot of foolish ideas into your head."

"John, have you read that book?"

"Have I read it? Did Sarah give me a moment's peace until I had read the wretched book? Have I had a moment's peace ever since, with everybody talking about it, and having hysterics over it?—Don't talk to me about that book, Ellen," said Dr. John half in fun and half in earnest.

"But what do you think of it, John," she demanded, disobeying his injunction promptly.

"Well, I'll tell you what I think about it if you like. I know I'm in the minority in my opinion, but that can't he helped. I think it was written by a very simple minded person—a woman. Yes, I'm almost certain John Smith is a woman. I wouldn't mind betting you a fiver that it's a woman, if you like to take me on. And I don't think the book is meant to be unkind or libellous at all. I think John Smith sat down at her desk, and wrote that book in absolute good faith, merely describing people as she saw them, putting in every smallest detail about them just as she saw it."

"But the second part," objected Ellen.

Dr. John laughed. "The second part ran away with her—that's obvious. The book suddenly took the bit in its mouth and bolted with John Smith, and she just sat back and held on like grim death and let it run. I confess that it amused me, Ellen—I know this is heresy in Silverstream, but it amused me immensely. It didn't strike me as a satire, nor could I find anything nasty in it. You can read it both ways, I know, especially some parts like the love scenes, but I'm pretty certain that John Smith intended nothing nasty. I'm pretty certain that it's just a simple story, written by a very innocent person—a person totally ignorant of the world, and worldly matters —perhaps even rather a stupid person."

"And who is it?" she asked him, thoughtfully.

"There you have me," the doctor owned, stroking his chin. "There, I admit, you have me cold. I have not the remotest idea who can have written that book, although, obviously, I must know the author quite well."

"She must be a local person," Ellen agreed, she had quite accepted the doctor's diagnosis of the author's sex.

"Of course she must be. And somebody who knows us all intimately. Everybody will tell you that the book is full of discrepancies, of course. Mrs. Carter says that it is quite wrong about her hair," said Dr. John with twinkling eyes, "and Mrs. Featherstone Hogg denies that she was ever in the chorus—"

"Was she?" enquired Ellen breathlessly.

"I'm sure I don't know, and if I did I wouldn't tell you," was the whimsical reply. "Bulmer says he's the soul of amiability, and Mrs. Dick doesn't feed her paying guests on congealed bacon fat, and I assure you here and now that I never prescribe castor oil for lead swingers— as a matter of fact I know a trick worth two of that— but all the same I am convinced that John Smith knows us all pretty well, and that, therefore, we must know John Smith."

"That's what I said to Mr. Abbott," Ellen agreed.

Dr. John was edging towards the door, he hoped that Ellen would let him go and have his lunch—it was after two o'clock and he was feeling somewhat empty—but she hadn't finished with him yet.

"You're not really anxious about Angela, are you?" she asked, following him into the hall.

"Not if you go away," he replied firmly. "I shall be

worried if you stay here. Lord! I wish I could get away from this abominable climate, and take Sarah—you're lucky."

"You wouldn't let Sarah come with us?" suggested Ellen hopefully.

"Kind of you," he said, struggling into his coat, and retrieving his hat from the stand, "very kind indeed, and of course I'd let her. But I don't think she'd go. Persuade her if you can. I'd miss her abominably, of course, but I'm all for it, if you can get her to go. I tried to send her away when she was ill, but she was twice as ill at the mere idea—"

"You were anxious about her, I know," said Ellen.

"Anxious? I was demented," replied the doctor. "I don't want anyone to go through that particular hell if I can help it. That's why I'm banishing you to Egypt." He was on the doorstep now, poised for flight—if only the woman would stop talking and let him get home.

"Why don't you send us to Samarkand while you're about it?" she demanded, with a deep chuckle. "I believe you're in league with your female John Smith."

Dr. John waved his hat at her, "Good! Splendid!" he cried. "That's the spirit—that's more like the good old Ellen King I know so well. Tell them all that you and Angela are off to Samarkand—and, Ellen," he added in lower and more confidential tones, "don't forget to order those riding breeches, will you? You'd look fine in them—"

CHAPTER XVI

The Drawing-Room Meeting

*B*ARBARA BUNCLE was a little late for the Drawing-room Meeting on Thursday afternoon. She had
been working at her new novel all the morning,
and then, just as she was in the middle of dressing, Sally
had appeared and had wanted to hear all about her adventures in town, and all about Virginia and the new clothes.
Barbara tried to talk and dress at the same time but she
was not used to it, having been an only child with no
sisters to initiate her in the art.

"That stocking's inside out," Sally told her, "and there's
a tiny hole in the heel. You had better give it to me to
mend while you put on your hat."

Barbara complied meekly, her new outfit had not
arrived yet, so she had to wear her old hat—the one that
looked so ridiculous upon her new hair.

"You can't go like that," said Sally frankly. "Haven't
you got any other hats at all?"

"None that I could wear," admitted Barbara sadly.

Sally put down the stocking which she had mended
neatly, and rummaged in Barbara's wardrobe. She unearthed an old black felt which Barbara had intended
to give to Dorcas, twisted it this way and that way in
her small capable hands, and finally crammed it on to
Barbara's head, back to front, and told her to go.

"You'll be fearfully late if you don't hurry," she said, just as if it were not her fault at all that Barbara was late. "Gran started hours ago. And I want you to listen to everything that everybody says and remember it all to tell me. I'd give anything to be there."

Barbara promised, and seized her umbrella, and fled, quite forgetting about the hat.

Mrs. Featherstone Hogg had arranged all her chairs round the drawing-room walls, they were filled with people. She herself was seated in the middle with a card-table in front of her, covered with a red cloth, and laden with writing materials. Beside her sat Mr. Bulmer wearing his gloomiest expression.

Mr. Bulmer's gloom was due partly to domestic difficulties which had arisen in the absence of his wife, and partly to the feeling that he looked a fool sitting in the middle of Mrs. Featherstone Hogg's drawing-room on a bedroom chair. He had tried to efface himself upon the sofa beside Mrs. Goldsmith, but Mrs. Featherstone Hogg had pounced upon him, and dragged him forth, and seated him at her side; and there he was, for all the world like an exhibit in a show—a secondary exhibit, of course, for Mrs. Featherstone Hogg was obviously the primary exhibit herself.

The Meeting had not yet started when Barbara arrived, so she was not late after all, or else the Meeting was late in starting. She slipped—as inconspicuously as possible—into a seat beside Sarah Walker and looked round the room.

Miss King was sitting near the window beside Mrs. Carter, and beyond them was Mrs. Dick flanked by two of her gentlemen paying guests—Mr. Fortnum and Mr. Black. (The latter was Barbara's supercilious young friend from the bank, of course.) Then came the three Snow-dons, Mrs. Greensleeves and Captain Sandeman, and Mr. Featherstone Hogg. Mrs. Goldsmith was alone upon the sofa but she filled more than half of it quite comfortably. She looked very solemn and important in a black silk cloak trimmed with astrakhan. Mr. Durnet was near the door, he was all in his Sunday clothes and was obviously quite bewildered to find himself in The Riggs drawing-room. I'm glad I didn't let Dorcas come, thought Barbara. Dorcas had been invited, of course, but she had shown no signs of wanting to attend the meeting, and Barbara hadn't pressed her in any way. Barbara felt she could bear the ordeal better if Dorcas were safely at home.

Barbara Buncle looked round the room and saw all her puppets (with a few exceptions) assembled together for the purpose of reviling their creator. She wondered if any other author had ever beheld such a curious sight. It would be exciting to write a play, Barbara thought, to see your creations put on the garment of mortality, to hear your words issuing from their mouths. But a play must always be a little disappointing, no actor can completely satisfy an author, there must be some discrepancy between the author's conception of a character and the actor's expression. This was far better than any play, for the actors were themselves. They couldn't act out of character if they tried, for they *were* the characters—as large as life and twice as natural.

A strange mist hovered before Barbara's eyes. Was this

Silverstream, or was it Copperfield? Was that Mrs. Horsley Downs, or was it Mrs. Featherstone Hogg?

Sarah Walker recalled her to reality—"I really ought not to be here because I'm not *in* it," she whispered, "John's coming later if he can possibly get away. Isn't it *funny?*" Barbara agreed that it was, and enquired after the twins' cold.

"Oh it's much better thank you," said their mother. "They are out to-day for the first time. I do like your hat, Barbara."

"Good gracious!" exclaimed Barbara, "I'd forgotten about my hat—what on earth can it look like?"

"Silence!" cried Mrs. Featherstone Hogg, and she tapped loudly on the card-table with a hammer.

"Ladies and gentlemen," said Mrs. Featherstone Hogg. "It is now ten minutes to four, and two of our—of our number have not come yet. There are other absentees, of course, but they have been unavoidably—er—prevented from attending. I will read their apologies later. But these two people have sent no word, they said they would come and I was expecting them. They are very important to our—to our cause. I refer of course to Colonel Weatherhead and Mrs. Bold. Does anyone know why they have not turned up?"

"Dorothea Bold has gone to London to stay with her sister," said Barbara in a small voice.

"How very strange!" said Mrs. Featherstone Hogg. "She might have let me know. Colonel Weatherhead promised to tell her about the Meeting. Well there is just the Colonel to wait for, then, and the point is shall we wait a little longer for him, or carry on without him?"

A babble of talk immediately broke forth as everyone present began to explain to her neighbour or to her hostess why it was absolutely necessary to wait for the Colonel's arrival, or to carry on with the Meeting at once. Barbara was swept into Copperfield (the new novel was all about Copperfield too, of course), she contemplated the scene with delight, she was a sponge, soaking up ambrosia.

Mrs. Featherstone Hogg consulted in undertones with Mr. Bulmer and then rapped upon the table. The Meeting relapsed into silence.

"Mr. Bulmer says I ought to have opened the Meeting by explaining that I am the chairman and he is the president," she said loudly. "But of course the Meeting has not been opened yet. I merely wished to ascertain whether everybody thinks we should start without Colonel Weatherhead or wait until he comes."

"Very unconstitutional," remarked Mr. Bulmer loudly.

"But look here," said Mr. Black (from the bank). "Look here, you don't need a chairman *and* a president, surely. I mean it's not usual. Either the chairman presides or the president takes the chair, I mean—"

Mrs. Featherstone Hogg took no notice of the objections and interruptions. She considered Mr. Black's objection foolish. It was her Meeting, and she would do as she liked about presidents and chairmen, she certainly was not going to take instruction from Mr. Black.

"Colonel Weatherhead is very important to us," said

Mrs. Featherstone Hogg, keeping firmly to the point, "and I consider we should wait until he comes."

"Why not telephone to the feller?" suggested Captain Sandeman, sensibly. "He's probably forgotten all about it."

The chairman considered this, and decided that it was a good idea, so Mr. Featherstone Hogg was sent to telephone to the Colonel and find out if he had started.

The Meeting waited patiently, all except Mr. Bulmer, who showed signs of strain. He had no use at all for Colonel Weatherhead, and considered that the business in hand could have been transacted quite as efficiently without the Colonel's presence. As a matter of fact he had the same feeling about two thirds of the people invited by Mrs. Featherstone Hogg. She had made a fool of the whole thing by asking old Durnet and Mrs. Goldsmith. The former was practically an imbecile in Mr. Bulmer's opinion—a good many people were practically imbeciles in Mr. Bulmer's opinion. He tapped irritably on the table with his fingers, and crossed and re-crossed his legs.

After some time Mr. Featherstone Hogg returned to say that the exchange could get no reply from The Bridge House.

"You should have told them to ring again," said Mrs. Featherstone Hogg crossly.

"I did," he replied.

There was nothing more to be done about the Colonel, so Mrs. Featherstone Hogg was obliged to start the proceedings without him. She rose from her chair and rapped upon the table with her hammer.

"Ladies and gentlemen," said Mrs. Featherstone Hogg, referring to her notes, which she had compiled that morning with considerable care. "Ladies and gentlemen we have met together to-day to discuss this book—*Disturber of the Peace*—which has been flung into our peaceful village like a poison bomb. Before the publication of this book we were all living together like a big happy family, but now there are rifts in the lute and the music is discordant and harsh. We have all suffered from the effects of this book—some in one way and some in another. I have no time to go into each individual case to-day, it is sufficient to say that all have suffered—that is why we are here. Books like *Disturber of the Peace* are a deadly menace to society. They undermine the foundations of English life. An Englishman's house is his castle, it is into the sacred precincts of this castle that *Disturber of the Peace* has entered, destroying the fragrance of the home, and violating its privacy. We of Silverstream must lead the way, it is our duty and our privilege to show England that the home is still a sacred spot and cannot be violated with impunity."

Mrs. Featherstone Hogg had marked on her notes, "Pause for applause." She paused hopefully.

Mr. Black was the only member of the Meeting who realised what was expected of him. He clapped feebly, but it is impossible to clap alone, so he left off almost immediately.

"There is only one thing to be done," continued Mrs. Featherstone Hogg, returning to her notes. "The author of this sacrilege—John Smith he calls himself—must be found. He must be dragged out of his hole like a rat, and punished severely, as an example to the world. It is to do this that we have met to-day." She sat down.

Mr. Bulmer rose somewhat wearily and said, "I was under the impression that I was president of this Meeting. The impression was evidently erroneous," and sat down.

The Meeting applauded loudly, but whether the applause was intended to encourage Mr. Bulmer, or to confirm him in his impression it is difficult to say.

Mrs. Featherstone Hogg bobbed up again. "I am sorry that Mr. Bulmer is not satisfied with the way the Meeting is being conducted," she announced in defiant tones. "I would like to remind him that we are here to-day to put our heads together and find John Smith. Small points of procedure are of secondary consideration compared with our main object. The Meeting is now open for discussion."

There was dead silence.

Mrs. Featherstone Hogg waited for a minute or two and then bobbed up again.

"Perhaps I haven't explained properly," she said. "The Meeting is now open, and anybody who has anything to say can say it now."

"I'd like to put in a word," said Mrs. Goldsmith, suddenly. "It's about my buns. It said in that book that my buns was full of electricity. I'd just like to say that's not true, and anybody who says it *is* true is telling lies. There's no electricity comes near my buns. I don't hold with these new electric ovens for baking, I don't. My oven's a brick oven, heated with an ordinary furnace, same as my father used. The dough's rolled by 'and.

There's no electricity comes near my buns, and no seconds neither. I use nothing but first grade flour in my bakery—there's people living not a hundred miles from here who couldn't say the same—and that's the truth," added Mrs. Goldsmith, leaning back and fanning her hot face with her handkerchief.

Mrs. Featherstone Hogg rapped on the table—"I'm sure it is very interesting to hear about Mrs. Goldsmith's methods of baking," she announced in patronising tones. "But I don't see how that is going to help us in our search for John Smith. We could all point out the horrible lies that he's written about us, if we liked, but what good would that do? I must ask the members of this Meeting to keep to the matter in hand or we shall be here all night."

"Perhaps I shouldn't have spoke up like I did," said Mrs. Goldsmith apologetically. "But it's hard to have people making wicked aspirations about my buns and lie down under it."

"Quite right too," said Mrs. Dick, nodding her head so that the ostrich feather round her hat waved like a milk-white pennon in the breeze. "Quite right too. Stand up for yourself, I say, for there's nobody else going to stand up *for* you. And while we're on the subject I'd just like to mention that if my guests are late for their breakfasts their breakfasts are kept hot—there's nobody in my establishment is asked to eat congealed bacon fat like it says in that book—Mr. Fortnum and Mr. Black will bear me out," she added firmly, looking towards the paying guests who had accompanied her to the Meeting.

"That's right," said Mr. Fortnum hoarsely.

"—And there's another thing," continued Mrs. Dick. "Just one more thing, and I'll have done, for I'm not going into the question of my mattresses in Mrs. Featherstone Hogg's drawing-room. It's enough to say that they're all good horse-hair mattresses every one of them, and anyone who says they're stuffed with potatoes is a liar—what I really want to say is this:—My guests are all respectable and well-behaved, and I've never had a gentleman of the name of Mason staying in my establishment, and if I did have, I'd have seen to it that he behaved as a gentleman ought. None of my gentlemen ever spent all night in a lady's garden playing on a mandolin. Mr. Fortnum plays the ukulele and very nice it is of an evening in the drawing-room and the other gentlemen singing—"

Mrs. Featherstone Hogg rapped on the table—

"Mr. Bulmer will now read out the apologies from the absentees," she said loudly.

"It ought to have been done at the beginning," said Mr. Bulmer crossly.

"I know, I forgot about it."

"You had better do it yourself."

"Very well," said the chairman, "if you don't want to do it, I will." She took up a sheaf of papers and cleared her throat. "Mrs. Bulmer is away from home and therefore regrets that she cannot be present. Dr. Walker is unavoidably detained, but hopes to come in later. Miss Pretty is in bed with a feverish cold, she much regrets that she is unable to be present at Mrs. Featherstone Hogg's Drawing-room Meeting, but hopes it will be a great success. (I am sure we are all much obliged to Miss Pretty for her kind message.) Colonel Carter has sailed for India and regrets that he is unable to attend. Major and Mrs. Shearer regret that owing to a previous engagement they are unable to accept Mrs. Featherstone Hogg's kind invitation to her Drawing-room Meeting. Miss Dorcas Pemberty regrets that she is unable to be present. Mrs. Sandeman is unable to be present as she is still in bed, she much regrets that she cannot accept Mrs. Featherstone Hogg's kind invitation. I think that is all, we can now proceed with the—er—proceedings," said Mrs. Featherstone Hogg, and she sat down.

"What are you going to do when you find John Smith?" enquired Miss King in her deep sensible voice. "It appears to me that you can't do anything at all. No reputable lawyer will touch the case with a barge pole."

"Leave that to me," replied the chairman of the meeting in a voice that boded ill for John Smith.

"I move that the vote of the meeting shall be taken on the point," said Miss King firmly.

Sarah Walker seconded the motion and Mrs. Featherstone Hogg was forced to ask for a show of hands. Hands were shown on the point, and it was found that the majority lay with Miss King. In other words they all wanted to have some say in what punishment should be meted out to John Smith rather than leave the matter entirely in their chairman's hands.

"I think we should send him to Coventry," said Isabella Snowdon, savagely.

"Poof—what would John Smith care for that," snorted

Mr. Bulmer. "A good ducking in the horse-pond is what he wants."

"It all depends on what sort of a man he is," Mr. Snowdon pointed out. "As Miss King so rightly says, no lawyer will touch the case—but there are other means of procedure."

"What means?" demanded Mr. Bulmer.

"Most men have a weak spot," replied Mr. Snowdon significantly.

"You mean we could find out something disgraceful about his past, and blackmail him?" enquired Sarah Walker, sweetly.

"I never mentioned blackmail," retorted Mr. Snowdon. "I merely said that most men have a weak spot. In dealing with a person of John Smith's calibre one cannot be squeamish. The man obviously needs a lesson. Find his weak spot and you have him at your mercy."

"What's it all about?" enquired Mr. Durnet suddenly in a piping voice. "What's it all about? Ella said we was going to 'ave tea. It's a long time coming."

"After the Meeting," shouted Mr. Black who was sitting next to the old man. "AFTER THE MEETING."

"Yes, eating. That's what Ella said," piped Mr. Durnet disconsolately, "But I don't see no signs of eating, nor drinking neither."

Mrs. Featherstone Hogg took no notice of the interruption. "You're all quite wrong," she said firmly. "John Smith ought to be horse-whipped, that's the only thing for a man like him. And horse-whipped he will be, if I have any say in the matter."

"You haven't," said Mr. Bulmer. "You are the chair-

man—or at least you are supposed to be the chairman—
and therefore you have no say in the matter beyond
giving a casting vote."

"If I had known that I wouldn't have been the chairman," replied Mrs. Featherstone Hogg with some heat.
"Do you mean to say that because I am the chairman I
have to sit here like a dummy, and not give the meeting
the benefit of my ideas?"

Mr. Bulmer did not attempt to answer this question,
perhaps his experience was insufficient to deal with such
a fine point.

"Who's going to do the horse-whipping?" he enquired,
passing on to safer ground. "Who's going to horse-whip
the man and probably find himself in gaol over the
affair? That's what I want to know."

"Colonel Weatherhead, of course," said Mrs. Featherstone Hogg calmly.

The entire meeting gasped with amazement.

"I'd like to see the fun," announced Captain Sandeman.

"So'd I," agreed Mr. Black, "but the Colonel's an oldish
man for a job like that, and we don't know what size
of a chap this John Smith will be. I'd like to know the
size of a chap before I said I'd tackle him—still I admire
pluck."

"It's a pity more people are not as brave as the
Colonel," said Mrs. Featherstone Hogg with asperity.
She had pondered for so long over the horse-whipping
business that she was now convinced in her own mind
that the whole thing was settled with Colonel Weatherhead. It would have been almost impossible to disabuse

her mind of the conviction that Colonel Weatherhead had agreed with alacrity to horse-whip John Smith. Fortunately, nobody present was in a position to try.

"I wouldn't mind taking him on if he was smaller than me," retorted Mr. Black, who felt that the chairman's remark was especially addressed to him, and resented the aspersion upon his personal courage. "But it wouldn't be the least use me undertaking the job if I couldn't be certain of getting the better of the chap."

Captain Sandeman was heard to murmur something, and was asked by the chairman to repeat his remark. It was obvious that she hoped he was a volunteer, he was young, and strong, and had broad shoulders, and his profession was militant.

"I just said—'First catch your hare'," said Captain Sandeman.

"Very pertinent too," remarked Miss Olivia Snowdon.

"Good Heavens! What's impertinent about it?" demanded Captain Sandeman indignantly. "I merely said—'first catch your hare'. It's a proverb. It means you can't punish the man till you've caught him. 'First catch your hare, then cook him.' You can't cook John Smith till you've bowled him over, can you? We aren't within a hundred miles of finding out who the feller *is* yet."

"I know, I know," soothed the harassed chairman. "Nobody said impertinent."

"Miss Snowdon did."

"I said pertinent," Miss Snowdon remarked scornfully. "Perhaps you do not realise that pertinent means to the point, it means the reverse of impertinent. The word has now lost its original meaning, of course—"

"Is it necessary to go into the etymological meaning of the word?" enquired Mr. Bulmer in a tired voice.

"I considered it necessary to explain my meaning to Captain Sandeman," returned Miss Snowdon, with some heat.

Mrs. Featherstone Hogg thought it was time to interfere. She rapped on the table with her hammer.

"We must really confine ourselves to the business in hand," she said sternly. "We keep on wandering away from the point—"

"It's the chairman's business to prevent that occurring," retorted Mr. Bulmer.

"I've been trying to," Mrs. Featherstone Hogg said, with pardonable irritation. "I've been trying to keep people to the point ever since we started. If you think you could do it so much better you had better be chairman and conduct the meeting yourself."

"God forbid!" exclaimed Mr. Bulmer.

"I'm only trying to help you all," continued the chairman in pathetic accents. "I've had you all here to-day to try to get to the bottom of this—of this distressing affair."

"And very kind of you it is, Ma'am," put in Mrs. Goldsmith who had determined to ally herself with her best customer at all costs. "Very kind of you to take all the trouble you have taken, and to have us all here to-day in your nice drawing-room—so it is. I propose a vote of thanks to Mrs. Featherstone Hogg," she added with sudden brilliant inspiration.

"Very unconstitutional!" exclaimed Mr. Bulmer.

"Very kind of you, Mrs. Goldsmith," said Mrs. Featherstone Hogg, with a defiant look in Mr. Bulmer's direction. "Very kind indeed of you, and I'm glad some-body appreciates my efforts, but the only thing is a vote of thanks comes at the end of the proceedings."

"Does it?" enquired Mrs. Goldsmith in an interested voice. "Well I never was at a Drawing-room Meeting before, so I didn't know. I've been to Quaker Meetings of course. My aunt who lives in Herefordshire is a Quaker, and we used to stay with her when we were young. And of course at Quaker Meetings you just speak as the spirit moves you, so I thought it was the same kind of idea—"

"Well, it's not," said the perplexed chairman. "If any-one has anything to say which will throw light upon the identity of John Smith we shall be only too pleased to listen to them, but if not I must request members to remain silent."

"How would it do if we all remained silent for ten minutes?" suggested Miss Isabella Snowdon, timidly. "Those who cared to pray for guidance could do so, of course, and the others could just concentrate upon the problem. The power of thought is so immense and so—so—er—powerful, I feel sure that we should gain some-thing valuable in that way."

"I didn't know this was going to turn into a séance, or I should have stayed at home," announced Mr. Bulmer, who was getting more and more irritable every moment.

"My sister never suggested a séance nor anything to do with spiritualism," cried Miss Olivia, rushing into the fray. "Concentrated thought is an entirely different matter—"

"The Meeting should have been opened with prayer,"

suggested Mrs. Dick, who had suddenly thought of this contribution to the debate.

"I think it would have been most unsuitable," said Miss King, firmly.

"When you've all finished quarrelling I would like to tell you about my idea," Vivian Greensleeves announced. There was something significant in her tone which quelled the rising storm. Everybody looked at her, of course, which was exactly what Vivian liked. She lay back with her legs crossed, smiling in a mysterious manner, and toying idly with the tassels on the arm of her chair. It was the first time that Vivian had opened her mouth since she had arrived, except to yawn once or twice in a ladylike manner behind her hand—she had been waiting, more or less patiently, until everybody present had made complete fools of themselves; she considered that she had now waited long enough, and was ready to contribute her quota.

"We shall be very glad to listen to your idea," Mrs. Featherstone Hogg announced graciously.

"Well," said Vivian Greensleeves, slowly. "I've been thinking it over ever since I read the book, and it seems to me there's only one person in Silverstream who is not caricatured in the book and held up to scorn, only one person who knows us all well enough to write about us and is not in the book herself. I think that John Smith is Mrs. Walker."

Everybody immediately turned and gazed at Sarah Walker. It would have taken a more brazen person than Sarah not to blush in the blaze of limelight suddenly thrown upon her.

"Oh!" she said.

"Oh no, it's not her," cried Barbara Buncle.

Mrs. Featherstone Hogg swallowed once or twice. There seemed to be a sort of lump sticking in her throat —possibly a form of excitement.—Why had she not thought of Mrs. Walker herself? Sarah had just the sort of perverted sense of humour which disfigured *Disturber of the Peace*. Sarah knew them all, she had opportunities of hearing things about her neighbours which are denied to the wives of stockbrokers. Sarah had ample time to write, for she was by way of being delicate and did not go about much. She made an excuse of her delicacy to abstain from such excitements as tea-parties and musical evenings at The Riggs. What more likely than that she stayed at home and ridiculed them all? Sarah went her own way, and lived her own life, she did not bow to the sovereignty of Mrs. Featherstone Hogg. Mrs. Featherstone Hogg did not like Sarah, she was pretty sure it was Sarah who had written the book.

Several other people seemed to be arriving at the same conclusion; Mrs. Carter was arguing loudly with Miss King; Mrs. Goldsmith was arguing loudly with Mrs. Dick; the Snowdons were whispering amongst themselves; Mr. Bulmer was glaring at Sarah like a gargoyle.

Mr. Bulmer was convinced that Mrs. Greensleeves had hit the bull's eye with her first shot. He disliked Sarah intensely, and, moreover, he knew that Sarah disliked him (Sarah never made any concealment of her likes and dislikes). Sarah was Margaret's closest friend, of course Margaret had told her all about him, and she had travestied him in her hateful book. The thing was obvious.

Mr. Bulmer plucked at Mrs. Featherstone Hogg's sleeve and whispered in her ear.

The chairman rose, and rapped upon the table.

"Mrs. Walker," she said solemnly. "It is my painful duty to ask you in the name of this Meeting whether or not you wrote the novel, *Disturber of the Peace*. Please do not let us have any prevarications, we desire the truth, the whole truth and nothing but the truth."

Sarah leapt to her feet, she was furious. How dared Mrs. Featherstone Hogg put the question in that way? As if she, Sarah Walker, told lies!

"I *will* tell you the whole truth," she cried, nerved by wrath. "I did not write *Disturber of the Peace,* but I wish I had. I wish I had the brains to do it. I think it is a very clever and amusing book, and I hope it will do you all good to see yourselves as others see you for once in a way. A set of smug hypocrites—that's what you are. It's a great pity there aren't more John Smiths about."

Having said her say, Sarah made for the door, and Barbara, who had had quite enough of the Drawing-room Meeting, got up and followed her. The remainder of the company was too astounded to move.

Barbara seized the door out of Sarah's grasp and closed it gently but firmly behind her. She heaved a sigh of relief—they had escaped without being torn in pieces—and pursued the flying Sarah down the stairs. In the hall was a tall familiar figure struggling out of its great-coat. Sarah flung herself into its arms and began to laugh hysterically.

"John," she cried, "John, John, John!"

Barbara stood on the stairs and gazed at them, open-mouthed.

"Sally dear!" cried the amazed Dr. John. "Sally dear, what on earth's happened?"

"They all think John Smith is me," cried Sarah, gasping for breath.

CHAPTER XVII

Inspiration

BARBARA BUNCLE rushed home and shut herself up in the small room which she had begun to call her study. She cast her hat and coat on to the nearest chair and seized her fountain pen. Words were yammering in her brain. They poured out onto the paper in an endless stream. The floor was gradually covered with sheets of closely written foolscap. It looked as if a snowstorm had been raging in the study when Dorcas came in to say that supper was ready.

"Go away, I'm busy," said Miss Buncle without raising her head.

"Now, Miss Barbara, don't be contrary," said Dorcas, firmly. "I've poached you an egg, and you can't go wasting eggs at two and eleven a dozen."

"Eat it yourself, then," suggested the author.

"I'll do no such thing," Dorcas replied. "Come along now, Miss Barbara, do. You hadn't much dinner you know, and I'm quite sure you didn't get no tea worth talking about at that old skinflint's party."

"I had none," said Barbara, raising a flushed face from her writing table.

"There," cried Dorcas triumphantly, "what did I tell you?"

"If you bring the egg here I'll eat it," said Barbara in

despair. "Only for goodness' sake go away and don't talk to me—"

Dorcas went away, she was beginning to get used to living in the house with an author. It was not comfortable, she found, and it was distinctly trying to the temper. Dorcas often thought with regret of the good old days when the dividends had come in punctually, and Miss Barbara had been an ordinary human being; taking her meals at regular hours, going up to bed as the clock struck eleven, and coming down for breakfast in the morning as the clock struck nine.

I believe hens would have been less bother after all, Dorcas thought, as she prepared a tray with the poached egg, a cup of cocoa, and two pieces of brown toast set out upon it in appetising array—Authors! said Dorcas to herself with scornful emphasis—Authors indeed!—Well, I'll never read a book again but what I'll think of the people as has had to put up with the author, I know that.—Preparing meals, and beating the gong, and going back 'alf an hour later to find nobody's ever been near them, and the mutton fat frozen solid in the dish, and the soup stone cold—and them ringing bells at all hours for coffee, "and make it strong Dorcas—make it strong!" and them writing half the night, and lying in bed half the day with people toiling up to their bedrooms with trays.—Authors—poof! Said Dorcas to herself—but I never could abide hens neither—and she took up the tray and marched across the hall and pushed open the door of the study with one foot, and crunched heedlessly over the foolscap covered floor, and dumped the tray down on the foolscap covered desk.

"Go away," said Barbara impatiently. Her pen was still skimming over the paper like a bird.

"Well I'm not going, then," Dorcas replied. "Not till I see you eat that egg and drink that cocoa with my own eyes, I'm not. For as soon as ever my back's turned you'll forget all about it."

Barbara knew she was cornered. She took up the knife and fork and made short work of the poached egg.

"I was hungry," she admitted in a surprised voice.

"Well, and what did you expect?" enquired Dorcas. "With no tea, and as much dinner as would fatten up a fly—anybody would be hungry, I should think. Drink up your cocoa, Miss Barbara, before it gets cold and nasty."

The meal was soon disposed of, Dorcas picked up the tray and made for the door—

"Oh, and Dorcas—"

"Yes, Miss Barbara."

"I'd like a cup of coffee about eleven—before you go up to bed—and make it strong, Dorcas."

"Yes, Miss Barbara," said Dorcas, she pulled a face at the author's bent back and shut the door firmly.

.   .   .   .   .

On Friday morning Barbara lay in bed just as Dorcas had expected. She was worn out with the spate of inspiration which had kept her chained to her desk until the early hours in the morning.

"Well, you do look a ghost and no mistake," Dorcas said, as she contemplated the recumbent figure of her mistress, and noted with dismay the dark smudges beneath Miss Buncle's eyes.

"I know," said Barbara, "I was writing nearly all night, that's why."

"You'd better take a few days off it," Dorcas advised, "or we'll be having Dr. Walker here, wanting to know what's wore you out like that."

"Oh, I can't do that," replied Barbara. "It's only just beginning to—to roll along smoothly, and Mr. Abbott's in a hurry for it. I must stick into it for a bit. Perhaps later on I might take a few days—"

"I'd be willing to try hens, Miss Barbara, if you're agreeable."

"Hens?" enquired Barbara, toying with her bacon distastefully.

"You give up writing and we'll try hens," wheedled Dorcas. "My nephew has a fine hen-farm in Surrey. He'd be willing to start us off with a few, and give us some hints—"

The author sat up in bed and gazed at her in amazement. "Dorcas, I could never give up writing *now,*" she said, incredulously (nor could she, the vice had got her firmly in its grip, as well ask a morphomaniac to give up drugs). "You don't know how exciting it is, Dorcas. It just sweeps you along and you've no idea of the time—"

"I guessed that much," interpolated Dorcas, grimly.

"And look at the money I've made," continued the complacent author. "A whole hundred pounds, and more coming soon, Mr. Abbott says. How long would it take to make a hundred pounds out of hens?"

Dorcas knew a little about her nephew's profits, and she was forced to admit, regretfully, that it might take years to make a clear hundred pounds out of hens.

"Well, you *see*," said Barbara triumphantly, "it would take years of work and worry to make a hundred pounds out of hens, and I can make it quite easily in a few months just by enjoying myself."

"I'm not enjoying myself."

"I know it's trying for you, but I can't help it, I really can't. When I feel it all bubbling over in my head it just *has* to come out, or I'd burst or something—you can have all my clothes if you like."

Dorcas looked at her in consternation—what new horror was this? Had the strain of writing all night deranged the poor lady's brain, or did she contemplate remaining in bed for the rest of her life, and having trays brought up to her?

"All your clothes, Miss Barbara?" echoed Dorcas.

"Yes, all of them," replied Miss Buncle, waving a negligent hand towards the wardrobe. "Take them all away, out of the cupboard and the drawers. You can give some of them to your niece if you like—or sell them. Do whatever you like with them, Dorcas, but don't bother me about it."

"You'll feel better after you've had a nice sleep," Dorcas suggested, anxiously.

Barbara yawned, "Yes, I am sleepy," she admitted, "I feel all empty and peaceful. I should think people feel exactly like this after they've had a baby—"

"Really, Miss Barbara, I don't know what you'll say next," complained the scandalised Dorcas.

Barbara giggled, and snuggled down in bed, "I'll sleep till lunch time," she announced.

Dorcas took up the breakfast tray and left the room—all was peace.

Barbara Buncle slept, and as she slept she dreamed that she was walking down the village street. There was a kind of misty radiance in the air, so she knew that this was Copperfield. She walked along with a springy step and her beautifully polished brown shoes hardly touched the ground. She was so happy—she was always happy in Copperfield. Everything always went right in Copperfield, people did as she wanted them to do, they were never rude about her book, they were never cross nor patronising. In Copperfield she had everybody under her thumb—even Mrs. Horsley Downs was obliged to obey her orders. Mrs. Horsley Downs couldn't walk across the street unless Barbara allowed her to. In Copperfield Barbara herself was just as she wanted to be, she was younger, and prettier and more attractive. People looked at her as she passed, not because she was a "sight", but because she was pleasant to behold. Her hair was beautifully dressed, her clothes were perfect, her petticoat never hung down below her skirt, her stocking never developed a hole in the heel—in fact she was not Barbara Buncle any more, she was Elizabeth Wade.

Elizabeth Wade it was, who tripped along the Copperfield streets that fine morning. Elizabeth Wade clad in a complete new outfit from Virginia's little shop. She was wearing the bottle-green coat with the grey fur collar and the little hat to match, and beneath the bottle-green coat was the jumper suit which went with it so beautifully.

Elizabeth Wade went into the bakery to buy buns.

"I can recommend these, Miss," said Mrs. Silver with

a smile, "these are full of electricity. Please let me send up a dozen for you to try, there will be no charge to *you*, of course, Miss."

Miss Wade gave her gracious consent and left the shop. How pleasant it was to be so popular! The sun was streaming down and filling the High Street with its golden beams, Elizabeth was dazzled by the brightness of the light. She closed her eyes for a moment, and when she opened them again she saw the Golden Boy. He was dancing along in the middle of the street playing on his pipe—lifting it up towards the sky and bending down again, first to one side and then to the other; bending and swaying from side to side, up to the sky and down to the ground, and all the time the music flowed from his pipe, a thin clear trickle of notes.

Elizabeth was not in the least surprised, why should she be surprised? He was her own Golden Boy, not the hybrid creature that had appeared upon the cover of *Disturber of the Peace*. He was her own Golden Boy, she had created him herself. He passed quite close to Elizabeth Wade, as she stood in the doorway of the bakery, and disappeared up the hill.

The bright light faded. Elizabeth rubbed her eyes and opened them to find her faithful slave standing at her bedside with a large tray. The sun was shining in at her open window and the birds were twittering blithely amongst the leaves of the ivy which covered Tanglewood Cottage.

"I've had a lovely sleep, Susan," said Elizabeth—Barbara stretching her arms.

"It's Dorcas," said that worthy in a humouring voice.

"It's your own Dorcas, Miss Barbara. Here's your dinner, sit up now and take it while it's nice and hot. Look, I got a little pigeon for you—isn't that nice now? And Mr. Abbott's just rung up on the telephone to say he's coming down this afternoon to see you, and here's a post card from Paris—it's come by air."

Barbara sat up the better to deal with this mass of information. Copperfield had vanished, and with it Elizabeth Wade. It was Barbara who held out her hand for the post card, not Elizabeth Wade. The post card was a highly-coloured photograph of the Eiffel Tower and written upon it in Dorothea Bold's large round hand was the following amazing message—"Enjoying our honeymoon tremendously. Love from us both. Dorothea Weatherhead."

"They're married, Dorcas," exclaimed Barbara.

"That's what I thought, Miss Barbara," Dorcas replied. (We must not blame Dorcas too severely. Post cards are fair game, and it was not every day that one arrived from Paris—by air mail too. It would have been scarcely human if Dorcas had not glanced at it as she took it from the postman—and Dorothea's hand was particularly round and clear.) "That's just what I thought they were," said Dorcas, "and a very nice couple they'll make. I expect it's *Disturber* that's done it."

"D'you really think it could be?" Barbara said, with her eyes like saucers. "D'you really think so, Dorcas? I *would* be glad if I thought that. D'you think they read my book and went straight off and got married? How wonderful it is!"

She lay back and thought about the mighty power of

the pen, quite oblivious of the fact that her nice pigeon was getting cold.

.   .   .   .   .   .

When she had thought about it enough, and finished her lunch, Barbara got up and had a hot bath. Her new garments had arrived—Virginia had kept her promise faithfully—and Barbara decided to wear one of her new frocks this afternoon. A bath seemed a fitting preliminary to the donning of the slinky, soft, wine-coloured creation which lay curled up in its neat brown box all padded out with rustling tissue paper.

When she had bathed, and dressed, and finished doing her hair, Barbara slipped the frock very carefully over her head and turned to look at herself in the long mirror which swung on a wooden frame beside her chest of drawers. She was quite startled at the change in her appearance—it was Elizabeth Wade who looked back at her from the quicksilver depths of the mirror (not Barbara Buncle at all). Elizabeth Wade with flushed cheeks and bright eyes enhanced by the deep red frock which swept in a pretty curve to her ankles, and added a couple of inches to her height.

The door-bell rang while she was still contemplating Elizabeth and she went downstairs to greet Mr. Abbott.

"You don't mind my turning up like this," Mr. Abbott said. "I had a slack afternoon and there were one or two things I wanted to talk to you about—"

He stopped suddenly and gazed at his hostess in surprise. He was a mere man, of course, and he had not the remotest idea what had caused the amazing difference in Miss Buncle's appearance. He only knew that she was much more attractive than he had thought, much prettier too, and years younger—

"I must have been blind," he said aloud.

"Blind?" enquired Barbara.

"Oh, I mean—er—I had some difficulty in finding your house again," explained Mr. Abbott, "couldn't have been looking where I was going or something—"

"Well, anyway, here you are," said Barbara smiling at him. She was full of self assurance to-day and happy in her mastery of the situation. She was Elizabeth of course, that was the reason for it. Elizabeth Wade always knew what to do and say on every occasion—how unlike Barbara Buncle!

"I've been working so hard," she told him, sitting down beside the fire and motioning Mr. Abbott to the sofa with a gracious wave of her hand. "—Do smoke Mr. Abbott, won't you—Dorcas is quite worried about me, she thinks it would be better if we were to try keeping hens."

"No, no!" laughed Mr. Abbott, taking a cigarette out of his tortoise-shell case and tapping it gently on his thumb-nail. "No, no, Miss Buncle. We're not going to let you off so easily. We're going to keep your nose to the grind-stone. There's no rest for the best seller, you know."

"Am I really a best seller?"

"Pretty good. The reviews have been very helpful—"

"Helpful!" cried Barbara in amazement. "Some of them said I was immoral and perverted."

"I know. It was simply marvellous," replied Mr. Abbott, holding out his cigarette and watching the smoke curl upwards with appreciation and content. "It really was simply marvellous. In my wildest and most optimistic moments I scarcely dared to hope that they would misread you to that extent."

"Then—then it was a good thing?"

"Couldn't have had better reviews if I had written them myself. The sales leapt up—"

Barbara was astounded. How strange people were! What an incredible sort of world this business of writing had opened up before her eyes!

"And how's Copperfield?" enquired Mr. Abbott. "Anybody found John Smith yet?"

"No."

"There are lots of people out for his blood."

"I know," said Barbara sadly.

"A Miss King called on me one day," Mr. Abbott continued with twinkling eyes, "I gathered that she was rather peevish at being banished to Samarkand. And she was followed by a Mr. Bulmer—a sour faced individual, who wanted a little talk with Mr. John Smith about his wife—"

"I know," said Barbara again. "It's simply dreadful the way they all go on. They had a Meeting here yesterday, and decided that I was to be horse-whipped, only it seemed rather difficult to get volunteers for the job."

Mr. Abbott laughed, "First catch your hare—" he said.

"Captain Sandeman said that too."

"Then Captain Sandeman is a sensible man. What about the new novel, Miss Buncle? How is it going?"

"Like mad," replied Barbara. "But of course it's all about Copperfield too. I don't know how to write about anything else—"

"Don't worry. You write what you feel you want to write, and never mind what Copperfield says. Copperfield ought to be flattered at being immortalised by your pen."

"Now you are laughing at me," said Barbara, provocatively. It was really Elizabeth who said it of course, Barbara would never have dared, but Mr. Abbott wasn't to know that his hostess had suddenly changed into a totally different woman.

"I never laugh at charming ladies," he told her.

They sparred in a friendly manner until Dorcas appeared with the tea. Dorcas approved of Mr. Abbott, he was a real London gentleman. To show her appreciation she had made some little cakes, and put on her best muslin cap and apron.

"Smart. That's what he is," Dorcas said to Milly Spikes who had got the afternoon off and was having a cup of tea with her in the kitchen.

"I like 'em smart," agreed Milly.

Dorcas was not very proud of her friendship with Milly Spikes. In fact she would not have admitted its existence. "She likes to come in now and then for a cup of tea," Dorcas would have said if anyone had hinted that she liked Milly. But Dorcas did like Milly all the same, and, although she frequently told herself that Milly was "low" and not her style at all, she was always very pleased to see Milly and to listen to her gossip. Milly knew everything that happened in Silverstream. She got all the village news from Mrs. Goldsmith who was her aunt; and the news about the gentry filtered to her ears (which were preternaturally alert, and occasionally glued to keyholes) through the medium of Mrs. Greensleeves. Mrs. Greensleeves was not as reticent about her affairs, and the affairs of her neighbours, as she might have been if she had taken the trouble to understand the mentality of her maid. The remainder of the Silverstream news was garnered by the indefatigable Milly in the kitchens and servants' halls of Silverstream, where, owing to her good-nature and amusing tongue, she was *persona grata* with one and all.

Milly's tales lost nothing in the telling, and it was "as good as a play" when she really got going, and imitated Mrs. Greensleeves' somewhat affected tones or described her rages which broke forth periodically when the tradesmen sent in their bills. She heartily despised her employer and spoke of her with contempt—a thing quite definitely "not done" in the opinion of Dorcas—

Dorcas was torn between her disapproval of Milly's stories and her enjoyment of their racy character.

"I s'pose you 'eard all about Mrs. Featherstone 'Ogg's Drawing-room Meeting," said Milly, helping herself to Miss Buncle's jam with a liberal hand. "Seems to 'ave been a sort of free fight from wot I 'ear. They all fixed on Mrs. Walker as being John Smith—"

"Well, they fixed wrong," interpolated Dorcas.

"I know that," said Milly calmly.

"And how d'you know that so certain?"

"Easy as A. B. C. I took a walk up to the Doctor's after supper last night an' 'ad a little chat with Nannie—you know Nannie Walker, silly old fat 'ead, ain't she? Well, Nannie says Mrs. Walker never does no sort of writing except the Doctor's accounts an' suchlike. She reads, and knits the twins' jumper suits. That's proof enough for me. A person can read when they're knitting, but they can't write, can they? Not unless they've got a double set of 'ands, they can't."

"A regular Sherlock 'Olmes, aren't you?" enquired Dorcas with a trace of irony in her tone.

"Well, I can put two and two together as well as most," replied Milly amiably, "and a good deal better than some. I found out more in 'arf an hour from the twins' old Nannie than all Silverstream sitting round The Riggs drawing-room the 'ole blessed afternoon. They 'ad old Mr. Durnet there if you'll believe me—wot on earth they 'oped to find out from that pore dotty old man is more than I can see. And in the middle of the Meeting the pore old soul ups an' says, 'When's my tea coming, that's wot I wants ter know.' Aunt Clarer said 'e did, an' I don't blame 'im neither. It beats the band, don't it, Dorcas?"

Dorcas was forced to agree that it did. She was beginning to wish she had not been so scornful about Mrs. Featherstone Hogg's Drawing-room Meeting. What a score it would have been if she could have said to Milly, "Ah yes, of course, I was there myself." How Milly's round eyes would have bulged at the news. But Dorcas hadn't been there, and she was beginning to get a little tired of Milly's second-hand account of the proceedings, so she changed the subject very successfully by remarking,

"That's a nice hat you've got on, Milly."

"*She* give it me," replied Milly with a wink. "Had me

eye on this 'at ever since she got it. She gave three guineas for it, if you please."

"Lor!" said Dorcas, looking at the hat with increased respect.

"It's too smart for 'er now she's after the Vicar," continued Milly. "That's 'ow I got it."

"I thought she was after that Mr. Fortnum."

"You *are* be'ind 'and," said Milly mischievously. "It's the Vicar now, and she's as good as got 'im too. Calls 'im Ernest to 'is face—an' 'e *is* earnest too. She thinks 'e's got plenty of money—"

"Well, he has, hasn't he?" enquired the thoroughly interested Dorcas.

"No 'e 'asn't," said Milly, lowering her voice confidentially, "everyone thought 'e 'ad money when 'e come, but Mrs. 'Obday says it's not true. She says the poverty of the pore young gentleman is beyond words. 'E goes about with 'oles in 'is boots the size of five shilling bits, and she spends all 'er time trying to darn 'is socks because 'e 'asn't a penny to buy new ones. Mr. 'Obday tol' me 'imself 'e 'as to put 'is foot down strong, or she'd be taking the scraps of meat out of their own mouths to feed the Vicar—fair gone on 'im Mrs. 'Obday is."

"Lor!" exclaimed Dorcas in amazement.

Milly had finished with the Vicar now, she emptied out the dregs of her tea and studied the cup carefully.

"Do mine, Milly," Dorcas said, handing over her cup to the amateur fortune-teller, "what's that big square looking thing, there?"

"Ooh, that's a wedding, that is! A wedding in the

'ouse. It 'ull be Miss Buncle—wot's the London gentle-man like?"

"Biggish man," said Dorcas thoughtfully, "nice eyes, dark hair, greyish over the ears—"

"That's 'im. See 'e's down there near the bottom of the cup—biggish man—"

"Where? Let's see," entreated Dorcas.

"An' that's a flitting—see, down the other side? Means you're going to move, that's wot that means—and those dots all over the place is money coming in—"

CHAPTER XVIII

A History Lesson

IT was decreed by the Powers that Be that Sally Carter was to have some instruction. Dr. Walker had been consulted and had given his opinion that an hour's study every morning would do Sally no harm. The truth was Mrs. Carter was finding difficulty in employing her grand-daughter. Sally was not domesticated, she disliked household toil, and the suggestion that she should help with the jam was met with a firm refusal. Sally had never made jam, she didn't know how to make jam, and she wasn't going to go into the kitchen and display her ignorance to the cook.

Mrs. Carter's habit was to rise about eleven, and what was Sally to do with herself until then? What Sally did was to wander about the damp garden and catch a cold in her head. So Mrs. Carter called in the doctor, and they put their heads together and decided that a little study—just an hour every morning—would do Sally less harm after her operation than mooning about and catching cold. "And she's woefully ignorant," Mrs. Carter said, shaking her beautiful grey curls in dismay, "I don't know what Harry has been thinking about, I really don't. He has kept the child with him all the time, roaming about the world.—A year in this school, and six months somewhere else, and then a governess for a bit until Harry found her making eyes at him and sent her away.—The poor child knows nothing, positively nothing. It is deplorable. Who can we find in Silverstream to teach the child? Who *can* we find, Doctor? You know *everybody,* of course, so perhaps you can help me."

"I wonder if Hathaway would take it on," said Dr. Walker thoughtfully.

"You mean the new vicar?" enquired Mrs. Carter in a surprised voice.

"Well, I don't know, of course," said Dr. Walker, cautiously. "He might not consider it for a moment—but then, again, he might. I happen to know he's not very well off, and he might be glad to make a little extra in that way."

"But my dear doctor, I thought he had plenty of money."

"So we all thought, but he hasn't."

"Are you quite certain?" asked Mrs. Carter incredulously.

"Quite certain. My information is from a reliable source," replied Dr. Walker. "Perhaps he has lost it all, like many unfortunate people in these troublous times, or perhaps he never had as much as rumour gave him. Anyway, there it is. Hathaway is a poor man, and a well educated man and he must have a lot of time on his hands," said the busy doctor, "and I can't think of anybody else at all."

The last argument clinched the matter as far as Mrs. Carter was concerned. She was really desperate. She sat down the moment the doctor had gone and wrote a little note to Mr. Hathaway (Mrs. Carter always wrote little notes), putting her difficulties before him, and asking him in a most tactful manner whether he could possibly spare an hour in the morning to initiate her granddaughter into the mysteries of Latin and History.

Ernest was somewhat startled when the little note reached him per Mrs. Carter's gardener. He wouldn't have minded coaching a boy, but this was evidently a girl—grand-daughters usually were—and it seemed just a trifle *infra dig* to coach a girl. On the other hand there was the money question, and the money question was troubling Ernest very badly at the moment. Three pounds a week had seemed quite a lot when he had started so gaily on his new *régime,* but by the time Mrs. Hobday's wages had come off it, and the weekly bills had been settled, there was nothing left over for such necessary items as the replacement of underwear, the soling of shoes, a pair of winter gloves, or seeds for the garden.—The Apostles and the Saints had lived in warmer climes, and under totally different conditions, of course—

After a few weeks, in which he vainly endeavoured to live below his income, Ernest began to wonder what would happen when his suits wore out, or if he had to call in the doctor, or see the dentist about his teeth. There was also his library subscription to think of—a mere nothing in the old days, but now a serious consideration. It must be met somehow of course, for it was absolutely necessary for a man in his position to have new books and keep abreast of modern thought. It was his duty to do so, and he would starve himself sooner than neglect his duty.

Ernest sat and thought about it for a long time, and then he rummaged about and found an old tobacco tin, and made a hole in the lid. Every week he tried to drop a few shillings into the box, and every week they had to come out again to meet some unexpected demand upon his purse.

He had told Mrs. Hobday that he would have much less money in future, and had asked her to be as economical as she could. She had taken the news very calmly. Everybody was losing their money nowadays. It was a pity, but it couldn't be helped. Why, just the other day Mrs. Hobday's own brother had lost all his savings in one fell swoop. It was rubber or something, Mrs. Hobday thought. "I tell you what we'll do, sir," she said helpfully. "We'll shut up the 'ouse, all except your bedroom and the study, and then we needn't have that girl, Karen, any more. A good for nothing slop of a girl she is! I'll manage the whole thing myself easy."

It had not been any part of Ernest's scheme to throw a girl out of work, but he realised that something pretty drastic must be done, unless of course—but he wasn't going to contemplate that for a moment, he would last out the year supposing he starved, supposing his clothes fell into rags. It was unthinkable to go crawling back to Uncle Mike with the admission that he had failed.

It is interesting to note that he was already thinking about the year, not as a term of probation, but as a definite task to be faced. Perhaps Vivian had something to do with this. He had begun to get interested in Vivian at this juncture—interested, but no more.

Some weeks after the dismissal of Karen he had to

speak to Mrs. Hobday again. He hated the job—hated it all the more because Mrs. Hobday was so frightfully nice, and had been so kind to him and so decent about it before. He put it off from day to day, brooding over it, and making himself utterly wretched about it, but at last he pulled himself together and went off to look for her. He found her making his bed.

"We must keep the bills down, I'm afraid," he said, feeling extremely shy and embarrassed. "D'you think if I had just an egg or something for my supper it would make any difference?"

"That's all right, sir," she replied, beating up his pillow with her capable work-stained hands. "I've been getting the best of everything, seeing you were a gentleman as has been used to it—so to speak. I'll keep the bills down to what you say. Only of course you're bound to notice a bit of difference. Stooing steak isn't the same as best steak and no amount of cooking will make it the same. And while we're on the subject, sir, Hobday was asking if you'll mind if I went 'ome nights. I'd take a bit less if I could get 'ome about six and cook Hobday's supper. I could leave your supper all ready, and you could 'eat a cup of cocoa for yourself. I'd be 'ere early in the morning to see to the breakfast of course."

Ernest consented, he was wax in Mrs. Hobday's capable hands.

"I 'ardly liked to ask," continued Mrs. Hobday. "But it would make a lot of difference if you really don't mind. You see my girl's been running up expenses—she's a good girl, Mary is, but she's young. She 'asn't the eye to pick out the best bit of meat at the butcher's. And then

Rosy's ill again an' that makes more work. She gets the bronchitis every winter, that child does. As soon as ever the wind comes cold it strikes 'er in the chest. I don't know what we'd do without Dr. Walker, he's such a kind gentleman, 'e was in seeing Rosy yest'dy afternoon. I took a run down 'ome just to see what was 'appening, an' I run straight into Dr. Walker, 'e's coming again tomorrow to see Rosy. Mrs. Walker was in too with a basket full of oranges and jelly and a bunch of flowers. Mrs. Walker would do you good just to look at 'er if you was ill, let alone what she brings."

"I don't think I know Mrs. Walker," Ernest said.

"She goes to church pretty regular too," replied Mrs. Hobday. "Except if the twins is ill, or anything—a tall slim lady she is, with brown 'air, and grey eyes, and 'er eyebrows go up and down a lot when she talks. You wouldn't forget Mrs. Walker once you'd talked to 'er—and the doctor's a fine man.—*Kind* that's what they are."

"You must go down to your home when you want," Ernest said (he felt vaguely that he could be just as kind as the Walkers), "especially when your child is ill. Don't mind about me. I'll manage quite all right. Your first duty is to your home, of course."

"Thank you kindly, sir, but I'll manage to run both 'ouses—that's nothing to me. As long as you've got your 'ealth you can do anything you set your mind to. That's what I always say. I've said it to Hobday often when 'e's been a bit down in the mouth about 'is work. You see, sir, Hobday's a boiler-maker by trade. 'E used to go to Bulverham every day, but the works is closed down now, and 'e's 'ad to take a job on the roads. Lucky to get it too. But Hobday gets a bit down in the mouth every now and then. 'When am I going to get back to me own work,' he says to me. I'm sorry for 'im, too. It's 'ard when you can't get your own work, isn't it, sir? Just like as if *you* 'ad to go for a schoolmaster or something— I hope you don't mind me making the remark, my tongue do run away with me sometimes."

"No, of course not.—Yes it is exactly the same, and I do feel very sorry indeed for your husband," said Ernest trying to answer all her questions at once and getting a trifle mixed up in the attempt.

That was only last week, and here was Ernest going for a schoolmaster just like Hobday. He felt even more sympathy for Hobday now that he knew exactly what it felt like to have to take up work which was not really your own line. Of course it was much worse for Hobday, because Ernest's was only a temporary thing. Now that he was definitely engaged to Vivian there was no question of carrying on with the experiment after the year was up. He must tell Vivian soon about his financial affairs, but there was no hurry about it. He had a lurking suspicion that Vivian would not understand the motives which had prompted his experiment in Poverty—she might even think him rather a fool.

Perhaps I *am* rather a fool, Ernest thought, wearing myself into a shadow quite unnecessarily. At any rate I don't seem to be much use at this job. His financial affairs had not benefited very much from the new arrangement with Mrs. Hobday. The few shillings he had saved on her wages went into the tin, of course, but they came out again almost directly to buy a new spade for the garden—and only this morning the kitchen kettle had developed a small hole in its bottom—it was extraordinary how the money dribbled away.

"I *must* teach that little girl," thought Ernest sitting down at his desk and taking up his pen to reply to Mrs. Carter. "There's nothing else for it—and I ought to be glad of the opportunity, ungrateful wretch that I am!"

But all the same he sighed, as he sealed up his letter, and gave it to the gardener who was waiting for a reply. It was rather a come down, after all his noble aspirations, to start teaching Latin and History to a little girl.

So far, little has been said about Ernest's aspirations, and the reason why he had accepted the living at Silverstream which was really rather a backwater and had, hitherto, been held by ancient or unambitious men. Ernest was neither ancient nor unambitious, but he felt that he could chew the cud of his learning for a while, and read and meditate, and, eventually, when he had got his somewhat chaotic ideas into order, he could write a book.

It was certainly quiet enough at Silverstream, and now that he was alone at night in the big empty Vicarage it was really rather eerie. Sometimes Ernest thought he heard strange noises and went round the house with a thick stick, and an electric torch looking for burglars, but it had never been burglars yet. It was just the old house creaking in the wind, and talking to itself about all it had seen, and the big cheerful families which it had sheltered and sent forth into the world.

Ernest made up his mind, at last, that he would give up his nocturnal rambles. They wasted his time and made him feel lonely, and it was unlikely—when you thought about it seriously—that any sane burglar would choose the Vicarage for his nefarious purposes, considering that the Vicarage was almost empty and contained nothing of the slightest value for a burglar to take. It was much more likely, Ernest thought, that a sane burglar would choose The Riggs which was glittering with silver plate, or The Firs which boasted a valuable collection of Eighteenth Century snuff-boxes. So he ceased to listen to the strange noises at night, and, after a little while, he ceased to hear them.

．　　．　　．　　．　　．

Sally was annoyed when she was informed of the arrangement with the Vicar. The idea of a grown-up woman like herself being sent back to the schoolroom like a troublesome child was galling in the extreme. But the whole thing was settled before she heard of it at all, and she was obliged to bow to the inevitable. Sally donned her most sophisticated garments, as a sort of mute protest against the indignity of it, and presented herself at the Vicarage punctually at ten-thirty. Her injured feelings were somewhat soothed by the Vicar's reception of her.

"Oh!" cried Ernest, leaping from his chair, "are you— I mean I didn't know—are you—are you Miss Carter? —I thought it was going to be a child." (His amazement and consternation were all that could be desired.)

"Gran treats me like one," replied Sally, taking command of the situation at once. "It really is most annoying —I suppose it's because Gran is so old herself."

"I suppose it is," agreed Ernest.

"Old people never seem to think that children grow up—they think you remain at the same age always. And of course Gran remembers Daddy being a little boy, and eating bread and milk for his supper, so I suppose it is difficult for her to realise me at all."

"I suppose it is," said Ernest again.

"People's brains work slowly when they get old. They don't pick up new impressions, you know. A doctor explained that to me once. It was very interesting indeed."

"Yes, it must have been," said Ernest helplessly. He was quite at a loss as to how he was going to begin the lesson. How on earth was he to start teaching Latin and History to this very self-possessed young lady? Lord's *Modern Europe,* which he had found and decided upon as being the very thing for his purpose, now seemed entirely inadequate support. So too, the Latin Primer which he had unearthed last night from a box of old books and carried down to the study with triumph and satisfaction. The young lady was taking off her gloves, she evidently expected him to start at once. Ernest ran his hands through his hair in despair.

Sally had begun to enjoy herself, she was fully aware of Ernest's dilemma.

"I had this at school of course," said Sally, taking up the well worn primer. "But I expect I've forgotten all about it by now. Do we start at the beginning?"

"Yes," agreed Ernest. "At least I don't know. Perhaps you would rather do some translations. The primer is rather dull. You see I didn't know you were—I thought you were—I mean I just got those books out because—"

"But I'm really very ignorant," Sally told him, opening her blue eyes very wide, and gazing at him innocently. "You'll be horrified when you find how little I know. I've forgotten everything I ever learnt." How blue her eyes were!

"Perhaps I might take off my hat," suggested Sally.

"Oh yes," he said, "yes, of course, do take it off if it's more comfortable."

Sally took it off, and gave her head a little shake so that her golden curls fluffed out round her head like a halo. Ernest had never seen anything so pretty in his life, he gazed at her with fascinated eyes.

"Well, I suppose we had better begin, hadn't we?" she enquired, sitting down at the table. "Yes I suppose we had," replied Ernest, trying to pull himself together.

"We mustn't waste our time," Sally pointed out.

Ernest agreed. He took up the Latin Primer and laid it down again—it was awfully dull.

"What about history?" suggested Sally. "I'm awfully ignorant about history, you know."

"We had better start with history, then," Ernest said.

"Everyone should know something about history, shouldn't they?" Sally demanded.

Ernest was sure that she was right. They opened Lord's *Modern Europe* and glanced through it together.

"I think this is too—too elementary for you," Ernest said suddenly, closing the book and looking at his pupil— he found it difficult not to look at her. And when he looked at her he could think of nothing except how pretty she was. He looked away again, and tried to collect his scattered wits. "Modern thought has progressed so enormously," said Ernest. "Dates are not considered so important nowadays, it's the background that really matters. It's understanding how the people lived, what kind of things they had to eat, and what they felt and thought."

"Dates are dreadfully dull," Sally agreed. "I never could learn dates. What you say sounds so interesting."

Ernest glowed, he said some more about it, elaborating his theory. They discussed the manner in which history should be taught. Meanwhile the time flew. It was half past eleven before they had decided where to begin.

"I'm afraid we haven't done much work," Ernest said guiltily as his pupil rose and pulled on her hat.

"We've cleared the ground," Sally pointed out. "It's most important to clear the ground. And you have found out how little I know—"

"Oh, but I haven't at all," Ernest assured her. "I mean you're so intelligent. So alive."

Sally liked being called intelligent and alive, it was better to be intelligent than clever (who had said that?) Sally rather suspected that she was both, and perhaps she was right. She went home quite pleased with herself, and told Gran that the ground had been cleared. Gran had had a peaceful morning so she was easily convinced that the experiment was a success.

CHAPTER XIX

Miss Buncle's Holiday

MRS. CARTER was expecting Barbara Buncle to tea, she was somewhat surprised when Elizabeth Wade arrived instead.

"My dear Barbara!" she said, peering at her guest shortsightedly, "My dear Barbara, what have you been doing to yourself? Not monkey glands, I hope."

"Just a new coat and hat, that's all," replied Barbara slightly dashed at her reception.

"And you've had your hair permanently waved," Mrs. Carter pointed out, "I must say it's a great improvement to your appearance. It always is an improvement to anybody with straight hair. Mine is naturally wavy, of course," she added defiantly—Mrs. Carter was trying hard to live down the wicked aspersions cast upon her hair by John Smith—

"How nice for you!" said Barbara, sighing.

"Sally has started lessons with the Vicar," said Mrs. Carter, changing the subject rather abruptly. "It is such a blessing for the dear child to have some definite employment in the morning when I am busy."

"With the Vicar?"

"Yes, he's very badly off—so Dr. Walker says. I don't know how Dr. Walker found out, except that he seems to know everything. Of course that's how Sarah got all the information for her book—although a great deal of it is incorrect—"

Barbara followed this disjointed and not altogether logical sentence with some difficulty. She seized upon the main point—or at least what she considered to be the main point.

"But Sarah didn't write it," she said firmly.

"How do you know? I'm perfectly certain she wrote it. Who else could have written it? Look at the opportunities she has. I'm certain the doctor tells her everything. I would never have Dr. Walker again if it were not for the fact that he understands my rheumatism so well. But I shall cut Sarah when I see her," added Mrs. Carter with satisfaction.

"She didn't write it," said Barbara again.

"Well, I'd like to know who did, then. You didn't stay until the end of the meeting, of course. We all decided that John Smith was Sarah Walker—it was unanimous, except for Ellen King, who always disagrees with everybody. Even old Mr. Durnet held up his hand—"

"I don't suppose he had the slightest idea what he was holding up his hand for," interrupted Barbara.

"Well, he held it up anyway—and wasn't it a clear proof of guilt getting in such a rage and dashing out of the room like a maniac without even saying good-bye to her hostess?"

"I did the same," said Barbara bravely. She had not realised until this moment that she had been guilty of a breach of manners. Ought she to have said "good-bye" to Mrs. Featherstone Hogg, and "thank you very much for having me"? I suppose I ought to have—thought

Barbara—but if I had thought that at the time I wouldn't have come away at all, I simply couldn't have done it before everybody, so perhaps it's just as well I forgot my manners.

"Oh, *you!*" laughed Mrs. Carter. "Nobody even thought of you. You could never have written *Disturber of the Peace*. Sarah Walker has brains. I don't care for the woman at all—never did. She has no idea of how a lady ought to behave. The way she hob-nobs with the village people and doesn't pay proper respect where proper respect is due! I never could understand what *you* could see in Sarah Walker—but she certainly has brains of a kind—"

Barbara was hurt, and amused, intensely relieved, and very much annoyed all at the same time. There was a queer bubbly feeling in her inside at the mixture of emotions. She felt inclined to shout, "Well, I did write it then, you silly old thing!" but she managed to stifle the inclination. She merely reiterated her conviction that Sarah had not written *Disturber of the Peace*.

"It's no use keeping on saying that, Barbara," said Mrs. Carter irritably. "If Sarah didn't write it, who did? Agatha Featherstone Hogg and I made a list of everyone we knew in Silverstream and went through it one by one, most carefully. Everyone is either in the book themselves—or else absolutely incapable of writing it. But in any case it doesn't matter much now, we shall soon know for certain whether Sarah wrote it or not."

"You will soon know for certain?"

"Agatha has a plan," explained Mrs. Carter. "At least the plan really originated with Mrs. Greensleeves. Agatha has merely adopted it and they are working it out together."

"And what is the plan?" Barbara asked breathlessly.

"Well, I can't tell you about it, because I promised Agatha I would tell nobody. Of course it wouldn't matter telling you, Barbara, but a promise is a promise. Personally I think the plan is a trifle risky, but Agatha will be careful."

"Goodness!" said Barbara feebly. She was alarmed at the news. If the plan had been Mrs. Featherstone Hogg's concoction she would not have worried so much—Mrs. Featherstone Hogg was vindictive but not subtle—Mrs. Greensleeves was of a different calibre, she was cunning and sly as a vixen.

"Yes," said Mrs. Carter with satisfaction, "yes, we shall soon know for certain whether or not it was Sarah Walker. Did you get a post card from Paris, by any chance?"

Barbara admitted that she had.

"Disgraceful! Positively indecent!" said Mrs. Carter, warming up again, "I don't know what the World is coming to, nowadays."

"I think it's nice that they got married," Barbara said, trembling a little at her temerity in contradicting her hostess.

"Nice!" exclaimed old Mrs. Carter. "It's certainly not *nice*. The word is misused nowadays to a ridiculous extent. The word *nice* means fastidious, discreet—was it either fastidious or discreet for two people, whose names are being bandied about the world in a third rate novel, to rush off to Paris together? I suppose they *are* married," added Mrs. Carter, in a tone which inferred that she had grave doubts on the subject.

"Dorcas was saying that they would make a very nice—er—I mean charming couple."

"Dorcas!" snorted Mrs. Carter, "what does Dorcas know about it? It's a great mistake to talk things over with servants, you shouldn't pay any attention to what Dorcas says."

"I don't, unless I agree with her," said Barbara simply.

The conversation was getting more and more unpleasant. Barbara longed for Sally to come in and rescue her. She wondered where on earth Sally was, all this time. Once Sally appeared upon the scene Mrs. Carter would cease talking about disgraceful marriages, for she was very careful what she said before her grand-daughter—quite unnecessarily careful considering Sally's knowledge of the world and its wicked ways.

"The amount of harm that book has done!" said Mrs. Carter, raising her eyes to the ceiling. "This dreadful hole-and-corner wedding, the Bulmers' home broken up and Isabella Snowdon's nightmares are all directly attributable to that book—not to speak of the discomfort and worry it has caused to people like Agatha and myself—"

Sally drifted in silently when tea was nearly over. She was all in brown to-day, russet brown like a November beech leaf. She sat down and sipped a large tumbler of milk with obvious distaste.

"Where have you been, Sally?" enquired her grandmother anxiously, "I hope you haven't been wandering about outside, it's far too cold for you to be out at this time of night."

"I was walking."

"Where did you go, dear? All by yourself?"

"I met Mr. Hathaway," said Sally, carelessly. "He came along."

"That was good of him," said Mrs. Carter. "Very kind indeed of him to take you for a walk. I hope you are not imposing too much on Mr. Hathaway's good nature."

Sally did not seem to think this required an answer, she sipped her milk, and crumbled a biscuit in her fingers.

"Don't make crumbs, dear," said Mrs. Carter. "You can ring the bell for Lily to take the tea away if you like."

Sally ceased crumbling and rang the bell for Lily without speaking. When Sally had stayed at The Firs as a small child it had been a treat to ring the bell for tea to be cleared away, and Gran seemed to think it was a treat still. These small things annoyed Sally—she knew it was silly to be annoyed, but she was annoyed just the same.

Barbara felt sorry for her to-day, she looked sad, and withdrawn—the child was suffering within herself. Perhaps she was fretting for her father. It must be frightful for her—Barbara thought. Half an hour of old Mrs. Carter's conversation had left Barbara somewhat worn— what must it be like to have nobody but Mrs. Carter, and Mrs. Carter all day long, and every day? Barbara remembered her promise to Virginia to keep an eye on Sally, and felt a trifle guilty. She had been so engrossed in her new book that she had not seen as much of Sally as she had intended.

"Sally must come and have tea with me again," she said.

"I'm sure the child would enjoy that," said Mrs. Carter, graciously. "Wouldn't you, Sally? Say thank you to Miss Buncle."

"Yes, thank you, Miss Buncle. I would like to come," said Sally with a wan smile.

She's ill—thought Barbara in dismay—she's pining away under our very eyes. I must try to cheer her up, poor little soul! Aloud she said—

"Well, what about to-morrow at four o'clock?"

    .   .   .   .   .

The following morning was damp and unpleasant. Barbara glued her nose to the window and tried to determine whether it was actually raining or not. She decided that in any case it was not nice enough to go out for a walk. This was annoying because she was taking a little holiday and she was therefore free to enjoy herself. The new novel had absorbed all her thoughts and energies for days, and she felt exhausted, and a trifle stale—"I shall take a holiday," she had said, throwing down her pen and shutting her desk firmly, and she was making herself take it. To-day was the second day of her holiday and she was already weary of it; Silverstream was a cold bleak place compared with Copperfield.

Barbara longed for the sunny atmosphere of her spiritual home where she could do as she liked, and say what she pleased, and nobody could contradict her unless she allowed them to do so; where there was no fear of anyone discovering who she was; and where nobody made secret and alarming plans to unmask John Smith—or, if they did, she knew beforehand exactly what they were and could foil them at will.

She wandered round the house getting in the way, and moving things about so that Dorcas couldn't find them when she wanted them.

"Why ever don't you go and write your story, Miss Barbara?" said Dorcas at last in exasperation.

"I'm taking a holiday," said Barbara peevishly.

"You don't seem to be enjoying it much," Dorcas said looking up from the kitchen table where she was rolling out the pastry for a pie. "It's not my idea of a holiday mooning round the house with a long face—"

"I wish I was dead," Barbara said. "I wish I had somebody to talk to, I wish—"

"You better go out, Miss Barbara," said Dorcas crossly. "What's the good of wishing you was dead, and then wishing you had somebody to talk to? You couldn't talk if you was dead. If you was to go out for a nice walk you might meet somebody to talk to, and I'd get on with my work—I'm behind as it is."

"I'll go for a fastidious discreet walk," Barbara said, "that's what *nice* means. Did you know that, Dorcas? Well it does. I'll go out for a fastidious walk if you like—it would be more discreet to stay at home with all the talk that's going on in Silverstream. I know now exactly what a wanted man feels like."

"A wanted man?"

"Yes, a man wanted by the police for murder or something. John Smith is wanted in Silverstream, you know, very badly wanted, and every time I walk down the

High Street I expect to feel a heavy hand on my shoulder, and hear Sergeant Capper's voice saying, 'I arrest you in the name of the law,' or whatever it is that they say to a wanted man."

"How you do rave on, Miss Barbara. Sergeant Capper would never arrest *you*."

"It would really be John Smith he was arresting," Barbara explained, sitting down on the edge of the kitchen table and watching Dorcas fit her neat oval of dough onto the top of the pie. "John Smith is wanted for the murder of Mrs. Featherstone Hogg's reputation—and Mrs. Carter's too of course—Sergeant Capper would have to arrest John Smith even if he didn't want to—"

"Get your 'at like a dear, Miss Barbara," Dorcas besought her. "The rain's off now, and it's nice and bright. I declare I don't know what I'm doing with you standing over me talking all that nonsense. I'm not sure now as I haven't gone and put sugar in the potatoes by mistake."

Barbara looked out of the window and saw that it had really cleared up, and the sun was struggling through the clouds. She went upstairs and put on her new coat and hat, and she took a new pair of grey gloves with fur gauntlets out of a drawer and put them on. She was wearing her new clothes every day now—it seemed rather extravagant, but she couldn't help it, she had taken a dislike to her old clothes for the new ones had opened her eyes to their frightfulness. They were scarcely worthy to be called clothes, Barbara thought, they were merely coverings for the body. She wondered how on earth she had ever worn them.

It was Elizabeth Wade—looking very Elizabeth Wade-ish—who issued forth into the fitful winter sunshine and went strolling down to the shops.

I might go in and see Sarah—she thought—as she passed the doctor's house. It would be rather nice—no, rather pleasant—to have a chat with Sarah. Sarah was about the only person in Silverstream except Sally who approved of *Disturber of the Peace,* she wasn't in it of course, but she was in the new novel. She was "nice" in it, of course, because Sarah *was nice*—not in the least fastidious, nor discreet but just nice. It gave Barbara a warm feeling in her heart when she remembered how Sarah had stood up for the much maligned *Disturber of the Peace* before all those old cats. Yes, she must certainly go in and see Sarah.

There was another reason urging Barbara to go and see Sarah, and a much more important one. Sarah was not "coming out" very well in the new novel. It was easier—Barbara found—to portray people who were a bit odd like Miss King, or catty and patronising like Mrs. Featherstone Hogg. Sarah was none of these things, and her portrait was rather "wishy washy" in consequence. She would take a good look at Sarah this morning and try to absorb her personality so that when she sat down at her desk to write about her there would be something to write about.

Sarah was embroidering a brown Teddy Bear on a blue linen overall for one of the twins. She had a slight cold, and the doctor had forbidden her to go out, so she was feeling a little bored and was delighted to see Barbara. Barbara was rather a dear.

"Goodness, you're all new!" she exclaimed. "How nice you look! How on earth did you manage to afford a new coat in these hard times?"

"I got a little money unexpectedly," said Barbara with perfect truth. She preferred to tell the truth if she could.

"I wish I had," said Sarah. "My relations are all frightfully healthy at present. Sit down near the fire, Barbara dear, wasn't that Meeting ghastly!"

Barbara agreed that it was.

"Mrs. Featherstone Hogg ought to be drowned," continued Sarah. "She really ought, and Stephen Bulmer, and the Greensleeves woman. Silverstream would be ever so much pleasanter to live in if they were all drowned. I still boil all over when I think of the way she stood up and asked me not to tell lies in front of everybody. I would have loved to tell them I had written the book just to see their faces. Ellen King is very nearly as bad, she got John all het up about *Disturber of the Peace* until I made him read it. Then, of course, he agreed with me that there was nothing disgusting about it. I can't understand Ellen King at all, she's usually such a sensible sort of person. I can't see anything in the book for her to make a song and dance about—can you?"

"No, I can't," said Barbara. She had not intended to be hard on Miss King, she liked her. The fact was that Barbara had always been of the opinion that Miss King found Silverstream a trifle dull, there was little scope in Silverstream for Miss King's energies and capabilities, and it had been with friendly intent that she had arranged an adventurous holiday for her in Samarkand.

"You've read *Disturber of the Peace,* of course," Sarah

said. "What a well chosen name it is! We have had no peace in Silverstream since it was published, have we? Don't you think it's amusing, Barbara? I laughed and laughed when I read it. I couldn't leave it and go to bed."

Barbara was intensely gratified, she preened herself inwardly.

"I suppose you think I wrote it?" asked Sarah with twinkling eyes.

"No, I don't," replied Barbara, "but the others do—I mean Mrs. Carter and Mrs. Featherstone Hogg and all of them. They've got some deep plan that's going to prove you wrote it. Mrs. Carter wouldn't tell me what the plan was, she had promised not to tell anybody, but she was full of it. I thought I'd better warn you."

"It was dear of you," said Sarah, "but I didn't write the book so they can't prove that I did."

"I know, but I didn't like the way she spoke of the plan, she looked sort of mischievous. I can't explain what I mean but it made my blood run cold."

"I don't give a damn for any plan made by Hogg and Carter," said Sarah naughtily. "It's bound to be futile and foolish—"

"But this is really Mrs. Greensleeves' plan, the others have only adopted it."

"That's different. Vivian Greensleeves hates me, for some reason. I know she hates me because she is always so frightfully sugary—and of course it was her suggestion that I was John Smith—and of course she doesn't like John Smith at all. John Smith was really very unkind to Vivian Greensleeves," said Sarah, sniggering a little, "that Romeo and Juliet scene with Mr. Fortnum and Mason was just a *trifle* beneath our friend Vivian—not very much beneath her, I fancy, there was just enough truth in it to be intensely galling."

"She's dangerous, Sarah."

"She's a snaky sort of person," Sarah said, wrinkling her brows, "but I don't see what she could do to me, I don't really see what she could *do.*"

Barbara didn't see either but she felt that something nasty was brewing.

The twins were just coming in from their morning walk as Barbara went away.

"Aren't they lambs?" said their mother proudly—and they really were like two little lambs in their white fur coats and caps. Each lamb was hugging tightly beneath one arm a very shabby disreputable looking Teddy Bear, more precious in the sight of its owner than all the other toys in the nursery put together. The Teddy Bears went everywhere with the twins, and shared their beds, and meals, and walks. They had been worn threadbare with love and kisses.

"Have they been good, Nannie?" Sarah asked.

"Very good," said Nannie fondly. It was her invariable reply to Sarah's invariable question—no matter how wicked the twins had been she always assured their mother that they had behaved like angels. She punished them herself of course, but she never "told on them." Nannie adored them, she had had them "from the month" and they were the joy and pride of her heart. Even their wickedness was of an endearing nature.

Barbara shook hands with the twins gravely, she was

never at her best with children. She was under the impression that children didn't like her, they always stared
at her so solemnly with their large innocent eyes. Her
relations with Sarah's twins were further complicated by
that fact that she never knew which was Jack and which
was Jill—for Sarah dressed them both alike quite regard-
less of their sex. It was so awkward not to know whether
you were addressing a male or a female.

"I can't think why John Smith didn't put them in his
book, can you?" Sarah said, "they're quite the loveliest,
darlingest lambs in Silverstream. Good-bye, Barbara dear,
and thank you for coming. I'll keep my wits about me
and look out for squalls."

.   .   .   .   .

Miss King was just going in at her own gate as Barbara
passed, and Barbara, although she would fain have
avoided the woman, was obliged to stop and speak to her.

"What horrid damp weather," Barbara said, wondering
what we would do without that safe topic of conversation. "And so warm and unseasonable, isn't it? I do hope
it will clear up and be nice and frosty for Christmas Day.
I like Christmas Day to be frosty, don't you?"

"It never is," Miss King pointed out.

"I expect we shall have a cold spell later," continued
Barbara. "After all this mild wet weather we are practically bound to. Don't you think so?"

"Well, it won't affect me, anyway," said Miss King
blithely, "Angela and I are off to Samarkand next week,"
and passed in.

Barbara was left outside, staring at the gate as if there
were something peculiar the matter with it.

CHAPTER XX

Chiefly About Sally

CHRISTMAS came and went, Silverstream went to Church and gave each other small, and somewhat useless presents just as it always did at this season of the year. Sally's history lessons progressed on unconventional lines. Mr. Hathaway had ordered from his library some of the modern books about historical people and they were reading them together. It was scarcely history in the accepted sense of the word, but it was much more interesting than Lord's *Modern Europe*. They read aloud in turn and discussed what they read, exchanging ideas, and getting to know each other pretty well in the process. Ernest learnt quite as much as Sally at these history lessons—not much history, of course, but there are other things just as important as history. The conversation was apt to wander off into other fields, and linger there until Ernest suddenly remembered that he was giving Sally a history lesson and they returned hastily to their book.

They went for several walks together (not many, because Ernest's garden claimed such a large proportion of his time and energy) they explored the little byways of Silverstream and the woods, and they visited Twelve-Trees Farm once or twice because Ernest wanted to see one of the farmer's sons, who had sprained his leg and couldn't come to church. Dick Billing served well as an excuse for a walk up the valley and the Billings were delighted with the new Vicar's kindness and attention. Of course, there was no need to talk about history during these occasional rambles.

Ernest was so innocent and inexperienced in worldly matters that he was able to keep Sally and Vivian quite apart in his mind. Sally was a pretty child and a charming companion of whom he was growing very fond. Vivian was the woman he was going to marry.

Sally began to like Mr. Hathaway very much. She had been rather scornful of him at first and had decided that he was "soft," but she soon revised her opinion. Ernest wasn't "soft," he was just "different." It took Sally a little time to understand him because she had never met anyone the least like him before. He was a new kind of being to Sally who was used to captains and subalterns and an occasional young man about town. Ernest had an entirely different point of view from these gay and self-possessed young creatures. His vocabulary was different, his character was different, his mind worked in a different way. But once she began to understand Ernest, she began to like him, and the more she understood him the better she liked him.

One morning—a few days after Christmas—Mrs. Hobday knocked discreetly upon the door while the lesson was in progress, and asked for three shillings to pay the laundry. Ernest found his old tobacco tin and peered into it.

"I'm afraid there's only two and threepence here," he

said regretfully. "I thought there was more, but, of course, I had to pay carriage on the books, hadn't I?"

"They can wait till next week," said Mrs. Hobday, who knew the secrets of the tobacco tin, and accepted this strange financial arrangement with the equanimity of her kind.

"No," said Ernest firmly, "you had better give them the two and threepence while it's here. Otherwise it will just fade away and the bill will be double next week. Tell them to add on the ninepence to their next account."

Sally was amazed at this poverty. She knew what it was to be economical, of course, and to go without a new hat when you wanted it very badly, for soldiers are proverbially poor; but she had never realised that you could be so short of money as this. Fancy not having three shillings wherewith to pay your laundry bill—how ghastly!

"It's awkward being so poor," said Mr. Hathaway to Sally, quite frankly and somewhat apologetically, when he had replaced the empty tin in his drawer. "I try to save a little in that old tin, but there's always something coming along that has to be paid. I was hoping to get my shoes mended next week."

Sally gazed at him with wide eyes.

"I don't mind really," he said, laughing a little at her distress, "it's rather fun pinching and scraping and trying to live on my stipend—it's like a game—"

How brave he was!

"Don't worry," Ernest continued, "I shall be all right— you mustn't look so sad about it, you know."

"You'll have the money for my lessons, of course," Sally pointed out.

"I oughtn't to take it, really," replied Ernest, "I'm afraid you're not learning much from me."

"Oh, I am!" declared Sally, "I'm learning lots. Gran ought to pay you ever so much for my lessons, and she ought to pay you every week, I shall tell her about it."

They discussed the question with the utmost frankness. Sally had been brought up with soldiers, a class which is completely frank as regards money. Having very little to come and go on, and knowing to a half-penny what each other is drawing in the way of pay, the Army Officer has no false pride about his financial affairs. Ernest was perfectly frank, also, because he had never been poor, and he was not really poor now. This poverty of his, as he had told Sally, was merely a sort of game. Sometimes it was a troublesome worrying sort of game, but there was nothing bitter, and real, and grinding about it. Poverty is easy to bear if it is only temporary, easier still if it is an entirely voluntary burden.

The next morning Sally appeared with an envelope containing two weeks' salary from Mrs. Carter for the instruction of her grand-daughter, which the said grand-daughter had extracted from Mrs. Carter with firmness and tact.

Ernest was quite pleased to see the money—which Sally assured him he had "honestly earned"—and not at all embarrassed at taking it from his pupil's hands. Together they placed it in the tobacco tin, and Ernest promised to have his shoes mended at once. It was high time he did something about his shoes, for he did not possess a pair without large holes in the soles, and these large holes let in the water most uncomfortably when he walked about the muddy lanes of Silverstream.

They were just settling down comfortably to a perusal of *Elizabeth and Essex,* by Lytton Strachey, when the door-bell rang and Mrs. Greensleeves was shown in to the study. Mrs. Greensleeves beautifully dressed in navy blue, with black fox furs, and a quiet but obviously costly black felt hat set at a jaunty angle on her elaborately waved hair.

Sally had no use for Mrs. Greensleeves, she had met her like that before, and her sharp eyes had sized up that wily lady the moment they had beheld her sitting at her ease in Gran's drawing-room and laying down the law to Gran and Mrs. Featherstone Hogg about *Disturber of the Peace.* And, besides her own infallible instinct, Sally had John Smith's word for it that Mrs. Greensleeves was no good.

It was, however, quite obvious to Sally that Mr. Hathaway did not share her views, and the views of John Smith, about his unexpected visitor. He seemed enchanted to see her and apologised profusely for being in the middle of a lesson. He was shy, and embarrassed, and meek, and propitiatory—almost as if he had been found out doing something wrong—and his excuses for Sally's presence were not altogether tactful. Sally was annoyed: she had every right to be here—far more right than Mrs. Greensleeves if it came to that—and she did not like being apologised for. She had ceased to think of these hours with Mr. Hathaway as lessons (except, of course, that Gran must pay for them), and it was humiliating to be shoved back into the schoolroom before Mrs. Greensleeves whom she disliked and despised.

"It doesn't matter at all," said Sally, seizing her hat and cramming it on her golden curls.

"Oh, but you mustn't go," said poor Ernest. "We have only just begun our lesson. Mrs. Greensleeves won't mind waiting, or coming back later."

Mrs. Greensleeves said she wouldn't dream of disturbing a lesson, but, unfortunately, she could not come back later, she merely wanted to speak to Mr. Hathaway privately for a few minutes. Perhaps Miss Carter would wait.

It appeared, however, that Miss Carter could not wait either, Gran would be expecting her and it was quite unthinkable to keep Gran waiting of course. She wasn't very sure whether she would be able to spare the time to continue her readings with Mr. Hathaway, Gran was getting old, and required a lot of attention.

Ernest gazed from one to the other in dismay, he was quite helpless in this sudden and unexpected dilemma. He was being paid for Miss Carter's lessons, and therefore it was his duty to give them to her at the appointed time, but how could he let Vivian go away when she wanted to speak to him? Vivian would be annoyed if he sent her away—besides they were engaged, so, of course, he wanted to talk to her.

Sally read him like a book—he was fairly easy to read —and departed in high dudgeon and walked about Silverstream for an hour. She wasn't going home, and she wasn't going to tell Gran about it until she had made up her mind definitely whether she was going to continue her readings with Mr. Hathaway or not—it sounded so much better to call them readings, and of course that was what they really were.

Sally walked quickly up the hill and into the woods. At that moment she was furious with Mr. Hathaway for being such a fool, and the next moment she was sorry for him for being such an innocent. "I wonder if they are engaged," she said aloud, slashing at an unoffending bush with her umbrella. "I bet they are engaged or he wouldn't have been so terrified of offending her. How could he be such an idiot as to fall in love with a horrible little cat like Vivian Greensleeves! She's years older than he is—five years older at least—and not a bit his style. She cares for nothing but clothes—"

A sudden thought struck her, and she stopped slashing and leaned against a convenient tree. Vivian Greensleeves would never marry a poor man. "She can't know he's so poor," said Sally to herself, "or she wouldn't want him." It was an amazing thought, amazing and comforting. It was a sort of loop-hole in the blank wall, it was a ray of sunshine in a dark place. Perhaps Vivian Greensleeves had heard—as all Silverstream had heard—that the new Vicar was a wealthy man, perhaps she didn't know that he had lost all his money.

Sally closed her eyes and thought about it deeply, she could think much better when her eyes were shut. She would save the poor young man from the clutches of Mrs. Greensleeves, she would save him in spite of himself. The only thing to be settled was *how* she was going to save him.

Thinking all this over and over inside her head, Sally

went home and was wonderfully docile and obedient to her Grandmother, drinking up her milk without a murmur, and sitting reading very quietly in the corner of the sofa for the remainder of the morning.

"May I go out for a walk, Gran?" Sally asked, when they had finished lunch and were drinking their coffee in the drawing-room. "It is so nice and sunny to-day, I feel a walk would do me a lot of good."

Mrs. Carter saw no reason why Sally should not go for a walk; she, herself, liked to sit down quietly, with a book after lunch, and sometimes she closed her eyes and snoozed for a little in a ladylike manner; but children were different, of course, and the doctor had said most distinctly that Sally was to have sunshine.

"I think you might, dear," said Gran, "perhaps Lily had better put on her things and go with you—"

"Oh, Gran! It's Lily's afternoon out," said Sally reproachfully.

This was an argument that could not be met, Gran would rather have gone for a walk with Sally herself than have filched an "afternoon out" from her admirable and highly efficient parlourmaid.

"Well, I suppose you had better go alone then," she said, with a little sigh, "I don't like you walking about alone, but it can't he helped. Don't go too far, dear, and don't overtire yourself or get your feet wet."

Sally promised to obey these dull injunctions with unusual docility and departed to call on Mrs. Greensleeves.

.   .   .   .   .

Vivian Greensleeves was in, when Sally called, she often took a little nap after lunch herself—there was nothing else to do in Silverstream except sleep. She had just composed herself comfortably upon her pink bed, and closed her eyes, when Milly came in to say that Miss Carter had called.

"Miss Carter!" exclaimed Vivian irritably.

"Mrs. Carter's grand-daughter," said Milly, "the young lady from The Firs."

"I know all that," said Vivian. "What does she want to see me for?"

Milly had no idea, Miss Carter hadn't said why she wanted to see Mrs. Greensleeves, she had just called.

"Well, I suppose I had better see her," said Vivian reluctantly. "Some idiotic message from the old lady, I suppose—curse her!"

She arose reluctantly from her bed and powdered her nose. She did this quite instinctively and not because she wanted to appear at her best before Sally Carter.

Sally was waiting in the drawing-room, she rose when her hostess appeared and they shook hands gravely. It crossed Vivian's mind that the Carter child was much younger than she had thought, she couldn't possibly be more than fifteen. The impression was due to the fact that Sally had donned an entirely different set of garments from those she usually wore. With the old blue school hat which had been stowed away in the bottom of her hat box for the last three years, and the belted waterproof, and the coloured woollen scarf wound round her neck Sally would have passed anywhere for a schoolgirl. Nor had she been content merely to lay aside her attractive and sophisticated clothes (Sally was nothing if

not thorough) she had laid away her grown-up manner
as well.

"I hope you don't mind me coming," she said shyly.

Vivian replied conventionally, that she was very pleased
to see her—she could not well do otherwise—and asked
her to sit down.

"Silverstream is awfully dull, isn't it?" said Sally opening her eyes very wide. "I expect you find it awfully dull
too, don't you?"

"Yes, I do," replied Vivian fervently. She wondered
what on earth the child had come for. Why didn't she
say what she had come for instead of sitting there gazing
round the room with those intensely blue and innocent
eyes?

"Have you a message for me?" she asked at last.

"Oh, no," said Sally. "No, I haven't. You see Gran
didn't know I was coming. I expect you think it's rather
queer me coming to see you like this—I just—I just
wanted to see you—" said Sally, looking down and twisting one of the buttons of her waterproof in an embarrassed manner.

Vivian smiled—she thought she understood now why
Sally had come. The child had evidently taken a fancy
to her this morning, one of those schoolgirl passions
which one reads about in psychological novels. And
wasn't it quite a natural thing that Sally should take
a fancy to somebody so entirely different from the dull
and stodgy people with whom she was surrounded? Of
course it was.

"It was nice of you to come," said the pleasantly flattered Vivian—even a schoolgirl's admiration was worth having in a place as dull as Silverstream.

"Oh, no, it was so nice of you to *see* me," replied Sally humbly.

"I'm sorry you are feeling dull here—I expect you had a much gayer time with your father, hadn't you?"

"Yes. There were parties in the winter, and we used to play tennis at school in the Summer Term. Daddy was always moving about, of course, so I went to lots of different schools."

"Rather nice," suggested Vivian to whom a constant change of scene seemed very desirable.

"In some ways," Sally agreed, "but I didn't learn very much, because I was just getting used to one kind of teaching when I moved on to something quite different. Gran says I am very ignorant for my age, so that's why I'm having lessons with Mr. Hathaway."

"I see," said Vivian, she was interested. It had seemed such a queer arrangement when she had broken in upon them in the middle of the lesson that morning. She had even felt a trifle—just a trifle—jealous. Perfectly ridiculous of her to feel jealous of infant like this. She had tried to find out from Ernest why on earth he had taken on the job of teaching Sally Carter but he had not given any satisfactory explanation of his reasons. Ernest could be very obstinate when he liked.

"It's very kind of Mr. Hathaway to spare the time," Vivian continued, when she had sorted things out in her own mind. "I suppose he is doing it to please Mrs. Carter."

Sally nodded, "Partly to please Gran, and partly, of

course, because he needs the money so badly," she told Vivian with childish frankness.

"Mr. Hathaway has plenty of money," said Vivian sharply. "You needn't think the money is any object to him. I expect your grandmother asked him to do it and he didn't like to refuse." It would be just like Ernest, she thought, to feel he was obliged to teach the child when Mrs. Carter asked him.

Sally shook her head sadly, "I know people think Mr. Hathaway is rich, but he's frightfully poor really. He's lost all his money you know. It's frightfully sad. I shouldn't think anyone has ever been so poor before."

"Nonsense," said Vivian, but all the same her heart missed a beat. Supposing the child was right? Supposing Ernest really *had* lost all his money and she had wasted all that time and taken all that trouble for nothing? "What makes you think he has lost all his money?" she asked, trying to make her voice sound casual but not succeeding in deceiving Sally's sharp ears.

She's horrified—Sally thought, hugging herself with delight at the success of her plan—she's trying hard not to believe it, but she knows it's true all the same. Aloud she said sadly, "Dr. Walker told Gran, and I know it's true because he hadn't enough money to pay his laundry bill until he got the money from Gran for my lessons. Oh, I do think it's sad, don't you, Mrs. Greensleeves?"

"It's more than sad—if it's true," replied Vivian in a strange voice—and I'll find out whether it's true or not before I'm a day older—she added to herself fiercely.

Sally had now discovered the black cat. This sagacious animal usually remained in the kitchen with Milly and the food, both of which he infinitely preferred to his official mistress. To-day for some reason, known only to himself, he was sitting on the black mat in front of the drawing-room fire, and, when Sally called to him invitingly, he stretched his back and walked slowly across the floor.

"Oh what a darling cat!" Sally exclaimed. "Is he yours? Puss, puss, puss—what's his name, Mrs. Greensleeves?"

She continued to praise and stroke the pussy's glossy back. He really was a dear, and she was intensely grateful to him for helping her to change the subject. She felt instinctively that she had said enough about Mr. Hathaway's poverty, enough to upset Mrs. Greensleeves and to place a thorny doubt in her mind. Mrs. Greensleeves would never know a moment's peace until she had found out definitely whether the staggering news was true or not, and that was all that Sally wanted. So she stroked the cat's ears and slid her small hand along his ridgy back until he purred like a miniature Rolls Royce.

"But his clothes are so—so *good*," said Vivian, who was too closely interested to abandon the subject.

"I suppose he got them before he was poor," said Sally naïvely.

CHAPTER XXI

Mrs. Snowdon's Memorial

*E*RNEST was delighted to see his pupil appear as usual the following morning, he had been afraid she would not come. She had been annoyed and offended, he knew, at the arbitrary way in which Vivian Greensleeves had cut short their lesson. Vivian shouldn't have done it, of course, and he shouldn't have allowed Vivian to do it, but he had been absolutely helpless at the time—a mere shuttlecock between the two. Looking back upon the scene Ernest decided that he had played a poor part, he should have been firm, he should have sent Vivian away and finished the lesson with Miss Carter; but he could not have done it all the same. It crossed his mind that Vivian had been a little inconsiderate, and somewhat domineering. Was he taking unto himself a domineering wife? St. Paul said that a woman should be obedient to her husband. Of course he was not yet Vivian's husband, she would be different when they were married. Strangely enough the thought of being married to Vivian had ceased to thrill him. Ernest wondered why. A week ago, ten days ago, the mere thought of being married to Vivian had been sufficient to send delicious shivers up his spine. It's just that I'm getting used to the idea—Ernest thought.

When the mystic hour of ten-thirty drew near, Ernest

found that he could not sit still. He went and looked out of the window several times—would she come, or was she really hurt and offended? How awful if she didn't come any more, if she discontinued her lessons! They had had such pleasant hours together, he liked to hear her reading, she had such a pretty voice, and he could look at her undisturbed—he liked looking at her.

If she doesn't come I shall go and call, Ernest thought, I was at fault about the whole thing and I must apologise. Perhaps if I apologise she will forgive me for being such a weak idiot. He left the window—impelled by a sudden idea—and went into the kitchen to find Mrs. Hobday.

"Oh, Mrs. Hobday," said Ernest. "If anybody calls while I am giving Miss Carter her lesson please say I am engaged. The lesson must not be interrupted."

"Yessir," said Mrs. Hobday. "I'm sorry about yesterday, I really am. But Mrs. Greensleeves was so obstinate and you 'adn't said nothing definite about not being disturbed. I really didn't know wot to do."

"I know, it was my fault, Mrs. Hobday," Ernest told her. "Entirely my fault—but you'll know another time."

"Oh, I will, sir," replied Mrs. Hobday. She won't get in again and worry the poor lambs—added Mrs. Hobday to herself—not unless it's over my dead body, she won't.— Mrs. Hobday was another who had no use for Vivian Greensleeves.

At this moment the door-bell rang, it rang so loudly that Ernest—whose nerves had been on edge all morning —nearly jumped out of his skin.

"That'll be Miss Carter now," said Mrs. Hobday taking off her apron.

"Don't bother, I'll answer it," Ernest told her, and he ran to open the door. Sally was standing on the step, she smiled in a friendly manner when she saw Ernest.

"Am I late?" she enquired.

"No, not a bit," replied the Vicar, "but I was so awfully afraid you wouldn't come—I couldn't help it yesterday—I'm such an ass—you aren't angry, are you?"

"I was, at the time," Sally admitted, following him into the study. "But I'm not now, not a bit." She stood and smiled at him.

What a darling! thought Ernest. He had a sudden feeling that he would like to kiss her—a most extraordinary feeling for a man who was engaged to somebody else—of course it would never do to kiss her, it would be a frightful thing to do. Sally held out her hand and they shook hands gravely.

"It won't happen again," Ernest said, "I've told Mrs. Hobday to say I'm engaged if anyone calls."

"No," said Sally. "No, I don't think it will happen again." She took up *Elizabeth and Essex* which was lying on the table with a book-marker in the place. "Shall I read first, or will you?" she enquired.

"You read," Ernest said, and he composed himself very happily and contentedly in his chair to watch her.

•   •   •   •

Several days later Ernest, taking a little stroll round the church-yard, was surprised and somewhat pained to see that a large pink marble sarcophagus had appeared as if by magic upon the Snowdons' family grave. He was the more distressed because the little church-yard had hitherto been happily free from monstrosities of this nature. It was such a pretty little church-yard, peaceful and beautiful, with several fine old trees lending dignity to the scene, and the river murmuring past as if it were singing an endless lullaby to the sleepers.

Ernest paused and hesitated—there appeared to be several men employed in giving the finishing touches to the regrettable erection. He decided to go and speak to them—perhaps even remonstrate in a tactful manner.—At any rate he could find out the meaning for its sudden appearance among the simpler and more tasteful monuments. As he drew near Ernest perceived that Mr. Snowdon was there himself, speaking to the men and giving them some instructions about the lettering. "PEACE BE ST—" had already been inscribed in large gold letters upon one side of the stone—it was a curious text to have chosen—Ernest thought.

An older—and wiser—man than Ernest would have turned back on seeing the perpetrator of the outrage, himself. Tombs and tombstones are delicate subjects for an outsider to intrude upon at the best of times, and Ernest was not as calm as he should have been to deal with a delicate subject—in fact he was extremely annoyed. What business had Mr. Snowdon to destroy the amenities of Ernest's pretty church-yard with his execrable taste? The thing was a perfect eye-sore.

He said, "Good afternoon," to Mr. Snowdon, and asked, somewhat unnecessarily, what was being done.

"I am erecting a memorial to my dear wife," said Mr. Snowdon in throaty tones.

"But there was already a memorial to Mrs. Snowdon here," Ernest pointed out.

"Merely a temporary one," replied the bereaved husband. "Merely temporary."

"It was a granite cross, wasn't it?" enquired Ernest, pursuing the subject unwisely.

"Yes," replied Mr. Snowdon briefly.

"A granite cross is usually considered a sufficiently permanent type of memorial. As a matter of fact I liked it better than this."

"Did you?"

Mr. Snowdon's tone proclaimed that he did not care whether the Vicar liked it or not. If Mr. Snowdon thought fit to change the granite cross for a marble sarcophagus, it was no business of the Vicar's—interfering man, poking his nose into matters that did not concern him.

Ernest walked round to the other side of the enormous slab and saw that the inscription here was finished. Mr. Snowdon had caused the words "REST IN PEACE" to be cut upon this side of his dear wife's memorial. The Vicar did not care for the wording at all, it had a Roman Catholic ring about it, his annoyance was in no way appeased.

"I suppose you have obtained permission to erect it," Ernest asked indiscreetly.

"I have," replied Mr. Snowdon.

Ernest sighed, there was nothing more to be done about the wretched thing. He was just turning away when the marble sarcophagus hit him once more in the eye—it literally got up and hit him. It was a ghastly thing. It was too appalling for words. It spoilt that whole corner of the church-yard.

"Do you think it is quite—er—suitable?" said Ernest, returning once more to the attack. "I mean it is so—so different from all the other stones, so—so very—er—large, and—and—and heavy. The stone sarcophagus has quite gone out of fashion, you know."

"You think so?" enquired Mr. Snowdon, with dangerous meekness.

"It really has," Ernest assured him, "perhaps you don't know the origin of the custom of covering the entire grave with a large heavy stone. It was used to keep wolves and jackals from disturbing the grave—" Ernest was warming up to his subject now, he felt that if he explained the whole thing carefully to Mr. Snowdon he might see the error of his ways and consent to have the pink marble atrocity removed and the granite cross restored. Vivian could have warned Mr. Snowdon that he was in for a lecture on memorials and their historical and religious significance, but Vivian wasn't there, of course. "They were at first confined to foreign lands," continued Ernest, "where wolves and jackals abounded, roaming about grave-yards and digging up bones. One can easily understand how the idea of the large heavy stone covering the entire grave was evolved. The idea was brought home by the Crusaders who had seen it during their travels, and the practice of covering the tomb with a stone memorial became fairly common in England. It died out, I am glad to say, and was only revived for a short period during the panic caused by the trial of Burke and Hare. You will, of course, remember that these men were found guilty of despoiling newly made graves in order to procure anatomical specimens to sell to students and hospitals. I feel convinced that the panic caused was out of all proportion to the facts of the case, but naturally bereaved relatives felt anxious to protect the graves of their dead from desecration. Those days are now past and modern taste leans towards a simpler form, it prefers to dispense with all that is superfluous and meaningless. The sarcophagus is both superfluous and meaningless—it is even more meaningless than usual in this case for I believe Mrs. Snowdon has been dead for some years—"

"Thank you," said Mr. Snowdon with elaborate sarcasm. "Thank you very much. I am sorry to interrupt your eloquence but *I* have other things to do. When I want to hear another sermon from you I shall come to church, but this one will last me for some time I fancy. Meanwhile perhaps you will be good enough to mind your own business and allow me to mind mine. If I choose to erect a certain type of memorial upon my family grave, I shall do so. *Good* afternoon, Mr. Hathaway."

Ernest retired, baffled and conscience stricken. He realised too late that he had been treading on delicate ground with elephantine feet. He had offended Mr. Snowdon without achieving his object. Ernest brooded over the matter as he went home. It seemed to him a very strange thing to take down a granite cross and put up a marble sarcophagus after a woman had been dead and buried for three years. What was the meaning of it? The lettering was different too, for the granite cross had borne the inscription, "She is not dead, but sleepeth." Ernest remembered it distinctly because he had liked it, he had thought when he read it that it was a beautiful idea to put our Lord's consolatory words to Jairus upon a memorial tombstone. They had a deep significance, they carried with them a promise—the promise of resurrection.

Ernest felt sorry these words were not upon Mrs. Snowdon's grave any more (he had a strange feeling that Mrs. Snowdon was sorry too), but this was by no means the worst part of the unfortunate affair, even the hideous erection itself was not the worst part of it, far worse than these was the knowledge that he had been tactless and indiscreet. Uncle Mike had warned him of the pitfalls of his calling—"Tread warily," Uncle Mike had said. "You may think they're fools, but *you're* a fool if you let them see it, and don't offend the 'Little ones,' whatever you do or you will be much happier and more comfortable at the bottom of the sea with a millstone round your neck." This much from Uncle Mike and, already, at the very beginning of his incumbency, he had offended one of his most important parishioners.

Ernest was so upset that he could think of nothing else, he mooned round the house for a bit, and finally decided to go and have tea with Vivian. He must talk it over with somebody and Vivian was obviously the person with whom to talk it over. He was going to marry Vivian, she was going to share all his troubles and worries; well, she could begin by sharing this one— thought Ernest. Besides of course he *wanted* to tell Vivian all about it, she was so sweet and womanly and sympathetic, and she knew a good deal about the world. She could advise him whether he should write to Mr. Snowdon and apologise, and if so what he should say. Perhaps between them they could concoct a conciliatory letter to Mr. Snowdon.

Ernest thought all this as he breasted the hill. He hadn't seen Vivian for several days, indeed he had not seen her since that dreadful morning when she had interrupted Miss Carter's history lesson. That was Wednesday, and to-day was Saturday—practically three days without a glimpse of Vivian! It was strange that he had not noticed this before. He wondered why she had not dropped in to see him as she usually did either in the morning, when he was working in the garden, or in the afternoon, when he was reading in his study. Perhaps she had been busy, or perhaps it was because the weather had been so dreadful—it had rained all yesterday and most of the day before, he remembered.

He found Vivian having tea in front of the drawing-room fire. It was a cosy scene. How nice that she was alone! Ernest went forward eagerly.

"Well, what do you want?" Vivian asked sharply. The mere sight of him caused her to boil with rage, for she had discovered that what Sally had told her was true. In fact once she begun to make enquiries it appeared that everybody in the village was aware of Ernest's financial difficulties, everybody except herself. The village was full of the most astounding tales of the poverty at the Vicarage. She was told about the enormous holes in his shoes (which could be seen to great advantage during the Litany) and about the even more enormous holes in his socks, which Mrs. Hobday was obliged to wrestle with because the poor gentleman could not afford new ones. She was even told that Ernest had invested in a pair of hair clippers and had endeavoured with startling results, to cut his own hair so as to save a monthly ninepence at the Silverstream barber's gentlemen's saloon. Nearly all the shops had tales to tell of poor Ernest's amateur efforts in economy. He bought broken rolls at Mrs. Goldsmith's and odd scraps of meat at Mr. Hart's, and the outside leaves of cabbages at Miss Clement's fruit and vegetable emporium. Mrs. Hobday had put him up to it of course, they told Mrs. Greensleeves, the poor gentleman would never have thought of things like that himself.

Thus it was that when Ernest walked into her drawing-room looking pleased to see her, and expecting her to be equally pleased to see *him,* Vivian's blood simply boiled with rage, and instead of welcoming him with open arms as Ernest had expected, she looked at him as if he were some new and particularly loathsome species of slug and enquired what he wanted.

"You haven't been to see me for ages," Ernest told her, slightly damped by this unusual reception.

"I've found you out, you see," replied Vivian, trying to speak calmly and not succeeding very well.

"You've found me out?"

"Yes."

"But I haven't done *anything,*" said poor Ernest.

"Oh no! you haven't done anything, have you?" demanded Vivian scornfully, "you haven't lied and deceived me at all, have you?"

"No, I haven't," replied Ernest with some spirit.

"You thought you had taken me in nicely, didn't you?" continued Vivian with rising heat. "Coming here and pretending to everybody that you were rich and strutting about in fine clothes, and all the time you haven't a penny —not enough money to have your shoes mended—"

"Oh, is that all?" said Ernest, beginning to see daylight through the fog, "I can explain that quite easily, you see—"

"Yes, that's all," Vivian interrupted furiously. "That's *all* and it's quite enough too—"

"But Vivian, if you would listen for a moment I can explain—"

"I don't want to listen to you any more, I've listened to you quite enough, I'm sick of listening to you—"

"But Vivian—"

"The idea of you coming here," she cried, "the very idea of you coming here and pretending to be so good and pious—a sort of saint on earth—and all the time you're nothing but an impostor."

"I'm not an impostor."

"You are an impostor, and a liar and a cheat. The very idea of you coming to propose marriage to me when you hadn't a single penny to bless yourself with. What do you think I want to marry you for? I suppose you think I would be happy and content to live all my life in a mouldy country vicarage, pinching and scraping, and counting every half-penny? Well you're mistaken, then. I suppose you think you're so good and wonderful that any girl would be proud to marry you and darn your socks for the rest of her life? Well, you're mistaken there, too—thoroughly mistaken. You bore me to death," said

Vivian vindictively. "Do you hear that—you bore me to death."

Ernest heard it, he could not fail to hear it, for Vivian's voice was loud and somewhat shrill. He found that his knees were shaking for he was unused to scenes of this kind. He gazed at Vivian with horror—was this really Vivian, this woman with the hard eyes and the shrill shrewish voice? Was this the same Vivian who had listened to him so sympathetically, who had brought him her troubles and doubts to be smoothed away? Was this the lamb that he had brought back with such pride and joy to the fold?

You bore me to death, Vivian had said. He bored her. Why then had she listened to him and encouraged him to talk to her? Why had she sought him out, visited him at the vicarage, invited him to her house, and, above all, why had she promised to marry him? It seemed a most extraordinary thing to Ernest, he could not understand it at all, he was utterly bewildered. He gazed at Vivian and decided that she looked strange, she looked like an unknown woman, he felt as if he had never seen her before.

"Then it was—it was because—because you thought I had money," he said slowly, his brain clearing as he spoke, "you said you would marry me because you thought I had money?"

Vivian didn't like it put quite like that, it sounded all wrong, somehow, as if *she* were in the wrong and not Ernest at all.

"People must have money, you fool!" she said with

slightly less rancour, "how do you suppose people can live without money?"

"They need a little, certainly."

"I need lots," Vivian said frankly. "It's only idiots and imbeciles who say that money isn't important. Money is the most important thing in the world. I would be perfectly happy with lots and lots of money—"

"And a husband who bored you," suggested Ernest, looking at her very gravely and waiting for her answer with some anxiety.

She laughed, a trifle hysterically, "With the Devil himself," she cried.

CHAPTER XXII

The Children's Party At The Riggs

*T*HE Featherstone Hoggs' Children's Party was fixed for the second week in January. They gave one every year, usually on Christmas Eve and a large and elaborately decorated Christmas Tree was the *pièce de résistance;* but this year, with all the excitement over *Disturber of the Peace,* and the Drawing-room Meeting, the Children's Party had slipped out of mind.

Mrs. Featherstone Hogg disliked the Children's Party intensely, she only gave it because it was the "right thing" for the most important lady in the neighbourhood to give a Children's Party, and because Lady Barnton from Bulverham Castle could always be induced to come to it and bring her small nieces when she could not be induced to come to any other of Mrs. Featherstone Hogg's various parties or At Homes.

Christmas Eve had passed, and there was no mention of a Children's Party. Mr. Featherstone Hogg had not forgotten about it, he liked the Children's Party (it was the only kind of a party he did like), but he thought perhaps Agatha had had enough to bear this year so he said nothing about it. Perhaps they might have one at Easter instead; by Easter Agatha would have settled down a little. He decided to leave it at that. He was astonished when Agatha reminded him about it, the first mention of it usually lay with him. In spite of Lady Barnton, Agatha always approached the Children's Party with reluctance. It was such a bore, she always said, it was so noisy, the children made such a mess—

So, when a few days after the New Year Agatha suddenly enquired with an amiable smile whether they were going to have a Children's Party this year, Edwin looked up from his marmalade with surprise (they were at breakfast).

"I thought you were too upset, Agatha," said Edwin with solicitude. "I wasn't going to bother you about it this year."

"One mustn't be selfish," Agatha replied, smiling wanly. "One mustn't allow one's own feelings to interfere with the enjoyment of others."

"No," said Edwin, a little dazed by this altruism.

"I shouldn't like the children to be disappointed just because I happen to be miserable."

"No," said Edwin again.

"Of course the little Bulmers are away—banished from their home all because of that unspeakable book," continued Agatha in languid tones. "But we could have the Walker twins and the little Shearers, and Mrs. Carter's grand-child (she's rather old, of course, and a pert, unmannerly sort of girl, but we shall have to ask her), and Lady Barnton and her nieces, and the Turners, and the Semples from Bulverham—"

Mr. Featherstone Hogg was pleased, he did not analyze Agatha's motives. It was enough for him that they were to have the party, and have it, apparently, without the usual fuss. It was nice that they were going to have it after all, he always enjoyed it. Children were so jolly, he liked them, and they liked him. Children did not look through him, nor snub him because he was small and insignificant as so many grown up people did. He was rather a "dog" with children and he enjoyed being a "dog". Last year he had dressed up as Santa Claus and had been a tremendous success, in fact the success of the evening. It was too late to be Santa Claus this year, of course, but he would think of something else to amuse them, something entirely new. Mr. Featherstone Hogg finished his breakfast hastily and went off to find the "list" which he kept securely from year to year amongst his papers in his meticulously neat desk.

They fixed the date there and then and the invitations were issued immediately. Agatha pointed out that schools usually started towards the end of the month, and Lady Barnton's nieces—at least the two elder ones—would be going away soon.

Sarah Walker was not altogether surprised when she found that her name was omitted from the twins' invitation to the Children's Party at The Riggs. She could scarcely expect to be invited after her somewhat discourteous exit from the Drawing-room Meeting. The invitation card bore the information that Mrs. Featherstone Hogg was having a Children's Party on the tenth of January and would be delighted to see Master and Miss Walker and Nurse. Well, anyhow Nannie would enjoy it—thought Sarah—even if the twins didn't. The twins were still rather young to enjoy parties and they had so few that they were apt to become over-excited and obstreperous. But Nannie would manage them (she managed them better than Sarah), and she would enjoy taking them and showing them off to the other Nannies. It was rather dull for Nannies in Silverstream, there were so few children. Now that the Bulmers had gone the little Shearers were the only other children in the place. Sarah had been glad when the Shearers came and she found they had small children and a Nannie that *her* Nannie approved of. Fortunately Nannie had friends in Silverstream, she liked the Goldsmith girls, and Dorcas, and she was not above an occasional chat with Milly Spikes; but Nannies are a class apart and these people— though well enough in their way—were not really congenial to her. At the Featherstone Hoggs' Party Nannie would meet several other Nannies, she would be in her element. It was therefore almost entirely for the sake of their guardian that Master and Miss Walker accepted the kind invitation of Mrs. Featherstone Hogg.

Dr. Walker had an urgent call to Bulverham on the afternoon of the Party so he could not convey his offspring to The Riggs as had been arranged. Sarah was obliged to order a taxi for them; it was rather extravagant, of course, but fortunately parties did not happen very often in Silverstream.

The twins were ready some minutes before the taxi arrived, and came into the drawing-room to wait.

"How sweet they look, Nannie!" Sarah cried, hugging them both at the same time.

Nannie agreed that they did. They were dressed in blue silk tunics embroidered with white daisies round the collars and cuffs. Their fair hair was bobbed neatly round their little white necks. They had white silk socks

and white buckskin shoes with small silver buckles.
Nannie was intensely proud of them, it was so unusual
to see twins—a boy and a girl—exactly alike. Nannie
enjoyed the distinction of having such charges, she was
openly amused and secretly flattered when people—and
other Nannies especially—could not tell them apart.
"They're not a bit alike really," Nannie would say, laughing a little at the joke. "I could tell which was which
in the dark."

"There's the taxi," said Sarah suddenly. "You had
better not keep him waiting, Nannie. Tell him to come
back for you at six, that will be late enough for them."

Nannie promised to remember to tell him, she envel-
oped the twins in their white fur coats, and shepherded
them into the taxi.

The party was just sitting down to tea when they
arrived. Nannie counted about fifteen children, there
were more grown-ups, of course. Mrs. Featherstone Hogg
welcomed the Walkers affably and found two seats so
that the twins could sit together—they were never happy
apart.

"What a dear little couple they are!" said Mrs. Featherstone Hogg.

Nannie smiled with a satisfied air, she had made a
rapid survey of the table, and discovered that there
wasn't a child in the room who could compare with her
two, not one. She stood behind their chairs and buttered
their buns for them and saw that they didn't eat anything
unsuitable. Lady Barnton's youngest niece had a fat Nannie and *she* stood behind her child's chair. Nannie looked
at the fat Nannie and decided that she was the right sort,

she made a tentative remark and the two were soon chatting together happily. The Shearer's Nannie was at the other side of the table looking after the Shearer baby who was only eighteen months—just old enough to want all he saw in the way of cakes and too young to be allowed to have them. Nannie Shearer's hands were amply full, trying to keep him quiet and feeding him with sponge cake.

"I never seen twins as alike as yours, are they girls or boys?" said the fat Nannie admiringly.

"One of each."

"Well, I never. I'm sure nobody could tell the difference if they were paid for it. I had twins once but they were both girls, and they weren't so like each other either."

Mrs. Greensleeves now appeared at Nannie's elbow, she had come to "help with the children." She spoke to Nannie in a friendly way and admired the twins.

"Did you make their little tunics?" she asked.

"Mrs. Walker made them," replied Nannie. "Mrs. Walker makes nearly all their clothes, she's a beautiful knitter too."

"I wonder how she finds the time," said Mrs. Greensleeves inquisitively.

Nannie didn't answer, she thought it was a silly remark to make. What else had Mrs. Walker to do but to make nice clothes for the twins? She had three maids and a nurse so there was no need for her to do a hand's turn in the house. Still, apart from her silly remark Mrs. Greensleeves seemed nice and she had a tall gentleman with her that Nannie rather liked the look of, and a tall lady. Nannie decided that they were a brother and sister, for they had the same kind of nose, slightly hooky.

Mrs. Greensleeves sat down beside the twins and talked to them. They were quite friendly with her, and Jack offered her a bite of his chocolate biscuit.

"Just pretend to bite it," Nannie advised her.

Mrs. Greensleeves pretended.

"Here," said the tall gentleman. "Is that a girl or a boy making up to you, Vivian? I don't mind so much if it's a girl—"

"I've no idea which it is," replied Mrs. Greensleeves, laughingly.

The children's tea was nearly over now, and the other Nannies were going downstairs to the housekeeper's room to have theirs. Mrs. Greensleeves suggested to Nannie that she should go with them.

"I'll look after the twins," she promised.

There seemed no reason why Nannie should not go. The twins were quite happy with Mrs. Greensleeves, they were moving into the drawing-room now, for some games, so there was no chance of the twins over-eating themselves upon unsuitable food while she was gone.

"You're sure it will be all right, Madame?" Nannie asked. "You won't let them get too wild, will you? If they're not happy you could ring and send for me, couldn't you?"

"We'll look after them," said the tall gentleman, "off you go and have your tea, Nannie."

Nannie went as far as the door and waited, they were quite happy, they had not even noted her departure. Somebody had started to play the piano and dozens of coloured balloons had been let loose on the floor. The children were all laughing and scrambling after them. She went downstairs to the housekeeper's room and joined the other Nannies. It was a cheerful and pleasant party.

Nannie was away about half an hour. When she came back up the stairs she heard the sound of musical chairs in the drawing-room—a few bars of music and then silence, and then loud shrieks, and then another few bars of music. Musical chairs was rather beyond the twins. Nannie hoped they hadn't been allowed to play, it was a rough game for tiny children—she hastened her steps. The door of the drawing-room was open, she stood in the doorway and looked all round the room for the two little blue figures.—She saw the Shearer children, and the Semples and the Turners, but where were Jack and Jill? In about a minute Nannie was certain that they were not in the room, Mrs. Greensleeves and the tall gentleman had also vanished. She wondered what on earth had happened—there was the possibility that they had fallen down and hurt themselves and had been taken upstairs to have a knee bandaged or something, but it didn't seem likely. Surely Mrs. Greensleeves would have rung the bell for her if anything had gone wrong. She began to feel a little nervous and frightened, perhaps it was silly of her to have left them, they were so small, but what could have happened to them here?

Presently she edged round the room and touched Mrs. Featherstone Hogg on the arm.

"Please, Madame, where are the twins? It's about time

I was getting on their things to go home. Mrs. Walker does not want them to be late."

Mrs. Featherstone Hogg seemed excited, her face was very flushed and her eyes were glittering strangely—almost as if she had been drinking, Nannie thought—

"Oh, they'll be all right," she said.

"But where are they?" demanded Nannie.

"Mrs. Greensleeves is looking after them. I think she and Mr. Stratton took them out for a run in Mr. Stratton's car."

"A run in his car," echoed the twins' guardian in dismay.

"They were too small to join in the games."

"But I should have gone too—Mrs. Walker wouldn't like it. Mrs. Walker will be annoyed about it—"

"They will be quite safe in Mr. Stratton's car. He and his sister are staying with Mrs. Greensleeves for the week-end."

"Oh, why did I leave them?" cried Nannie. "And it's so frightfully cold and damp. When will they be back?"

"Mr. Stratton will probably take them straight home," said Mrs. Featherstone Hogg. "You had better go home too, and then you will be there when they arrive."

Nannie was aghast, how could she possibly go home without the twins? She couldn't possibly. Mrs. Walker would be furious, and with good cause. She began to explain all this to Mrs. Featherstone Hogg. Meanwhile the musical chairs was continuing with its maddening pauses, the noise was increasing. Nannie had to shout louder and louder to make herself heard above the din.

"I can't help all that," said Mrs. Featherstone Hogg,

interrupting Nannie's explanations and lamentations
crossly. "If they're so precious you shouldn't have left
them."

She left Nannie there gaping, and swept across the
room to speak to Lady Barnton.

The whole thing was utterly beyond Nannie's compre-
hension; such a thing had never happened to her before
in all her years of Nannie-hood. She turned it over in
her mind and decided to telephone to her mistress for
orders. Mrs. Walker would probably be angry about it
but that couldn't be helped, it was too serious to be hidden or glossed over. She made her way out of the hot
noisy drawing-room and hunted about the house until
she found a telephone. It was in Mr. Featherstone Hogg's
study, but Mr. Featherstone Hogg was playing with the
children so he was not there. Nannie was so panic-
stricken by now that she would not have cared for half
a dozen Mr. Featherstone Hoggs, she rushed to the telephone and gave the doctor's number in a trembling voice
—"If only the doctor is back," she prayed. "Oh God,
please let the doctor answer it."

Unfortunately the doctor was not back. Mrs. Walker
answered the 'phone, and Nannie was obliged to explain
the whole thing to her mistress. She explained exactly
what had occurred as clearly as her state of mind would
allow her—"I shouldn't have left them," she wailed down
the telephone. "But really they seemed all right, and I
never thought of anything like this. Never."

"It's not your fault at all, Nannie," said Mrs. Walker
in a peculiar voice. "I was an absolute fool to let them go,

I should have thought of it—oh Nannie, nobody would *harm* them, would they?"

"Harm them!" cried Nannie.

"Never mind," said Mrs. Walker. "I'll come straight up and see Mrs. Featherstone Hogg at once. You had better wait there till I come. Try to find out where they've gone."

"How?" enquired Nannie. "Who shall I ask?"

"I'll come at once," Mrs. Walker said. "Wait for me in the hall," she rung off.

Sarah was shaking all over with fright—but she tried to pull herself together. No good to collapse now, she must get her babies back first. If only John had been here, he was so strong and dependable; but there was no knowing when John would be back, she must tackle the matter herself. She kept on assuring herself that they wouldn't dare to harm the twins, they were just doing it to frighten her, of course, that was all. If only I had somebody to go with me—thought poor Sarah. Who could she get? Ellen King would have been the person, but Ellen King had gone, and Margaret had gone, and Dorothea was honeymooning at Monte Carlo. There was Barbara Buncle of course—Barbara was a nice kind creature and it was she who had warned Sarah that some deep scheme was being laid to her undoing. If only I had taken it more seriously—Sarah thought, as she lifted the receiver and gave Barbara's number—

Barbara was writing when Dorcas came to say that Mrs. Walker had rung up. She laid down her pen and went to speak to Sarah.

"They've done it, Barbara," said Sarah's voice in her ear.

"Done what?"

"They've stolen the twins. I thought I had better let you know. I'm going straight up to see Mrs. Featherstone Hogg."

"Good gracious!" said Barbara, trying to take in the situation, and make up her mind what was to be done.

"Unless they return the twins immediately I shall get the police," Sarah continued in a queer hard voice. "But I don't want to do that if I can get them back without. Nobody could do them any harm, could they, Barbara. It's just to frighten me, isn't it?"

"It's just bluff," Barbara assured her. "It's just bluff. We'll get them back at once. Don't worry, Sarah—or at least don't worry more than you can help. It will be quite all right when I've seen Mrs. Featherstone Hogg. Wait for me and we'll go up together and make her.—No, you *must* wait for me," she added, as Sarah began to say she couldn't wait a single moment. "It will be much better if you wait for me—I'll run all the way—I can't explain now but I can make everything all right."

She rushed upstairs and dragged on her clothes anyhow. Dorcas was waiting for her in the hall.

"Lor', Miss Barbara, you're never going out now?"

"Yes," said Barbara breathlessly. "I'm going up to The Riggs. If I'm not back in two hours you can ring up your friend Sergeant Capper and tell him to search for my dead body in the cellars—where's my umbrella, Dorcas? Where on earth's my umbrella?"

"In the stand, of course. But, oh, Miss Barbara, what

do you mean? For goodness' sake don't go and do nothing rash, now—"

"It's all right," Barbara told her, fumbling with the safety chain on her front door. "It's all right, Dorcas. I don't suppose they can do anything to me, really. I was just joking—just joking, Dorcas. Don't worry. I'll be back in an hour or an hour and a half—"

She fled down the path. Poor Sarah, it was frightful. It must all come out now, of course. She must tell Mrs. Featherstone Hogg that *she* was John Smith—not Sarah at all, and then they would give Sarah back her babies. She ought to have owned up before; but who would have thought the plan would have been such a fiendish plan as this? Of course it was all a gigantic piece of bluff, but still—

The road into the village had never seemed so long. Barbara ran, and walked, and ran again. She pictured Sarah's agony of mind, she wondered if it would have been better and quicker to ring up Mrs. Featherstone Hogg and explain matters over the telephone—perhaps it would have been better. On the other hand it might not have been so efficacious. Better to do the thing thoroughly, as it had to be done. Better to face it out in person—more difficult of course, but braver, to walk into the august presence and say, "I'm John Smith so please give Sarah back her babies at once—"

As she neared the doctor's house she expected to see Sarah waiting for her on the doorstep ready dressed to fly to the rescue of her twins. But there was no sign of Sarah, the house was perfectly quiet, the door was shut. Barbara rang the bell and waited impatiently. It seemed hours before Fuller answered the door. (Fuller was the doctor's parlour-maid, she had been with the Walkers for years. She knew Barbara well, of course.)

"Oh, Fuller!" said Barbara breathlessly. "Isn't Mrs. Walker ready?"

"Mrs. Walker's engaged," said Fuller. "She said I was to ask you to wait a few minutes in the drawing-room."

Barbara was amazed at the information that Sarah was engaged. What could be so important as to engage her at this critical moment with night coming on and the twins lost?

"Who is it, Fuller?" she enquired as they passed the door of the study.

"It's a strange lady," whispered Fuller. "Not a Silverstream lady. I never saw her before—Miss Stratton her name was."

"Fuller! D'you think it's all right?" asked Barbara anxiously. "I mean she couldn't *do* anything to Mrs. Walker, could she?"

"Lor'!" exclaimed Fuller, startled for once out of her propriety. "Lor', Miss Buncle! You don't reelly think anyone would 'arm the mistress, do you?"

They paused outside the study door and looked at each other with wide eyes. Miss Buncle's nerves had been completely upset by the kidnapping of the twins, and the distressing knowledge that it was her fault. It would be her fault too if the stranger did Sarah bodily harm. She visualised the stranger stabbing Sarah between the shoulder blades and escaping out of the study window; she visualised Sarah lying on the floor in a pool of blood, breathing her last. Miss Buncle frequently bemoaned the fact that she had no imagination, but one feels she must have had a little to visualise such a terrible scene in the placid atmosphere of the doctor's hall. The atmosphere was not so placid as usual to-night, of course, even Fuller seemed a little upset, and not quite her ordinary machine-like self. Barbara wondered if Fuller knew about the twins; she probably did.

"Couldn't you go in, and *see?*" suggested Barbara in trembling accents. "Do go in, Fuller. You could pretend you were going in to draw the curtains or something—"

"The curtains have been drawn *hours,*" said Fuller. "But perhaps I could go in and say you had come, Miss."

"Yes, oh yes, *do,* Fuller," entreated Barbara.

She remained outside the door while Fuller went in, and waited, trembling. She heard Fuller say, "Miss Buncle is here, Madame," and Sarah reply, "Please ask her to wait in the drawing-room, Fuller." A strange, rather high-pitched voice added, "We have nearly finished our business—may I use your telephone?" then Fuller came out again and the door was shut.

"It's quite all right, Miss," Fuller said in a relieved tone. "They're signing papers on the doctor's table." She led Barbara to the drawing-room, made up the fire and left her to her own devices.

Barbara was bewildered. It was so queer for Sarah to be transacting business with a strange woman instead of dashing up to The Riggs to rescue her twins. What could be the meaning of it? Sarah had sounded absolutely frantic when she had spoken to Barbara on the telephone. "I can't wait a moment," she had said, and here she was calmly signing papers on the doctor's table, and making no attempt to do anything about the twins. I suppose I must just wait—thought Barbara helplessly—it wouldn't be any use me going up to The Riggs without Sarah. Besides, she said I was to wait.

She walked about the room, restlessly; counting the patterns on the carpet, and, when that was done, looking at the photographs. More than half the photographs depicted the twins at various stages of their short career—the twins in long clothes, the twins in short clothes, the twins in practically no clothes at all, the twins standing on a staircase in jumper suits, the twins playing in the garden in overalls. In no case could Barbara determine which was which.

"Goodness!" said Barbara aloud. "Goodness, how I wish she would come! It's worse than waiting at the dentist."

She decided to shut her eyes and try to remember all the furniture in the room, perhaps that would pass the time and keep her from going mad. There's the piano, thought Barbara, and the cabinet with the Dresden figures, and the two armchairs near the fire, and the chesterfield of course. And there's a nest of tables near the door, and a lacquer screen—

"Are you ill, Barbara?" said Sarah's voice suddenly. She had come in quietly and found Barbara sitting there with her eyes shut and murmuring to herself—no wonder she thought Barbara was ill.

"Oh Sarah!" cried Barbara, opening her eyes and jumping up out of her chair. "Thank goodness you've come at last. I'm John Smith."

"So am I," smiled Sarah with remarkable calm.

"But I really am," cried Barbara, seizing her arm and shaking it fiercely. "I wrote the book, Sarah, do you hear? We've only got to go up to The Riggs and tell them that I'm John Smith, and not you at all, and they're bound to give us the twins immediately."

"It's sweet of you, Barbara," said Sarah affectionately. "It really is perfectly sweet of you to think of it, but they'd never believe you, for a moment, you're such a rotten liar, you know. But you're an absolute lamb to think of doing it. I'm not John Smith either, of course, but they've got it firmly fixed in their heads that I am and nothing will convince them otherwise. So the only thing—"

"But, Sarah, if I go and tell them that I am John Smith—I am, really and truly."

"It's all right. It's all settled," said Sarah. "They are sending the twins home at once."

"Thank goodness!" exclaimed Barbara, sinking back in her chair with a sigh of relief.

"Yes, they only wanted me to sign a paper saying that I apologised for all the things I had said about them, and that they were all quite untrue—"

"And you signed it?" gasped Barbara.

"Of course I signed it," said Sarah laughing. "D'you think it mattered to me what I signed so long as I could get Jack and Jill home safe and sound? I just signed my name wherever the woman told me to sign it, and she went away quite pleased. She's a friend of Vivian Green-sleeves and Vivian had evidently roped her in to the plan without giving her much idea of what it was. She was quite decent really—I don't think she liked her part very much."

"You signed a paper saying you were John Smith?" enquired Barbara again in bewildered tones.

"Yes, I told you, Barbara," replied her friend. "I signed everything she had with her. I signed a letter to the publisher as well. She telephoned to her brother from here and he said the twins were all right and he would bring them back in about twenty minutes."

"But Sarah, you signed a letter to the publisher?"

"Yes, Barbara, I did. Mr. Abbott will be surprised when he gets it, but I don't expect it will worry him much. I expect publishers often get letters from raving lunatics, don't you?"

"What did it say?"

"Oh, I don't know. I didn't read it very carefully. Just that I wanted my novel suppressed or something—*my* novel mark you!"

"It's really mine," Barbara told her. "I had better go and see Mrs. Featherstone Hogg and explain it all."

"My dear, it's not necessary. They're quite pleased now and the twins will soon be back. I'd really rather you didn't go and muddle it all up, if you don't mind. You see nobody would believe you and it would complicate matters."

"It would clear matters up."

"No, it wouldn't," Sarah said firmly. "It would complicate the whole thing, and I might not get the twins back or something.—I wish I hadn't been such a fool as to let them go to that party. I should have smelt a rat when they didn't invite me—"

"Who could have thought—"

"Nobody except Vivian Greensleeves, it's exactly the sort of plan she would think of.—I wonder if Mrs. Featherstone Hogg is giving her something for doing it. You will notice that Mrs. Featherstone Hogg is keeping well out of it all herself."

"You could have them up for kidnapping," suggested Barbara wildly.

"I don't think so," replied Sarah, wrinkling her brows. "They've been pretty wily about the whole thing, you know. Vivian and Mr. Stratton took them for a run in his car—it's a new car, the sister told me, and he's very proud of it—we couldn't prove that he had any intention of not bringing them home. As a matter of fact I expect he would have brought them back safely whether I signed the beastly papers or not—but I wasn't going to risk anything. I wonder what I had better do about telling John. Shall I tell him or not? He would be frightfully angry, of course. What would you do about it if you were me?"

Barbara had no idea what she would do if she were Sarah, she was completely bamboozled by the whole affair.

"Perhaps I had better tell John about it," continued Sarah thoughtfully. "He might hear a garbled version of it from somebody else."

"Yes," said Barbara dazedly. "Well, I think I'll just go home now, Sarah. Dorcas will be worried, and I can't do any good here—"

"You might wait until they come—until somebody comes," said Sarah quickly, "just in case of—of anything.

I'm upset, I'd hate to wait here all alone with nobody to talk to. Nannie will be back in a minute or two—I telephoned to her that everything was all right, the poor soul was completely flummoxed—"

"No wonder!" exclaimed Barbara.

The twins arrived first. The bell rang, and Fuller discovered the two little figures on the doorstep. They ran into the house, quite happy and full of excitement at their unusual adventures. They had no idea, of course, that their mother had aged about ten years in their absence.

"Me an' Jack had a lovely d'ive," cried Jill.

"I 'ike Bob," said Jack. "He gave me a chockit."

Sarah swept them into her arms and hugged them ecstatically, they were both a little surprised at the fervour of her embrace.

"You're squashing my nose, Mummie," said Jill reproachfully in a muffled voice.

"Well, I think I'll go home now," Barbara said. "You'll be all right now, won't you?"

"I haven't half thanked you," said Sarah, raising a flushed face and tear-filled eyes. "You're a real friend, Barbara dear. It was splendid of you to come so quickly and to think of that plan of yours. I'd have let you do it, if it would have got my babies back any quicker, but it was easier the other way. Perhaps some day we shall know who John Smith really is."

"It's me," said Barbara in a last despairing effort. "It really is me, Sarah. Really and truly."

"We wrote it together, didn't we?" Sarah said, smiling and nuzzling into her babies' necks like a mother-cow. "And Jack and Jill helped too—didn't you my precious loves? You filled Mummy's pen for her so that she could write funny stories about Mrs. Featherstone Hogg?"

"I got a paper yat out of a c'acker," cried Jack, escaping from his mother's arms and jumping up and down in front of her, "I got a paper yat out of a c'acker."

"I got a fistle," shouted Jill, "Mummie I got a lickle fistle—"

Barbara went away and left them—there was nothing more she could do. Sarah didn't need her any more, Sarah was perfectly happy.

CHAPTER XXIII

Miss Buncle's Day In Town

*B*ARBARA BUNCLE had been bidden to lunch at the Berkeley with her publisher. It was the most exciting thing that had ever happened to her, she was excited for days beforehand.

Even Sally—who was deeply immersed in important affairs of her own—was aware that Barbara was unusually animated and gay.

When the great day arrived, Barbara decided to go up to town early and combine the outing with a shopping orgy, she therefore arrived at the Berkeley with weird shaped brown paper parcels hanging painfully upon every finger—a solecism of which Elizabeth Wade would never have been guilty.

Mr. Abbott had been waiting for ten minutes, and he was surprised to see her with so many parcels, but she was so flatteringly pleased to see him that he forgave her all her sins immediately. He led the way to a table, which he had reserved, near the window, and sufficiently far from the band to make conversation possible, and helped the waiter to disentangle Barbara's fingers. Then they sat down and the lunch began.

Barbara enjoyed it all tremendously. She was Elizabeth most of the time, of course, for this was an Elizabethan sort of party—having a *tête-à-tête* lunch at an expensive restaurant with a distinguished looking man—but some-times she was Barbara for a few minutes, and then she felt a little shy, and awkward, and humble.

Mr. Abbott was very attentive. He had become increas-ingly attracted by Miss Buncle and to-day she was at her best. Her appearance was a credit to him, her conversa-tion intrigued him. You never knew what Miss Buncle was going to say next. At one moment she seemed a sophisticated woman of the world, and the next she seemed as innocent and confiding as a child. Mr. Abbott could not know that he was really entertaining two ladies to lunch at the Berkeley, that two ladies were laughing at his jokes and his light badinage—so appropriate to the occasion.

The conviction had been growing in Mr. Abbott's mind that Miss Buncle was the woman he had been wait-ing for all his life. She was attractive to look at, she was good-tempered and full of fun and she was obviously extremely healthy. He found her amusing and provoca-tive. She was clever enough, but not too clever (Mr. Abbott did not like a woman to be better off in the way of brains than he was himself, Miss Buncle wasn't). Last, but not least, there was something very fresh and inno-cent about her which appealed to Mr. Abbott immensely.

It sounds very matter of fact put like this, but Mr. Abbott was a matter of fact business man. It was his nature to weigh the pros and cons before he decided upon anything important. He was tremendously attracted by Miss Buncle but he was not exactly swept off his feet by her charms—perhaps he was rather old to fall in love in a headlong fashion, perhaps he was rather old to be swept off his feet—

Mr. Abbott decided that he would wait until he had the manuscript of the new novel in his hand before offering the author his heart. Whether or not Miss Buncle accepted him—and he had no idea what her feelings were—the proposal was bound to unsettle her mind, to knock her off her balance, so to speak. Once the new novel was completed he did not mind whether there was another John Smith or not. If she wanted to write she should write, and if she did not want to write she need never write another word—he would be her dividends. But he did want just one more John Smith, and he wanted it soon, for the amazing sales of *Disturber of the Peace* were waning now and it was the right moment to publish another novel from the pen of John Smith— "There is a tide in the affairs of men, which, ta'en at the flood, leads on to fortune." Mr. Abbott felt that it would be a thousand pities to lose the tide.

"And what is the new novel to be called?" enquired Mr. Abbott with interest.

"Well, I thought of calling it *The Pen is Mightier*——" Barbara said confidentially, "but I don't mind if you can think of something better—at least not very much," added Barbara, not altogether truthfully, for she would mind a good deal if the new novel had to be called something else. She was rather pleased with the name, it expressed her deepest convictions—had she not seen in the last few months what a mighty weapon the pen could be?

"I like the name," replied Mr. Abbott. "Of course I

haven't read the novel yet, but I like the name. How soon can you let me have it?"

"It's nearly finished."

"Good," said Mr. Abbott smiling.

"But I don't know how to finish it. I've come to a stop," said Barbara, tasting her Pêche Melba and deciding that it must have come straight from Paradise.

"Bad," said Mr. Abbott, frowning.

"I've thought and thought," said Barbara with a sigh. "Sometimes the whole thing seems the most awful rubbish, and I feel like throwing it in the fire."

"No, no!" exclaimed Mr. Abbott anxiously. "No, no—that would never do. Don't do that on my account. It's just that you are stale."

"I suppose I am," said Barbara sadly.

"All authors get stale," said Mr. Abbott with a comforting smile, "even the very best of best sellers. I tell you what. Send it to me, if you like, and I'll read it over. I might be able to make a suggestion which would help you."

"Would you really?" said Barbara, brightening up at once. "Would you read it and see what you think? Wouldn't it be a fearful bother for you, Mr. Abbott?"

"It would be a pleasure," he replied gallantly.

After lunch Mr. Abbott took his guest to see a film which was said to be "The Most Stupendous and Utterly Amazing Production of our Time." Mr. Abbott was stupendously bored at the amazing production, and he was glad to note that Miss Buncle was also bored. He was glad, not because he liked to bore his guests with stupendous productions, but because it showed more unmistakably than anything that had gone before that Miss Buncle was the right woman. If *His Wonderful Pal* bored Barbara Buncle, she would do. Most of the women round them and a good many of the men were following the hair-raising adventures of *His Wonderful Pal* with tense interest. In a way Mr. Abbott admitted that it *was* amazing.

It was amazing that anybody could have contemplated the filming of such a thing and of course the sum spent upon the production was stupendous—he didn't need the programme to tell him that—but the story was so puerile that it would not have contented an average child of ten years old. It was simply an excuse for scenery and love scenes.—*He* cheated at cards—at least *they* said he had, and everybody thought he had except "His Wonderful Pal." *She* believed in him, of course, but *He* told her he couldn't possibly marry her until he had vindicated Himself. To vindicate himself he had to visit the court of the Great Mogul (nobody knew why he had to do this, and most of the audience was too drugged by the really amazing scenery to have any critical faculty left).

"His Wonderful Pal" followed him at a discreet distance to watch over his safety, and passed through incredible adventures in the jungle, carrying them off with a sang-froid beside which the sang-froid of Elizabeth Wade paled into insignificance. "His Wonderful Pal" arrived at the court of the Great Mogul just in time to save her lover from the machinations of a man in whose truth and loyalty *he* had never doubted—it was *her* woman's instinct that warned her he was No Good. Most people with two eyes in their head would have seen from the very beginning that the man was No Good (what could you expect of a man with a wall-eye and a black gap in his front teeth?), but the lover trusted him implicitly in spite of these indications of a black heart and was very nearly in the soup.

The arrival of "His Wonderful Pal" at the court of the Great Mogul was accompanied by earthquakes, and tropical thunder and lightning, and the Great Mogul's Palace fell down, column by column, and crushed everybody to death—except, of course, the lovers. These fortunate survivors were quite oblivious of the fate of the Great Mogul and his myrmidons, nor did they make any attempt to succor the wall-eyed traitor who was pinned by the leg under a fallen column and was expiring in agonies. They left him to his well-deserved fate and escaped together through alligator infested swamps, and tiger infested jungles, and carried on intermittent, but harrowing love scenes—on one occasion whilst being pursued by a rogue elephant.

Her sang-froid had disappeared by now, but not her permanent wave, and she wept huge oily tears and declared that if *he* didn't marry her she would throw herself over a cliff—which had most conveniently appeared in the middle of the jungle—and thus end her useless and miserable existence. . . .

"Do people really behave like that?" Barbara whispered to Mr. Abbott.

"God forbid!" replied that gentleman fervently. "Shall we go?"

Barbara nodded, she had forgotten that a nod cannot

be seen by one's companion in the gloom of a picture house.

"Would you like to go out?" Mr. Abbott repeated after a minute or two. During this time "His Wonderful Pal" had almost thrown herself over the cliff but not quite, of course. *He* had just managed to catch her in time and the two were now locked in a frantic embrace. . . . A woman sitting just in front of Mr. Abbott was sobbing openly into her handkerchief. . . .

"Yes, let's go," whispered Barbara.

They went as quickly and silently as they could, stumbling over people's umbrellas and treading on innumerable toes. Everybody was furious with them for blocking out the scene at the most critical, or at any rate one of the most critical moments in the drama.

"Whew!" said Mr. Abbott, as they emerged into the cool bright air of day. "Whew, what an experience. I feel quite battered. What about a cup of tea?"

Barbara thought it would be nice, and they found a small tea-shop, requisitioned a small table, and gave their order.

"I could never think of anything like that," Barbara said, as she drew off her gloves and put them on an empty chair—she was referring, of course, to the incredible adventures they had just witnessed.

"Thank God for that!" exclaimed Mr. Abbott reverently.

"I have no imagination, you see," Barbara continued sadly, "I can only write about real things—things that really happen, I mean. How do people think of things like that? They must have quite different brains from ordinary people."

"Yes," said Mr. Abbott vaguely. He was watching Miss Buncle demolishing crumpets and his admiration at the feat was intense—what a digestion she must have! His lunch was still lingering in the region of the second button of his waistcoat, yet he was sure he had eaten no more than she had—

"I've no idea how people think of things like that," continued Mr. Abbott, when his surprise had somewhat abated. "I wish they didn't, don't you? Perhaps they dream after a visit to the Zoo and a heavy supper of toasted cheese."

Barbara laughed, and then sighed. "It would be rather nice to be able to write things like that. People seem to enjoy them—I suppose if they cry it does mean they're enjoying themselves?—and there would be no chance of people recognising themselves and being cross about it. I don't know what I shall find to write about when I have finished *The Pen Is Mightier*——"

"Copperfield played out?" enquired Mr. Abbott sympathetically.

"Just about it, I'm afraid."

"Don't worry, something will turn up. Take a little holiday after *The Pen Is Mightier*—— You really deserve a little holiday, you know."

CHAPTER XXIV

"The Pen Is Mightier——"

*T*HE *Pen Is Mightier——* was waiting for Mr.
Abbott when he got home from the office next
day. He tore it open eagerly, he was quite excited
about it. Miss Buncle was an enigma to Mr. Abbott, both
as a woman and as an author. Sometimes he felt he understood her quite well, and sometimes he felt that he
did not understand her at all. He hadn't the remotest idea
what her new book would be like—it might be the most
appalling rubbish, or it might be a best seller. Mr. Abbott
was rather afraid that *Disturber of the Peace* was a sort
of fluke and that Miss Buncle might never write another
word worth reading, but he might be quite wrong of
course, he hoped he was quite wrong. He settled down
comfortably to read.

The Pen Is Mightier—— was still "all about Copperfield," just as Miss Buncle had said. Mr. Abbott recognised the same characters in it as had appeared in *Disturber of the Peace,* but there were new characters too:—
Mr. Shakeshaft, the Vicar, Miss Claire Farmer, a grand-
daughter of old Mrs. Farmer (who had worn a wig and
put pectin in her famous damson jam) and Mrs. Rider,
the doctor's wife.

Mr. Shakeshaft was depicted as a serious, devout young
priest, deeply in the toils of Mrs. Myrtle Coates, who sup-

posed him to have a great deal of money. Mrs. Myrtle Coates had appeared in the pages of *Disturber of the Peace* (Mr. Abbott remembered the character distinctly), she was, in modern parlance, a "gold digger," and had been mixed up with an unpleasantly second-rate young man. This new embroglio with the Vicar of Copperfield was no credit to Mrs. Myrtle Coates, she led him on in a shameless manner, and then threw him over at the last minute, because he had lost all his money in a bank smash. So much for the Vicar and Mrs. Myrtle Coates.

The main theme of the book was concerned with the fortunes and misfortunes of Elizabeth Wade—Miss Buncle's other self. Miss Wade wrote a book, and the story of Miss Wade's career as a novelist was the story of Miss Buncle's own extraordinary experiences. Miss Wade wrote a book and placed it with Messrs. Nun and Nutmeg (the name made Mr. Abbott roar with laughing). This spicy firm published Miss Wade's book and it immediately became a best seller. The book was "all about" Copperfield, and Copperfield was annoyed or pleased according to how it found itself in Miss Wade's book. Miss Wade's book, which was entitled, *Storms in a Teacup,* by J. Farrier, was discussed and criticised very harshly by the Copperfieldians—at least by those of them who had no discernment, the others saw genius, which, of course, was clearly proved by the absolutely unprecedented sales. The theme was unusual, and intriguing. Mr. Abbott had never before read a novel about a woman who wrote a novel about a woman who wrote a novel— it was like a recurring decimal, he thought, or perhaps even more like a perspective of mirrors such as tailors use, in which the woman and her novel were reflected back and forth to infinity. It made your brain reel if you pursued the thought too far, but there was no need to do so, unless you wanted to, of course. So much for the main theme.

The character of Mrs. Rider, the doctor's wife, was clearly and sympathetically drawn. Mr. Abbott liked her immensely. She was really a charming creation. Mrs. Rider was suspected of being the author of *Storms in a Teacup,* and had rather a thin time of it in consequence. She was the victim of an absurd and altogether incredible conspiracy, hatched by the Myrtle Coates and Horsley Downs lot, to prove her authorship of the book. Mr. Abbott was rather doubtful about this incident, he wondered whether Miss Buncle would mind if he suggested its deletion. The kidnapping of the Rider baby was rather too improbable and unconvincing, even for a novel like *The Pen Is Mightier——,* which most people would take for farce. He decided to think it over carefully, and speak to Miss Buncle about the kidnapping business.

The Pen Is Mightier—— was a complicated sort of book, it had so many threads. There was the Myrtle Coates thread, and there was the conspiracy against Mrs. Rider, and there was the main theme all about Elizabeth Wade and her book, and besides these there were several smaller threads all intertwined one with the other in a decidedly ingenious manner. Mr. Abbott disentangled them in his own mind—Mr. Horsley Downs had cast off his fetters and was having a much better time of it than he had in *Disturber of the Peace.* He amused himself very pleasantly and innocently by taking actresses to lunch at the Berkeley. (This must have been added last night for it bore the authentic stamp, and the ink was still blue.) The Gaymers, the Waterfoots, and Miss Earle took subsidiary places in *The Pen Is Mightier——*. They had been dealt with faithfully in Miss Buncle's previous book. The Gaymers' divorce was touched on lightly; the Waterfoots sent post-cards from Rome to say that they were exploring the Forum and found it intensely interesting; and Miss Earle and Miss Darling were "seen off" to Samarkand accompanied by the good wishes of their friends.

All these stories merged into each other, but they were really distinct stories and Mr. Abbott surmised that they were true—or very nearly true. He could vouch for the complete and almost terrifying veracity of the Elizabeth Wade story, and his own portrait, labelled Mr. Nun, amused him immensely—Barbara was always kind to people she liked—

The book was very like *Disturber of the Peace,* but it was handled more firmly, it was better, funnier, more even in texture. Miss Buncle's writing had come on a lot, and yet it had not lost the extraordinary simplicity which some people had taken for satire. Mr. Abbott was delighted with *The Pen Is Mightier——*

Towards the end Miss Buncle had gathered in her threads with a cunning hand, and they were all gathered in and finished off neatly except the main thread of all. Elizabeth Wade was left—as it were—hanging in the air. It was this that stumped Miss Buncle—how was she to finish off Elizabeth Wade, seeing that Barbara Buncle was by no means finished off?

Mr. Abbott saw the difficulty. The book required something to round off the main theme and complete it, something definite. It was the more difficult, of course, because *The Pen Is Mightier*—— was all true, there was no fantastic element in this book like the Golden Boy in the latter half of *Disturber of the Peace*. It was all true, therefore the *dénouement* must be true also, otherwise the result would be inartistic.

Mr. Abbott sat and thought about it for a long time, and then he smiled. He saw the end of the book quite clearly, and it was an end that satisfied him—he hoped sincerely that it would satisfy Miss Buncle. He found a sheet of foolscap and outlined his idea for the completion of *The Pen Is Mightier*——, it did not take him long for it was only an outline, of course, and he made it as bare as possible because he did not want it to appear as if there had been a strange hand at work in the completion of Miss Bunce's book. The letter which he enclosed with the manuscript and the notes, took him much longer to write, and he re-wrote it several times before he was satisfied with its wording. Then he packed up the whole thing and sent it back to Miss Buncle per registered post.

Mr. Abbott reflected, as he procured his receipt at the Post Office, that this was—perhaps—a unique way of proposing to a lady. He hoped Miss Buncle would take it in the right spirit and appreciate its fine points; he hoped that she would do it justice in her book. It was all to go into the book, of course, that was the whole idea:— Elizabeth Wade's confession to her publisher of having got stuck with her new novel: Mr. Nun's offer to read it, and his suggestion for the end, coupled with a proposal of marriage to the fair author. *The Pen Is Mightier——* would end with the wedding of Mr. Nun and Miss Elizabeth Wade—no better ending could be possible. It finished off Elizabeth in great style and it was just the sort of finishing off that *The Pen Is Mightier——* required.

　　　•　　　•　　　•　　　•　　　•

Barbara Buncle was delighted with Mr. Abbott's sug- gestion for ending her novel, she saw at once that it was exactly what she needed. Wedding bells would make an artistic *finale*—how clever Mr. Abbott was to have thought of it!

It was not until she had digested the foolscap sheet, and laid some tentative plans for Elizabeth's wedding, that she turned to Mr. Abbott's letter, and discovered that he had sent her a proposal of marriage. The letter was not long, it merely said that he hoped Mr. Nun's suggestion would meet with Elizabeth's approval. He realised, he said, that everything in the book was true, and he hoped that the end would be no exception to the rule. Could she—he enquired, and the words were underlined lest she should fail to perceive their significance—could she pos- sibly see her way to making his suggestion for the ending of her book come true? The letter concluded with the information that he would come over on Friday after- noon for her answer.

Barbara was amazed, she read the letter several times before she could convince herself that it really meant what she took it to mean. She was absolutely staggered at the idea of anybody wanting to marry her. Mr. Nun had fallen in love with Elizabeth Wade, of course,—what more natural considering the charms of that fortunate woman?—but for Mr. Abbott to confess to a like passion for Barbara Buncle was the most incredible thing on earth. She had long ago decided that Mr. Abbott was quite the nicest man she had ever met, he was reliable, and kind and loyal, she had trusted him and leant on him when everybody had been so unkind about *Disturber of the Peace,* and he had not failed her. She had never before had a proposal of marriage in any form, but she realised—in spite of her inexperience in such matters—that Mr. Abbott's proposal was unique. It was delicate, it was flattering, it was clever. Of course, Mr. Abbott was a very clever man, she had realised that at their first interview when he had been a complete stranger to her. He was now her friend and she valued his friendship tremendously—but could she marry him? It was such a surprise that he should want her to marry him, she had never thought of such a thing for a moment. This is so sudden—Barbara thought—and smiled at the aptness of the hackneyed phrase.

I can't marry him, I can't possibly—Barbara thought. And yet she wouldn't like to lose him, to lose his friendship and his support. If she refused to marry him would he continue to be her friend? It would never be the same, of course, there would always be that feeling of embarrassment between them. The mere idea of losing Mr. Abbott's friendship filled her with dismay. She began to wonder if she could possibly marry him, she began to think she might.

Dorcas brought in the supper and found her reading and re-reading Mr. Abbott's letter.

"What do you think of marriage, Dorcas?" enquired Barbara, in a conversational tone.

"It's that Mr. Abbott!" Dorcas exclaimed, dropping the toast-rack in her excitement. "I knew it, Miss Barbara. I just knew it. It was in my cup—a wedding in the house and a biggish man looking towards it. That's Mr. Abbott I said—I really did. Oh, Miss Barbara, I'm so glad!"

"But Dorcas, I haven't made up my mind—" cried poor Barbara in dismay.

"No, Miss Barbara, of course you haven't. But it *will* be lovely—Fancy seeing you a bride, all in white with orange blossoms in your hair! Oh, and he's such a nice gentleman too. So free and easy. I will say this for Mr. Abbott, he knows what's what, he does. Oh, Miss Barbara, how happy I am."

"But I haven't decided anything—I probably won't marry him at all, Dorcas. I've got to think it all over—nothing is settled yet—"

"No, Miss Barbara, of course not. It would never do to jump at him, it wouldn't be proper at all. But I can't help thinking about the wedding. I *do* like weddings, don't you, Miss Barbara? We can turn out this room for the reception, and have a buffet across the corner. I shall get one of Miss Goldsmith's girls to help: she wouldn't mind giving me a hand, an' it would be ever so much nicer than having a stranger, don't you think so, Miss Barbara? And the twins is just right for pages—the doctor's twins—all dressed up in white satin and carrying your train—"

It was hopeless to argue with Dorcas, Barbara gave it up in despair.

"Well, anyhow, you're not to say a word to anybody,"

she said firmly. "I haven't decided anything, and I won't be rushed like this. It's a dead secret, Dorcas. Every bit as dead as *Disturber of the Peace.*"

"I won't say nothing," Dorcas promised. "Mum's the word, Miss Barbara. But you won't mind me thinking about it, will you? I couldn't promise not to think about it, not for ten pounds, I couldn't."

"Well, don't talk about it anyhow," Barbara said.

Dorcas sighed, there was lots more she could have said about the wedding, but she supposed it was no use trying to say it. She had thought of several most important points to discuss with Miss Barbara, but if Miss Barbara would not discuss them she must just hold her tongue. She took up her tray with manifest reluctance and turned to leave the room.

"Oh, and Dorcas," said Barbara. "I shall be writing late, to-night, so don't forget my coffee."

"You'd much better go to bed, Miss Barbara," said Dorcas sensibly, "there'll be no more need for you to write now that you've got a husband to keep you."

. . . . .

In spite of the fact that she had got—or was possibly going to get—a husband, Barbara wrote all night. The end came out beautifully. There was a touching scene in the garden when Elizabeth accepted Mr. Nun's heart and hand. It was summertime, and Mr. Nun came for his answer dressed in tennis flannels, with a light blue blazer enhancing his manly charms. Elizabeth was sitting in the arbour, and Mr. Nun was so impatient to get to her, that he vaulted lightly over the hedge and came to her across the grass. Elizabeth was coy, she placed her finished manuscript in his hands and said: "Reginald, dearest, there is my answer," and left him in the arbour to digest it at leisure. Reginald read the end at top speed and found that it gave him his heart's desire—he rushed into the house to claim his bride.

All Copperfield was bidden to the wedding and all Copperfield came with alacrity—even Miss Earle and Miss Darling were summoned from Samarkand to attend.—Elizabeth was loved and admired and respected in Copperfield. Nobody had the slightest idea that she was J. Farrier, that much discussed author of *Storms in a Teacup,* and there was no reason why anybody should ever know now. The wedding had done away with the need for the dramatic exposure which Barbara had been toying with reluctantly. The wedding was a far nicer ending than the dramatic exposure of J. Farrier. Thus it was that all Copperfield came gladly to Elizabeth's wedding, bearing gifts, and the villagers erected a triumphal arch. The wedding was solemnized in the little church of St. Agatha's by the sad-faced Mr. Shakeshaft, who could not help comparing the good fortune of Mr. Nun with his own blasted hopes. It was a brilliant wedding, the sun shone upon the bride, and the birds burst into song as she appeared at the church door after the ceremony, a radiant vision in spotless white.

All Copperfield now repaired to the bride's charming house for the Wedding Breakfast, and each and all of the assembled guests proffered congratulations and good wishes in characteristic phrases. It was a little like the last scene in a Christmas Pantomime where all the characters appear to make their bow.

Barbara finished *The Pen Is Mightier*—— just as the clatter of the milk-cans sounded in the road. She laid down her pen and went to the window. Dawn ought to have been breaking over the hills, but it was doing no such thing, and would not be doing any such thing for another two hours at least. The milk-cart was the only thing to be seen through the leafless trees. It was drawn up beneath the lamp-post so that the milkman could see which can was the right one for Tanglewood Cottage— a poor substitute for the breaking of dawn which Barbara felt was her right.

She yawned and stretched herself for she was very stiff and cramped. The joy of achievement—and what an achievement—buoyed her up, so that she did not feel tired at all, but she was very hungry. Dorcas would be coming down soon, thought Barbara, she would get Dorcas to boil an egg for her—perhaps two eggs—and then she would go to bed and sleep till tea-time, for she must be fresh and rested when Mr. Abbott arrived.

Writing all that about Elizabeth's wedding (her own wedding, really, for was she not Elizabeth?) had made the idea of marrying Mr. Abbott seem quite familiar. It was not surprising and alarming any more. She had been rather foolish to be so perturbed at the idea. There was nothing to be surprised and alarmed at in a wedding, people got married every day, and they continued to be much the same as before. Marriage did not alter people much, as far as Barbara could see.

Elizabeth had gone forward bravely to meet her fate, the sun had shone upon her and the birds had sung with joy, she was actually married now—Elizabeth was actually married.—She wasn't Elizabeth Wade any more, she was Mrs. Reginald Nun, and soon,—or perhaps not exactly *soon*, but someday—Barbara would be Mrs. Arthur Abbott.

CHAPTER XXV

Miss Buncle and Mr. Abbott

*B*ARBARA carried out the first part of her plan with the greatest ease. She ate her lightly boiled eggs and endured, with meekness, the scoldings of Dorcas. Then she went to bed and fell immediately into a deep and dreamless sleep. She awoke at two o'clock and found the sun shining. It was ridiculous to remain in bed any longer. She was refreshed by her sleep, thoroughly refreshed, but she found that she was somewhat restless and apprehensive. She must get up and move about. She must go out or something—anyhow it was quite impossible to remain in bed. The meeting with Mr. Abbott which had seemed a mere detail when she was divided from it by the gulf of sleep had suddenly assumed a terrifying guise. He would be here in two hours—in less than two hours—and he would want an answer to his proposal. Would Mr. Abbott propose again by word of mouth? Perhaps he would propose in the dashing manner of Major Waterfoot—how dreadful that would be! What on earth would she do if he fell on his knees before her, and declared in trembling accents that he could not live without her another moment. (Barbara could not quite *see* Mr. Abbott doing it, but you never knew.) Elizabeth might have managed such a scene with success, she would have known exactly what to do, of course, but Elizabeth was married now—Elizabeth could not help her. Elizabeth had managed her own love affair with consummate ease, she had placed her novel in Mr. Nun's hands, and had said, "Reginald, dearest, there is my answer." It was all very well for Elizabeth to do things like that, Barbara couldn't. To start with Barbara could not imagine herself addressing Mr. Abbott as "Arthur," she supposed she would have to if she were going to marry him, but it would take her some time to get used to it.

Barbara was dressed by now, and there was still an hour before Mr. Abbott was expected. She decided to go for a walk—a good sharp walk would be the best cure for her unsettled nerves.

"You're never going out, Miss Barbara!" Dorcas exclaimed, when she appeared downstairs with her hat and coat on. "What if the poor gentleman arrives before you get back?"

The words gave Barbara a sudden idea—it was such an excellent idea that she wondered why on earth she had not thought of it before.

"Give him this, Dorcas," she said, dumping the fat untidy manuscript of *The Pen Is Mightier*—— on the kitchen table. "If he comes before I get back just give him this from me, and tell him I left it for him to read."

"But he'll be wanting to see *you*," said Dorcas, reproachfully. "He won't want to sit down and read all that rubbish the moment he arrives. Really, Miss Barbara, you might have a little consideration for the poor gentleman, I do think."

"Just give it to him," said Barbara, and she disappeared

hastily out of the back door. There was no time to be lost. Mr. Abbott might arrive earlier than he had said, and it would be dreadful if he arrived before she had made good her escape.

She ran down the garden and squeezed through the gap in the fence and made off across the fields towards the church.

It was five o'clock before Barbara could make up her mind to return to Tanglewood Cottage, and even then it took all her courage. She crept into the hall like a burglar, and peeped in at the half-open door of the drawing-room. Mr. Abbott was sitting in front of the fire having tea, he looked very happy and quite at home in Barbara's drawing-room. He was just pouring out a second cup when he looked up and saw his run-away hostess.

"Don't be frightened of me," he said, smiling at her in a friendly manner, "I'm warranted not to bite."

Barbara laughed, it was so reassuring, so utterly different from what she had expected.

"Let me offer you some of your own excellent tea," Mr. Abbott continued, waving the tea-pot at her hospitably. "You must be cold and hungry. Dorcas informs me that you had no lunch. It is really very naughty of you to go out without your lunch and wander about in the cold, and get chilled to the bone. When we are married I shall not allow you to do such silly things—we *are* going to be married, aren't we, Barbara, dear?"

"Yes," she said, "I think so. At least if you really want to be. I'm quite happy like this."

"Of course I want to be," replied Mr. Abbott, ignoring

the latter half of her remark. "I want to be married very much indeed. Do come and have some tea, Barbara."

She sat down rather gingerly at the other side of the fire, and accepted the cup which he had poured out for her. So far all had been well, and she was nearly sure now that Mr. Abbott was not going to kneel down and break into impassioned speech—what a mercy it was that he was such a sensible sort of man!

"This is cosy," said Mr. Abbott, "I'm very happy. I hope you are happy too. We suit each other exactly, and I am very fond of you, Barbara. I will be very good to you, my dear—don't be frightened of me for goodness' sake," he added quickly. "Have some hot buttered toast."

Barbara was not really frightened, it was impossible to be frightened of Mr. Abbott any more. He was so nice and friendly—just the same as he always was, only nicer and kinder. She ate quantities of hot buttered toast, and felt much better. She began to feel quite safe and happy. She began to feel that some day—perhaps quite soon— she might manage to call him Arthur.

They discussed *The Pen Is Mightier*—— and Mr. Abbott told her that he thought it was even better than *Disturber of the Peace*. The only thing he was at all doubtful about was the kidnapping of the Rider baby. People didn't kidnap babies in this country, Mr. Abbott said, and it seemed a pity to introduce one improbable episode into an otherwise probable, and even veracious chronicle of everyday affairs.

"But it did happen," Barbara pointed out. "It all happened exactly like that, except that it was really twins."

Mr. Abbott gazed at her in amazement.

"It's all true, every word," Barbara continued. "Mrs. Greensleeves did it—Mrs. Myrtle Coates, you know—just as I wrote it. I could never have imagined it because I've got no imagination at all."

"Well I'm jiggered!" said Mr. Abbott, heavily.

"Truth is stranger than fiction," added Barbara with a satisfied smile. She was pleased at having thought of this exceedingly apt proverb, it was almost as good as "the pen is mightier than the sword," and would have done almost as well as a title for her book—almost as well, but not quite.

Of course Mr. Abbott could say no more about the improbability of the episode. An episode that has actually happened in real life cannot be said to be too improbable for a novel. So Mr. Abbott abandoned the subject, and, after suggesting one or two minor alterations, he asked if he might take the manuscript away with him to-night and put it in hand at once. He had brought the contract with him and Dorcas could be called in to witness Barbara's signature, if she approved of the idea. Barbara agreed and summoned Dorcas from the back premises.

The contract was a very different contract from the one which Barbara had signed for *Disturber of the Peace*. John Smith was a best seller now—or at any rate as near to a best seller as made no odds. Miss Buncle was to get a large sum in advance, and excellent royalties as well. It was a good contract even for a best seller, but Miss Buncle never looked at it. She took up Mr. Abbott's fat fountain pen and enquired where she was to write her name.

"But you haven't read it!" exclaimed Mr. Abbott in surprise.

"I suppose it's just the same as before, isn't it?" asked Barbara. "Why should I bother to read it over if you say it's all right?"

Mr. Abbott was touched at her complete confidence in him, but somewhat startled at her ignorance of financial matters. She evidently quite failed to realise that her stock had gone up since *Disturber of the Peace* had been published, and that her market value had increased a hundredfold. It was a good thing—he thought—that she would have him to take care of her in future, and see that she was not swindled out of everything she possessed.

Dorcas signed her name upon the contract with a considerable amount of heavy breathing, and returned to the kitchen with all speed. She was busy roasting a duck for their suppers, and she was rather anxious about it. How awful if it "caught" while she was signing their stupid papers—something to do with the wedding, Dorcas supposed. She, also, had not bothered to glance through the contract, but that was chiefly because of the duck.

There was only one thing which had to be decided immediately. Mr. Abbott was a little anxious as to how Barbara would take it, he approached the subject with all the tact he could command.

"I like the way you've finished *The Pen Is Mightier*——," he told her, with an ingratiating smile.

"It was your idea entirely," she told him.

"I mean I like the manner in which you have carried out my idea," he explained. "The wedding is excellent, and all Copperfield coming to the feast is a delightful touch—one of the best things you've done, Barbara—it is delicate farce (if such a thing can be)."

"Farce!" said Barbara somewhat perplexed at the word, "but it's not funny at all. At least it's not meant to be funny, I didn't mean—"

"I know, I know," he said. "Never mind. It doesn't matter about that. Everybody will like it immensely and that's the main thing. What I want to put before you is this, the end of your book is going to be true in essentials, but we can't make it altogether true—I'm explaining it badly," he cried, running his hand over his smooth hair, and looking at Barbara in a harassed manner. "I mean we can't have our wedding here in Silverstream."

"Why not?" Barbara enquired, she had already begun to look forward to the wedding. It was to be the same as Elizabeth's wedding—or as near that ideal ceremony as possible. Of course you could not arrange for sunshine and bird-song in Silverstream as you could in Copperfield. Barbara realised that, and bowed to the inevitable like the philosopher she was; but she did want her wedding to be at the same church, and to be attended by the same people as Elizabeth's wedding, and she did want to appear before the inhabitants of Silverstream as a pure white bride.

"Why not?" enquired Barbara again, for Mr. Abbott hadn't answered her the first time. "Why can't we have our wedding here in Silverstream, and everything just like Elizabeth and Mr. Nun?"

"Well," said Mr. Abbott. "Well, you see, Barbara, the moment we publish *The Pen Is Mightier*——, everyone in Silverstream will know that you are John Smith. They couldn't help knowing it, if they tried, because Elizabeth Wade is Barbara Buncle to the meanest intelligence, and

Elizabeth Wade wrote *Storms in a Teacup,* and *Storms in a Teacup* is *Disturber of the Peace.*"

Barbara saw—"Fancy me not noticing that!" she said, sadly.

"It's a pity but it can't be helped," said Mr. Abbott.

"I suppose you couldn't keep back *The Pen Is Mightier*—— till after the wedding, could you?"

"I could," agreed Mr. Abbott, "and I would too, if that would be any use. We could quite easily be married before the book is published, but there's another thing to be thought of. Don't you see what will happen when you send out the invitations to the wedding with my name on them? Wedding invitations usually have the name of the bridegroom inscribed upon them, don't they?"

"Yes, what will happen?"

"Everybody will say, 'Mr. Abbott'—who on earth is Mr. Abbott? Is he the publisher fellow? How is it that Miss Buncle knows Mr. Abbott so well?"

"Of course they will," said Barbara sadly. "How clever you are! Far cleverer than me. I would never have thought of that until it had happened."

"Not clever at all," Mr. Abbott said, preening himself a little—it really was very pleasant to be appreciated at one's true worth.—"Not clever at all, Barbara, dear. It is just my business brain. Your brain runs on other lines. Now, I could never have written *Disturber of the Peace,* and *The Pen Is Mightier*——," said Mr. Abbott with perfect truth. "People are made differently (and how fortunate that they are, what a dull world it would be if we were all alike!). One person can do one thing and another person can do something else. Together we shall be complete, invincible, perfect," said Mr. Abbott ardently and he leaned forward, and laid his hand on Barbara's knee.

It was a strong, comforting, safe sort of hand. Barbara rather liked the feeling of it lying there on her knee—she smiled at him.

"You see how it is," he continued, "I should have loved you to have a beautiful wedding like Elizabeth's but it simply can't be done. Directly Silverstream realises that you are John Smith your life will be a burden to you. They can't do anything very desperate, of course, but they can make things extremely unpleasant—"

Barbara knew that he was right, she would have to leave Silverstream. She found that she did not mind very much. She had lived in Silverstream all her life but the last few months had been too great a strain upon her nerves, she was not happy in Silverstream. The reason for her unhappiness was not far to seek, she never had a moment's real peace. She never knew when somebody was going to pounce upon *Disturber of the Peace,* and tear it to bits; she never knew when somebody would stop her in the street and denounce her as John Smith; she felt positively sick every time the telephone bell rang in case somebody had found her out. Barbara felt that it would be a great relief to get away from Silverstream and leave all her fears, and all her troubles behind.

She loved Copperfield, of course, but the books were finished now and Copperfield was fading from her mind. She could no longer enter Copperfield at will, the door was shut—she had shut it herself, of course, but she could not open it again.

"Will you be very sorry to leave Silverstream?" Mr. Abbott asked her, sympathetically.

"No," said Barbara, "I don't really think I shall mind very much."

"Good," he said, smiling and rubbing his hands.

CHAPTER XXVI

Colonel and Mrs. Weatherhead

*T*HE Weatherheads returned to Silverstream about the beginning of March. They had had a delightful time at Monte Carlo and had settled down into married harness with the greatest of ease. The Colonel was delighted with his pretty, agreeable wife, and had no idea that he was completely under her thumb.

Barbara was the first person in Silverstream to call upon the newly married couple. She had always liked Dorothea Bold, and she was anxious to see what Dorothea Weatherhead was like. What had marriage done to Dorothea? Besides, it was something to do, to walk down to the bridge and call. It would take the best part of an afternoon and would serve to kill time. Barbara was very restless these days, she couldn't settle to anything.

The Weatherheads had taken up their abode in Cosy Neuk, whilst The Bridge House was being altered to suit their requirements. They were delighted to see Barbara Buncle and asked her to stay to tea. They told her all their news, first about their adventures at Monte Carlo and then about the alterations at The Bridge House. It was being painted and papered from attic to cellar—they told Barbara—and a bow window was being thrown out on the south side of the drawing-room.

"I may tell you that's my idea entirely," said Colonel

Weatherhad with no little pride. "The room was dull and cold. A south window will make all the difference."

Barbara complimented him on his sagacity.

"It's convenient being so near at hand," said Dorothea, chipping into the conversation, "Robert can keep an eye on the workmen and see what they are doing. You've no idea how it keeps them up to the mark to have a man after them. They never pay any attention to a woman."

"It was only because Dorothea wanted somebody to chivvy the plumbers who were doing her drains that she consented to marry *me,*" put in the Colonel chuckling.

"Yes, that was the reason," agreed Dorothea, "you really ought to get a husband, Barbara. They're quite useful if the drains go wrong, or if you want a bow window built out."

"My drains never go wrong," Barbara replied, smiling inwardly, "and I couldn't possibly afford a bow window. Besides nobody would want to marry *me,* would they?"

They both protested vehemently, but insincerely, at her modesty. Barbara was aware of the insincerity of their protestations—her writing had made her perspicacious of her fellow creatures—and she hugged herself with delight to think of their amazement when they heard—

"And how's Silverstream?" enquired Dorothea, as she sat down behind the tea-table, and arranged the cups with her pretty plump hands.

Barbara told her that Silverstream was just the same as ever.

"Not entirely," said Colonel Weatherhead, chuckling and winking at his new wife. "Been a bloodless revolution at The Riggs, hasn't there?"

"Now don't be naughty, Robert," Dorothea entreated him. "I'm sure Barbara wouldn't be interested in nasty gossip about poor little Mr. Featherstone Hogg."

"I'm dashed sure she would be," returned the Colonel.

"Of course I would," cried Barbara. "It's too cruel to rouse my curiosity like that. I insist on hearing all about it."

"You tell her then," Dorothea said.

"Well, it's not very much really. It's only rather funny when you know the Featherstone Hoggs, and know how the poor little feller has always been kept in order, and squashed on every occasion. Dolly and I saw the little feller in town one night at that new smart restaurant in Mayfair—'Silvio', or something. He was dining *tête-à-tête* with a young lady and enjoying himself tremendously. He was far too much taken up with his fair companion to see us."

"She looked like a chorus girl," Dorothea put in, "frightfully made up, and the least possible amount of clothes. I don't know what 'Agatha' would have said if she had seen 'dear Edwin' and his companion that night."

They were in the middle of tea when Sarah Walker arrived to pay her call. She kissed Dorothea and told her that she was a wicked woman—

"The idea of keeping us all in the dark like that!"

"It was all very sudden, you know," replied Dorothea blushing prettily.

"You must blame me, if there's any blame going," said the Colonel. "The whole thing was entirely my fault and I'm not a bit sorry, either."

"You dreadful soldier-men," said Sarah, shaking her

head in dismay. "You're a wild, dangerous lot, and no mistake."

"I'm going to have an At Home," announced Dorothea, changing the subject abruptly, "you and Barbara must both come, and help me with it. I don't want Silverstream to feel done out of its Wedding At Home."

Sarah wrinkled her brows, "It's sweet of you, Dorothea, but I don't think I will. You see Silverstream doesn't like me much at the moment. They all think I'm John Smith."

"They think you are John Smith?" enquired Dorothea in a bewildered voice. "Who on earth is John Smith?"

"That's just what everybody wants to know—or at least they did until they fixed on me."

"But who is he? What has he done?"

"You don't mean to say you haven't read the book?" exclaimed Sarah in amazement. "I thought everybody in the whole world had read it—*Disturber of the Peace,* by John Smith," she added, on seeing that her hostess had no idea what she was talking about, "You've read it, haven't you, Colonel?"

"Oh, I know now!" cried Dorothea. "It's that book Mrs. Featherstone Hogg was so furious about. Robert read it just before we went abroad. He said there wasn't much in it—didn't you, Robert?"

"Not very much," said Robert, uncomfortably.

"I bought it in London to take abroad with me," continued Dorothea, "but the queer thing was it disappeared —so I never read it after all."

"Disappeared?" enquired Sarah with interest.

"Yes, vanished completely. I put it in the top of the

lunch basket to read it in the train, and when I opened the basket it had gone—wasn't it odd?"

"Very odd indeed," Sarah replied, "but I really wouldn't bother about it any more, if I were you. As the Colonel so rightly says there is not much in it."

Colonel Weatherhead looked at her gratefully—what an eminently sensible, charming, and agreeable woman Mrs. Walker was! Just the very friend for dear Dolly— the friend he would have chosen for her himself.

Barbara left the tea party early. She was expecting Arthur to supper, and she was pleasantly thrilled at the prospect of seeing him. She had not seen Arthur for nearly a week, he had been so busy trying to get all his business cleared up and put in order so that he could take a nice long holiday with a clear conscience. And, besides the pleasure of seeing Arthur again, there was another pleasure in store to-night, Barbara was looking forward to it immensely. Arthur had promised to bring with him an advance copy of *The Pen Is Mightier*——. The book was going to be published quite soon now; in fact, as soon as certain important arrangements had been completed.

As she walked home, Barbara thought about the Weatherheads very contentedly. It was obvious that their marriage had been a success, they both seemed very happy. The Weatherhead marriage was her most successful achievement—or perhaps it would be more correct to call it the most successful achievement of *Disturber of the Peace*. They had done exactly what they were told, and made no fuss about it whatever. She felt a proprietary interest in the Weatherheads.

Next to the Weatherheads in order of merit Barbara put Miss King and Miss Pretty. They had departed to Samarkand just after the New Year. At least they had said they were going to Samarkand. Barbara was in some doubt whether their flight south had really ended in Samarkand, for the post cards which had arrived in due course, and had been displayed on the mantelpieces of Silverstream, seemed to be views of the pyramids, varied by an occasional sphinx. Barbara had always been led to believe that these interesting and ancient monuments were exclusively Egyptian.

Margaret Bulmer was also one of the successes achieved by *Disturber of the Peace,* but in an entirely different manner. Margaret had returned from her long visit to her parents, looking ten years younger, to find a much more considerate and agreeable husband. The truth was that Stephen had missed her quite a lot, the house had not been nearly so comfortable without Margaret to oil the wheels of the domestic machinery. Stephen was determined to take no risks, and he laid himself out to be agreeable to his wife. Moreover an old shed at the bottom of the garden had been converted into a very comfortable writing room for Stephen, so he was able to carry out his researches into the character and attainments of Henry the Fourth without being disturbed by the noise of his offspring and dependants. The house was more comfortable for everybody now that there was no longer the need for complete and absolute silence. Mr. Bulmer's writing room was all the more necessary because the children had been thoroughly spoilt by their grandparents during their long visit. They were now a pair of ordinary, healthy, noisy children and no longer little white mice. All this was directly attributable to the influence of *Disturber of the Peace,* so that although Margaret had not actually followed her prescribed destiny and eloped at midnight from her bedroom window with Harry Carter, Barbara felt quite justified in claiming Margaret as another success.

And lastly there was Mr. Featherstone Hogg. Barbara was so glad to hear that he was really having a nice time. She liked Mr. Featherstone Hogg, he had always been kind to her. Barbara liked to repay kindness with kindness so she had given him a nice time in *The Pen Is Mightier——.* A chance remark of old Mrs. Carter's anent Edwin's unfortunate penchant for the stage, coupled with her own experiences at the Berkeley, had shown Barbara in what way Edwin could be entertained (she might not have imagination but she was certainly ingenious), and it appeared that she had chosen well for him. She had entertained him exactly as he liked to entertain himself. Barbara was glad.

CHAPTER XXVII

Sally's Secret

*T*HE next morning was fine and sunny, Sally came dancing in to see Barbara with a copy of the *Daily Gazette* in her hand.

"Look," she cried, "look, Barbara! John Smith has written a new book. It's coming out next week. Oh, I am excited about it, aren't you, Barbara? I wonder what he's written about this time. It's called *The Pen Is Mightier*—— doesn't it sound thrilling? No pen could be mightier than John Smith's, could it?"

Barbara tried hard to register surprise, she decided that she was not a born actress. Fortunately Sally was too full of her great news to notice Barbara's attempts. She did not wait for answers to her various questions. Sally rarely expected answers to her questions, and Barbara knew her well enough now not to bother about finding any. By the time you had found an adequate answer Sally had flitted on to something quite different.

"Gran rang up Mrs. Featherstone Hogg," continued Sally delightedly. "She shut the door of the library so that I shouldn't hear what she was saying, but she was so excited and talked so loud, that I heard quite clearly in the hall. They are both ordering copies of it to be sent to them the moment it comes out. They hope it will give them some clue to John Smith.—Are you ordering a copy, Barbara? You had better do it soon. The first edition will be sold out directly. Will you lend me your copy to read if Gran sits on hers? Oh, I do think John Smith is marvellous!"

"You're going to marry him, aren't you?" enquired Barbara wickedly.

"Oh, that was just my nonsense," said Sally, actually blushing, "you mustn't take all I say for gospel truth, Barbara dear. When I'm excited I just gas on, and say all sorts of rubbish. How could I possibly want to marry a man I've never even *seen*?"

"It does seem impossible. But of course you know exactly what he's like, and that makes a lot of difference. Big and strong—isn't he—with a humorous mouth and piercing eyes and long tousled hair—"

"You're teasing me now. What a horrid person you are! Do be good, Barbara, and I'll tell you a secret. It's a frightfully important secret too.—I'm in love."

"Not really? Not with John Smith?"

"Silly, it's true. I'm engaged," Sally said, fishing down the front of her jumper and displaying a ring set with diamonds. *"Now* will you believe it's true?"

Barbara was forced to believe such indubitable evidence, she was suitably impressed.

"We're going to be married directly I hear from Daddy. I've written to tell Daddy all about it—Oh Barbara, he's a marvellous man!"

"I know. You always said he was."

"Not Daddy (although of course he's marvellous too). I mean Ernest's marvellous—Mr. Hathaway, you know.

Barbara, he's too sweet for words. I adore him. Of course I've been in love before," continued Sally, looking very wise and experienced, "but never the least like this—this is the real thing. We're just waiting now for Daddy's letter and then we'll get married and live happily ever after."

Barbara looked at her in distress. "Sally dear," she said anxiously. "I don't think your father will consent to your marrying Mr. Hathaway. He's very nice, of course, but he's so frightfully poor—what would you live on?"

"That's just the amazing thing, my dear. He's not poor at all. He's written and told Daddy exactly how much he has, and it's lots," said Sally, opening her blue eyes very wide. "He gave away all his money for a whole year just to see what it was like to be poor. He's so *good,* you know Barbara. His ideals are so wonderful. I shall never be able to live up to Ernest's ideals."

"Of course you can if you try.

"Yes, perhaps," Sally agreed, "If I try very hard—but isn't it wonderful, Barbara? Isn't it just like a novel to fall in love with a poor man, and then find he's rich beyond the dreams of avarice?"

Barbara agreed, she hugged Sally and told her how frightfully glad she was.

Sally was rather young of course, but she had seen more of the world than many older people and she was quite capable of managing her own life. Barbara had always thought Mr. Hathaway a nice young man—rather serious perhaps, but Sally would liven him up. It seemed very suitable, and she thought that Sally would be happy. She was in a condition of mind to believe that marriage was a desirable state.

"And you'll come to the wedding, won't you, Barbara?" Sally said, disengaging herself from Barbara's embrace.

"If Barbara Buncle still exists, Barbara Buncle will be there," replied that lady. (And that's really rather clever of me—she thought—because I shan't *be* Barbara Buncle any more, I shall be Barbara Abbott. It's a pity I shan't be at the wedding of course, but I can't be, so it's no use thinking about it.)

Sally's news was really astounding, she could hardly believe it was true. She wished she had known about it before so that she could have put it all into *The Pen Is Mightier*——. It would have added considerable interest to the story of Mr. Shakeshaft if she had married him off to his pupil—just like Swift and Stella, Barbara thought regretfully. There might even have been a double wedding at St. Agatha's. No, the wedding was Elizabeth's and Elizabeth's alone. It would never have done to filch any of the glory from Elizabeth; but the story about Mr. Shakeshaft being a rich man after all—a sort of prince in disguise—was a distinct loss to *The Pen Is Mightier*——. Why didn't I think of it? sighed Barbara. I have no imagination at all. It would have finished off Mr. Shakeshaft so happily and made Mrs. Myrtle Coates look even more of a fool. It is, of course, the obvious end, only I was too blind and stupid to see it.

"What *are* you thinking about Barbara?" demanded Sally.

"I'm wishing I had a little imagination," replied Barbara. She was always truthful when it was possible so to be.

"Never mind, old thing! We can't all be John Smiths," said Sally, squeezing her arm affectionately.

CHAPTER XXVIII

John Smith

THE *Pen Is Mightier*—— arrived in Silverstream. It seemed that practically everybody had ordered copies in advance. By twelve o'clock Mrs. Featherstone Hogg was on the telephone summoning her forces.

"Of course it's Barbara Buncle," she said to Mr. Bulmer. "Who would have thought that frumpy little object would have the audacity to write such wicked books? You've read the new one, I suppose, *it's worse.*"

"I've glanced through it—just glanced through it casually," replied Mr. Bulmer, who had had his nose glued to the pages of *The Pen Is Mightier*—— ever since it had arrived. "The novel is not worth *reading.*"

"Of course not," agreed Mrs. Featherstone Hogg. "I just glanced through it too, just to see whether I could find any clue to John Smith's identity, and it's perfectly plain now."

Mr. Bulmer agreed.

"I'll call for you in the Daimler in about ten minutes," added Mrs. Featherstone Hogg. "We can't *do* anything to her, I suppose, but we can go down to Tanglewood Cottage and have it out with her."

Mr. Bulmer agreed with alacrity.

Mrs. Featherstone Hogg rang up Vivian Greensleeves and arranged to pick her up on the way; the Weatherheads were invited but refused; Mrs. Carter agreed to meet the others at the gate, so too, the Snowdons.

Mrs. Featherstone Hogg could not think of anyone else to ask, she did not want people like Mrs. Dick and Mrs. Goldsmith—they only complicated matters. She had made the mistake of asking too many people to her Drawing-room Meeting and she was determined not to repeat it. Of course it was a great pity that Ellen King was not here—

Mrs. Carter was coming out of her gate as the Daimler drove up to Tanglewood Cottage and disgorged its occupants.

"Isn't it awful?" cried Mrs. Carter, hastening towards the others. "Isn't it perfectly awful to think I've been living next door to him—to her—to John Smith I mean—all this time? I never was so mistaken in anyone, it just shows how *deep* she is."

"I always considered Barbara Buncle half idiotic," agreed Mrs. Featherstone Hogg.

"The books in no way disprove your opinion," gasped Miss Snowdon, who had just arrived upon the scene, very breathless, with her father and sister in tow.

"That's what I think," agreed Mr. Bulmer. "They're idiotic books."

"Hullo!" exclaimed Vivian Greensleeves (who had been looking about her while the others talked), "look at that. What does that mean?" She pointed to a large white board which was fixed securely in a tree near the gate. They all looked at it, and saw that it bore in new black lettering the announcement:

TANGLEWOOD COTTAGE

THIS DESIRABLE RESIDENCE FOR SALE

THREE BEDROOMS. TWO RECEPTION. BATHROOM.

H. & C.

(*Apply* MRS. ABBOTT, c/o Abbott & Spicer,
Brummel Street, London, E.C.4.)

"She's going away," Mr. Snowdon suggested.

"Can you wonder?" cried Mrs. Carter. "What sort of a life would she have in Silverstream after this?"

"I wonder who Mrs. Abbott is," said Vivian.

Mrs. Featherstone Hogg was shaking the gate fiercely. "It seems to be locked, she's frightened out of her wits, I suppose."

"Quite likely," agreed Miss Snowdon.

They all gazed up the drive. Vivian pointed out that there were the wheelmarks of a large car in the soft ground. They were quite recent wheel marks.

"Who can have driven in?" Mrs. Carter wondered.

"She's probably bought a car," said Mr. Bulmer.

"Barbara Buncle!" cried Mrs. Carter incredulously. "The woman is as poor as a church mouse."

"Is she," said Mr. Bulmer sarcastically. "Is she really? She must have made hundreds out of her first novel, and even more out of the new one."

"Hundreds out of that rubbish?" cried Mrs. Featherstone Hogg.

"Yes, hundreds. It's just those trashy novels that make money, nowadays," said Mr. Bulmer bitterly. His bitterness was caused by the fact that *Henry the Fourth* was now completed, and was going the rounds of all the Publishing Houses in London, and returning every few weeks, to its author, with the sure instinct of a homing pigeon.

"Well, it's no use standing here all day," said Vivian Greensleeves, crossly.

They agreed that it was not. Mrs. Featherstone Hogg shook the gate again, but with no result.

"We could go in through my garden," suggested Mrs. Carter. "There's that gap in the fence—Sally uses it. I shall have it blocked up immediately, of course."

It was an excellent idea, and the whole party turned to follow her.

At this moment another car drove up and was seen to be the doctor's Alvis. Sarah had also procured a copy of *The Pen Is Mightier——*, and had spent the morning reading it, and discovering its authorship. She had given the doctor no peace until he had agreed to bring her down to Tanglewood Cottage in the car.

"They'll kill her," she told him, with exaggerated concern.

Dr. John didn't think that they would actually kill Miss Buncle, but he agreed that it might be as well to go down and see what was happening.

"Hullo!" said Sarah, stepping out of the car, "everybody seems to be calling on John Smith this morning."

"Did you ever know such a wicked deception?" cried Mrs. Carter.

"Who would ever have thought it was Barbara Buncle?" cried Miss Isabella Snowdon.

"Barbara told me about it months ago," replied Sarah nonchalantly.

"She told you she was John Smith?"

"Yes, months ago" (but of course I didn't believe her, added Sarah to herself).

The whole party stood and gazed at Sarah in amazement. They had so much to say that they couldn't find words to say anything at all.

"Well, never mind that now," said Mrs. Carter. "Come along—this way—through my garden."

They followed Mrs. Carter through her gate, and down the somewhat muddy path that led to the gap in the fence. Dr. Walker and Sarah came last, by themselves. They were not strictly of the party, they were merely here to see that nothing happened.

"What are you going to say, Agatha?" enquired Mrs. Carter, rather breathlessly of Mrs. Featherstone Hogg.

"Words will be given me," replied that lady, confidently, as she squeezed through the fence in the wake of the fat Miss Snowdon.

They approached the house through the shrubbery where Barbara had had her "feu de joie." The trees were budding now, and there were some early daffodils amongst the long grass; but the party had no eyes for the beauties of Spring, they were one and all engaged in framing cutting sentences to hurl at John Smith. They couldn't *do* anything, of course, but they could say a good deal.

They approached the house in silence, and stood in a little group upon the lawn. They stared at the house, and the house stared back at them with closely shuttered windows. It wore the unmistakable, forlorn look of a deserted nest.

Barbara Buncle had gone.

THE END

DATE DUE